LIES OF THE WICKED

B. L. LEWIS

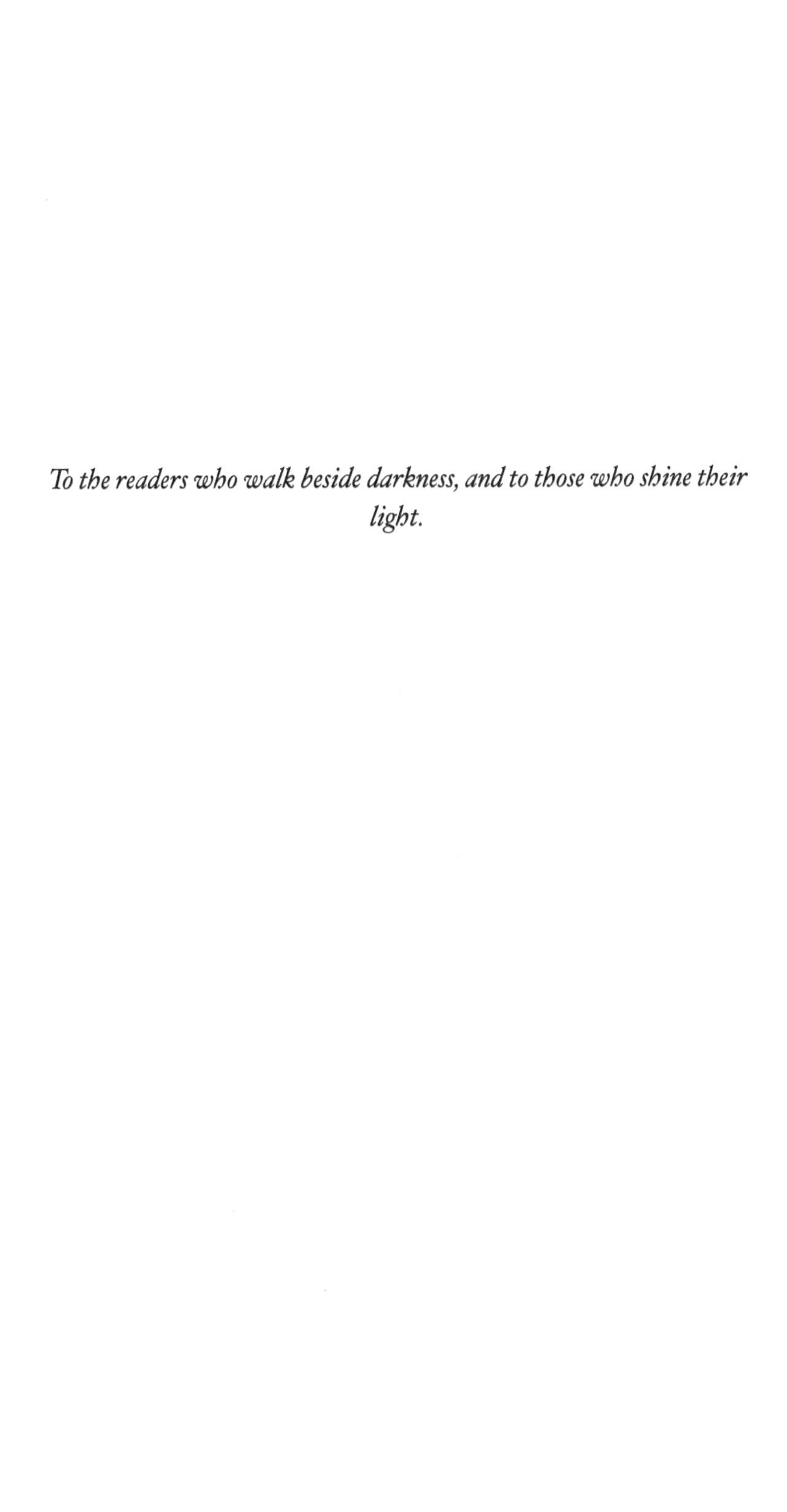

To the readers who walk beside darkness, and to those who shine their light.

CONTENT WARNING

Sexually explicit, open-door scenes. Panic attacks. Newborn relinquishment. Violence, death, gore, and arson. Animal death. Traumatic birth (brief mention). Fetal loss. These warnings are provided in an effort to be empathetic to all readers; mental health is important. This book may not be suitable for all audiences, discretion is advised.

MAP OF ANDERA

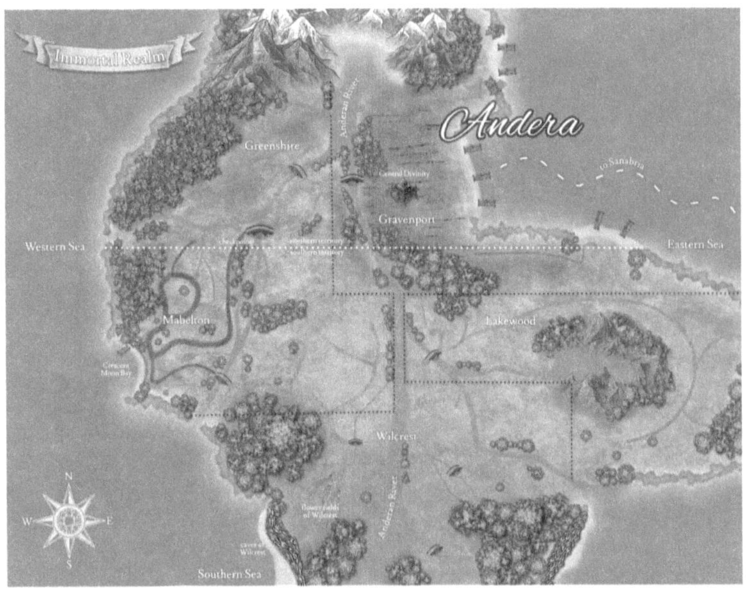

Map: https://inkarnate.com/p/7mOvYa

PRONUNCIATION GUIDE

Andera: Anne-dare-a
Sanabria: Sahn-ahb-riah
Thessa Skiafer: Thess-a Ski-a-fer
Shovak: Show-vack
Leora: Lee-or-a
Noam: No-ahm
Emiel: Em-eel
Soren: Sor-en
Jussal: Juss-ul
Eiliana: IL-ee-ana
Echidna: Eck-eed-na

DEFINITIONS

Anvil: a large metal block used for blacksmithing.
Tome: a large book, often times scholarly.
Grimoire: a spellbook.
CSA: Central Secondary Academy.
Secondary school: is similar to high school.
Tertiary school: is similar to college.
Immortal: non-human; witches and demons in this story are considered immortal with a thousand-year lifespan.
Summoning Day: the day an immortal turns eighteen; they receive their magic, bestowed via a physical gift from the goddess.

MAGICAL SYSTEMS

& THEIR SUPREMES

Celestial: Madame Morganna
Botanical: Madame Hearthling
Elemental: General Valstrom

PROLOGUE

SEVENTEEN YEARS AGO

Insects buzzed—the true minstrels of night.

A cloaked female hid in a shadowed alleyway, wearing a body that did not belong to her. Rain beat down, drenching her and the baby bundled in her arms.

She peered around the corner, narrowing her focus on the two soldiers pacing before sky-high gates. In her own tongue, she whispered, *"Vashi nolathi tavini moofinith."*

One thump sounded ... and soon another.

Swiftly, she approached the sleeping guards to place the newborn between them. Piercing cries hummed through her borrowed ears. Strange instincts begged her to coddle the child—feelings she had to ignore.

Dashing back down the dark alley, she glanced over her shoulder, reciting her spell in reverse. When the soldiers wake, they wouldn't recall how they fell. There'd be nothing but a wailing witchling consuming their thoughts.

A poor abandoned thing, they'll think.

The cloaked female ran until her unfamiliar limbs collapsed, then she crawled.

AS THE SUN ROSE, A MIDWIFE NAMED GENEVIEVE YAWNED awake.

She shuddered at the insect skittering down her arm and flicked it away. Tucked between rubbish bins, she wrinkled her nose, unsure why she'd slept in the alley behind a smelly fish market.

Rubbing her eyes did nothing to retrieve her memories. Had she stopped for mead after work?

Perhaps one too many again, Genevieve.

Rising on uncertain legs, she inspected her soaked cloak for clues.

Nothing.

After peering beneath it, her breath hitched. There was blood splattered on her white apron—demon blood.

LECTURE NOTES FROM THE ART OF BLACKSMITHING III:

Bladesmithing is an entirely different craft.

Daggers are complicated. Thessa set the scalding blade atop her anvil and gripped the hickory handle of her hammer. Swinging in an arc motion, she beat the edges flat. Iron striking iron reverberated around the workshop, filling her ears with a familiar, steady drum.

Bang.

Bang.

Bang.

The incessant noise had a way of drowning out every miserable thought she had—until it stopped.

She sifted beneath her tool-ridden workbench for some gritty parchment. Sanding was just as brutal as hammering, but not as loud. Swiping away, she filled her mind with lecture notes to pass the time.

If a blade is not smooth, consider it unfinished. The correct angle will remedy any imperfection.

Professor Shovak, with a belly and beard as oversized as his heart, eventually checked in. "Another dagger, Thessa?"

She kept sanding. "You say this like it's a bad thing. Would you prefer a spiked collar like Sebastian's making?" she asked, her voice tart.

Professor Shovak laughed. "I suppose that's the nature of an assessment which lacks specificities, but no, it's not a *bad thing*. In fact, quite the opposite. A smith can make several different things fairly *or* focus on one and make it well. Let it be well then." He tapped her workbench with a soot-stained finger before meandering over to the next student.

Once her dagger was smooth, Thessa strode to the forge.

The strongest of steel is forged by the hottest of fires.

Dagger clamped and ready, she pushed it into the flames —her favorite part. The forge roared by way of greeting, warming her balled-up cheeks. When her blade burned as bright as a star, she pulled it free, plunging it in the oil bucket by her feet.

Quenching the metal is for hardness, strength, and resistance.

After cooling and cleaning it, she went back to her workbench, wrapped the hilt, and sharpened the point. By the time she'd looked up, only a few students remained.

Despite the heat of the workshop, and the sweat coating her skin, a shiver ran down her spine. Finishing this blade meant she was finished with Central Secondary Academy.

Thessa paced towards Professor Shovak with her dagger in hand.

He stood. "Ah, is it ready?"

She shook her head. "As ready as it can be." Six hours was all the time he'd allotted for this final assessment.

"Of course, of course. Let's see what you've come up with."

Professor Shovak took her blade and began his ministrations, examining each edge before poking the tip. It was sharp enough to draw a drop of his Elemental blood—red hued with bright blue flecks. Before Thessa could apologize, he'd gripped the hilt, hoisting her blade in the air for his *true test*. Accustomed to his theatrics, she stared with anticipation as he stabbed his abused desk.

Will it fall?

Together they watched her dagger stand, unfaltering.

She wiped her forehead in relief, smearing soot and sweat across it.

Professor Shovak beamed. "Excellent work Thessa, just excellent. You'll make quite the bladesmith ... if you so choose to be."

She smiled back. "All thanks to you. Will you be at the ceremony tomorrow?"

"You can thank me, but it's your work. And yes, of course, all professors will be in attendance."

Thessa scanned the filthy workshop one last time. "I'm going to miss this place the most. I mean it. Thank you for everything."

"How kind, this shop will miss you much the same. You've certainly shined among all this soot."

She grinned.

"Alright, I have grading to do." He gestured to the students' work surrounding his desk. "Go on and get some rest before the big day tomorrow."

❦

OPENING THE DOOR TO HER PRIVATE CHAMBER, THESSA'S pulse wavered.

The entirety of her short immortal life had been reduced to piles. The blankets she'd collected over the years, once layered so thick over her windows that they blocked any trace of light, were crumpled in one corner. Twenty-seven handcrafted daggers were shoved into another; clothes that hardly fit were bunched beside those.

The blade renderings pinned along her walls still needed unpinning.

It all had to go.

Completion of secondary school meant she was finally free to leave Gravenport, except leaving meant parting with most of her things. And since there'd be no family or hidden fortune to find when school ended, *things* were all she had.

Despite wishing the years away, and hating the capital she grew up in, her panic brewed. Trying to remember her steps from the school healer, Thessa closed the door and breathed.

A FORGOTTEN LESSON FROM PRIMARY SCHOOL:

Brightly colored creatures are typically poisonous. Stay away from those.

A jarring knock sounded and Thessa shot out of bed. "Who's there?"

"Thessa, open the door."

Rolling her eyes at the sound of that voice, she asked, "Must I?"

"Why didn't you tell me you were leaving the capital?"

Half-awake, she dragged her feet to the door. "Why are you here?"

"So that's it then?"

She opened the door, waving Kellan inside. "Why are you doing this in the hallway?"

He blew past her, running fingers through his thick, golden hair.

She closed the door, diverting her attention to the handle. His crystal-blue eyes had trapped hers too many times before.

They were like the surface of the sea, flecked with light; whereas hers were dark blue, like the deepest part—devoid of any.

"Well?" He had the nerve to question her.

Thessa took a breath before facing him. "I'm not doing this."

"Then why open the door?" he asked, tilting his head. "You really weren't going to say goodbye?"

She narrowed her gaze. "What difference does it make?"

"You could've told me you were leaving Gravenport. I thought—"

"You thought what?" He ended their relationship two months ago, shortly after his shift into an Elemental. "Shouldn't you be seeing to Asteria?" She arched her brow as high as she could manage it. "Or is it Lilith now?"

He was entering the Elemental Training Program soon where plenty of other females were ready and waiting for his attention.

"Thessa." Her name drifted too easily off of his lips. "Despite your beliefs, I do care about you."

Lies.

"There's no reason for you to be here," she reminded him.

He stepped closer and said, "Stop avoiding me." The noxious smell of cedar and smoke rolled along with him.

"You're infuriating." With her back flush against the door, she swallowed whatever was building in her throat.

Kellan raked his gaze down to her chest. "You're infuriating, too."

"Please leave."

He grinned, flicking his eyes to hers. "Without a proper farewell?"

Thessa was going to snap. "Now."

A small laugh escaped his lips; the sound was so arrogant.

Gripping the handle—trying not to rip it off—she spoke through her teeth. "If you ever cared about me, you'll just *go*."

He remained still. The fire inside his unflinching gaze threatened to smolder her where she stood. Kellan had a way of making every second feel like an eternity.

She opened the door. "Goodbye."

Brushing the pad of his thumb along her lips, he whispered, "That's it?"

She dropped her chin in an effort not to bite off his digit.

He clicked his tongue in disapproval. "Then may I ask why you're still in your sleeping tunic? It's hardly covering your breasts, and you know how much I love them."

Thessa barked up at him, "You're unbearable."

He shook his head. "Fine. I'll see you at the ceremony. *Which* you should consider getting dressed for."

"What time is it?"

"A quarter to ten."

Disbelief tumbled through her. She'd overslept. "What? I need to get ready." She shooed him out.

He placed a flat palm on her door. "You can at least tell me where you're going."

Ignoring the throb inside her chest, she told him about the work-and-board program in Mabelton. Why she gave Kellan anything—why she'd given him *everything*—she wasn't sure. She'd been as foolish as they come.

As he went to leave, she blurted, "Wait."

He turned, arching a brow as if his prayers were about to be answered.

"Could you take my boxes to the Administration Office on your way out? There's a space for donations." Package delivery was the least he could do for the perpetual reminder that her heart belonged nowhere. After stuffing all her pertinent belongings into a single duffle bag last night, she'd divided the rest between two boxes, for some other orphan.

In answer, Kellan returned, stacking and scooping up her boxes. He made it look easy, but he was also the size of her door frame.

"Thank you ... for taking them." She wanted to be clear that it was the only thing she was thankful for.

"Of course. I'll see you soon."

Thessa scrunched her face and closed the door, recounting every horrid detail about the day she'd met him. He'd transferred during her second year—straight from the underworld as far as she was concerned. Between whispering sweet nothings in her ear, his blazing eyes, and puckered lips, he'd been too lustrous to dismiss.

Little had she known he only snared her before unleashing his poison. It was the same toxin he'd used on many females, like the several he'd bedded during their so-called relationship. But, desperate for love, or something like it, she'd always forgiven him.

It'd been two years of torture bound by lust and lies.

Shaking off Kellan's captivation for the last time, she rushed to leave.

LECTURE NOTES FROM REALM RULES & METHODOLOGY:

Red cloaks are worn to respect our fallen Supremes for their Blood Sacrifice—a power so vast it dissolves the witch.

Thessa concealed her annoyance behind star-dusted lids and soot-stained lips. The lip color matched her hair and dress. She slid on pointed clogs, tossed her scarlet cloak atop her shoulders, and left her private chamber.

◈

"This may signify the end, but a commencement represents the beginning. Much like the phases of our moon, this ceremony symbolizes the eternal cycle of impermanence and growth. I'd like to formally welcome everyone to the 177th Annual Commencement Ceremony for Central Secondary

Academy." He paused, smiling as the green and gold banner unfurled behind him, the letters CSA were inked on the center.

The crowd applauded until he gestured for silence. "As chancellor, it is my pleasure to grant this achievement upon our students in front of friends, family, and faculty. We hope you'll all join us in the courtyard for continued celebrations after the ceremony. Now I'd like to announce our guest speaker, your Celestial Supreme, Madame Morganna."

The crowd roared as she stepped up to the stage.

Beyond the podium were rows of faculty members wearing elaborate red cloaks. The scarlet hue was worn by all witches in this realm, except the Supremes, who wore robes specific to the hue of their magic.

"Thank you, Chancellor Dulameer, the pleasure's all mine." When Madame Morganna stood at the podium, her presence was ethereal as ever. The sun bounced off her ivory skin and soaked into her silver hair. Her pearl-colored robes glistened as bright as her smile. Rows of silver bangles along each wrist sparkled and clinked as she waved. She was a shining moon, among a sea of blood.

Madame Morganna scanned the crowd of hundreds before silencing them with a white-tipped finger. "Two centuries ago, the Immortal Realm was forged by the Blood Sacrifices of our fallen Supremes. As we honor your path ahead, let us not forget our past. We'll begin today by honoring those who crafted our sanctuary from the cruel, Mortal Realm." The Celestial Supreme brought her hands into prayer. "Please join me in a moment of silent gratitude."

The crowd of red hoods bowed like a blood-wave crashing against a moonlit shore.

It was minutes before she began again. "This academy was

founded to bolster the next generation of witches, so ask yourself today, what will you bring forth to this new world? Just remember, the possibilities are as unique and infinite as our stars."

The Celestial Supreme scanned the auditorium before raising both arms up. "Everyone, please rise." Her opalescent magic swirled toward the ceiling, forming thick clouds overhead. They grew and grew, filling the entire auditorium. Without help, it was a release of magic only a Supreme could muster.

"A divine future to all," she shouted before dropping her arms, bangles clanking along the way.

The room went wild as her clouds exploded into a mist of shimmering stars.

Soon after, each student called to cross the stage and accept their Scroll of Achievement. There were cheers after each name, likely her classmates' families, proud enough to hoot like owls.

Thessa's chest hollowed as self-pity crept in. She tried to remind herself there were other orphans here today, although that trick never worked. She shifted her weight side to side until her name was called through the enchanted amplifier.

"Ms. Thessa Skiafer."

Like her final dagger, she would not falter. *Not here*, anyways. Breathing in for courage, she stepped on stage and made her way toward the podium. From the corner of her eye, a faculty member rose from their seat. Her self-pity molded to joy when a burly man, without his filthy work apron on, stood tall and whistled with two fingers.

The moment she made eye contact with Professor Shovak, tears welled in her eyes.

Arriving at center stage, she met the gracious hands of

Chancellor Dulameer and accepted her Scroll of Achievement.

Once all the students made it through, festivities continued in the courtyard. The pomp and circumstance would go on for hours, but she had a carriage to catch.

4

LECTURE NOTES FROM IMMORTAL GENETICS:

The purest of bloodlines are rare, that is part of what makes our Supremes, supreme. Since marriage has never been restricted between the three bloodlines, parental designation is no longer a reliable method of power prediction.

Thessa sent a silent prayer to the goddess as she sprinted toward the gates of the Central Divinity. At least the gravel beneath her clogs provided enough traction in the pouring rain.

"Everything alright?"

She halted to answer, knowing better than to dismiss an Elemental guard. "I'm trying to make it to the work-and-board carriages."

Their scarlet uniform remained pristine and dry. It was typical for Elemental soldiers to use their air-magic for protection from rain or snow, creating a sphere around themselves. Meanwhile, she was drenched. Tucking her duffle bag beneath her cloak had only helped one thing: her duffle bag.

They dismissed her. "Better hurry then."

As I was trying to do.

She nodded and pressed onward.

Other than fish markets, the gravel processing factories took up most of the capital. Sand from the coast and gravel from the riverbank were mixed and melted here. The final product made up the foundation of houses and roads. It was sold locally or shipped, while the profits funded resource distribution across Andera. The same resources she'd depended on—until now.

There was one more corner to turn.

"Do you need help?" Another soldier cut off her pursuit, their arm outstretched across her chest.

Had she not been stopped four times already, she'd be there. Thessa grumbled, "I'm trying to make it to the carriages."

They dismissed her.

Gravenport had not always been so rigid. She learned fear had washed over the capital a century ago, after the UnResting—when demons found their world. The battle for domination that followed spared no side of deaths. The fear of future infiltrations had set in like a plague, evolving the capital into the unyielding regime of fire-spewing witches it was today.

Elementals in Andera had to complete a mandatory ten-year training program in the capital. While that may feel like a snippet of time to an immortal, Thessa craved freedom from the capital she was born into. Whatever witch she may be, she wished not to be an Elemental. She'd not leave Gravenport, to be shuffled right back.

After bending the final corner, the bells on the clock tower chimed.

Noon.

Her heart jumped.

There was no time left.

The confirmatory clang of iron rang in her ears as guards pushed the gates open with their air-magic. She could see the carriages approaching, readying to exit.

Thessa skidded to a stop with no breath left and waved her arms in a panic. "Stop!"

The soldiers on gate duty whirled to face their predetermined threat. They formed a diamond pattern as their spheres of air-magic fused into one, approaching her like wolves on prey. Magic swirled away from the three soldiers in back, casting a net of air so wide that it covered the gates, carriages, and herself.

Storming the gates of the Central Divinity was a quick way to draw the wrong kind of attention. Aside from city services, it was the army's training center and home of the Supremes. There's a lot to protect beyond those gates, and impress, considering the Elemental Supreme was also the General of the Elemental Army.

She froze in both terror and amazement. To maintain a personal sphere was usual magic, but emanating their power outward like that was an expenditure. The soldiers in back held their arms steady, each maintaining their portion. Rain battered the shield, trickling down the sides of it like a glistening globe.

The soldier in front had her fire-fingers focused on Thessa as she shouted, "Back up from the gates."

She did as she was told. Elementals were the superior line of magic. Blessed with both flame and air, not even rain could douse their fire.

Their power stemmed from the highest and lowest parts of the universe: the heavens and the underworld. The blue hue was a combination of air at its coldest peak and flame at its hottest point. Air fueled the flames with oxygen and gave them force to launch, while the warmth of their fire kept the air from icing over ... as long as the witch willed it. It was a magical game of give and take; one could easily burn up or freeze.

Immortal does not mean indestructible.

She stopped studying the magic on display and reached a trembling hand into her pocket. Pulling out her carriage ticket, she waved the crumpled, damp piece of parchment high.

The guards' arms went down, releasing their shield. The soldier in front shook her head while the driver in the first carriage shouted, "She rides with us."

Thessa tipped her head back, relieved to feel raindrops on her face once more.

Walking up to the first carriage, she was greeted by the driver. "Greenshire or Mabelton dear, plenty of space in each."

"Mabelton."

Greenshire's snow-capped mountains gave way to the gorging river slicing through Andera. Mabelton was just south of there. She'd read about the cobblestone streets filled with various shops, vendors, eateries, and taverns, all wedged between quiet neighborhoods and Crescent Moon Bay.

The driver jerked his head toward the rear carriage. "Other carriage, go on now." He eyed the guards before looking back to Thessa. "And don't mind them. Only performing their blessed duties."

"I know. Thank you, sir."

After handing her ticket over, the driver of the Mabelton

carriage pointed toward the cabin. "There'll be one stop along the border for checks and watering the horses. We'll arrive by dusk."

Two steps inside, a soldier slammed the door behind her.

She'd always thought the name *ego-mental* better suited the line of witches. Something about their training period turned them all into repugnant pyromaniacs.

To be expected, the three passengers stared blankly at her. There were two bench seats facing each other, the upholstery matched the dark jacquard fabric draped along each window. Noam and Rhetter, two orphaned and inseparable males she'd known for too long, sat on one bench, and an unfamiliar female sat alone on the other. Her complexion and eyes were the color of chestnuts. Her hair was tightly coiled with short pieces falling in front, while the rest was pulled back into a neat bun.

Thessa's hair was far from neat after her sprint in the rain. She removed her hood and swiped some flyaways behind her ears.

Noam and Rhetter waved briefly, as if they'd never met. She'd known them since primary school and didn't bother asking how they'd got there so fast. They began assembling the same board game they were always playing—Dungeons and Serpents—leaving no extra space between them.

As if noticing the same thing, the lone female waved her over.

Thessa removed her soaked cloak and duffle bag, then plopped down beside her. "Thanks."

As the wheels rolled, she unscrewed the vial around her neck.

The Botanical witch from the school infirmary had taught her *breathing techniques* a few years ago. He'd said there was no cure for her wound, rather, collected lavender buds from the school gardens—*for an herbaceous form of balance during times of need.*

She'd carried the flower, dried in a small vial around her neck, ever since. It was hardly a remedy, bladesmithing was her preferred medicine, but as the minutes passed, her tension eased well enough.

Thessa turned to see the female staring at her. "Hi?" she asked it like a question, screwing her necklace back together.

"Hi, I'm Leora, Leora Saint Jamith. What's your name?"

"I'm Thessa."

"You smell divine, I love lavender."

Thessa tucked the pendant underneath her tunic. "Thank you, but it's not meant to be perfume."

"I see that," Leora answered. "Well, you're welcome to rest, I just didn't think you could over this tumultuous tale—" Leora cocked her head towards the males while widening her eyes.

"I suppose you're right." Thessa extended her voice across the cabin. "It's hard to relax with all this jabber about sea serpents."

Rhetter stuck his tongue out at Thessa.

Thessa countered with the same.

Leora and Noam cackled.

On their journey south, Thessa learned more about Leora, while tuning out the males. To her relief, Leora had no problem weaving their conversation. She said she was from Captiva, a southern port city on the eastern continent which specialized in trade. Her father was in the business of exporting steel—Thessa smiled at that part—and her mother owned a small business for naming stars.

Silver lined Leora's eyes at the first mention of her parents. She gave endless details about them, especially their love for each other.

Leora went on to say that during her final semester at Chrisnol Academy, northern Gravenport's private boarding school, she received a letter from her parents. They'd sent word to expect their arrival at the local dock in time for her Commencement Ceremony.

"I wasn't sure why it was taking them so long. I thought maybe the trade winds slowed their trip. I know Elemental captains are only so strong, but my dad would've tapped into his power. He could've helped." Leora went on to tell Thessa she thought they'd still make it in time, that they'd be there when she walked across the stage, and their vessel was just late. The way Leora had explained it, Thessa could tell hope was still radiating inside her.

Leora continued, "After the ceremony, I ran in circles looking for them, but they weren't there. I found the chancellor and told her they were missing. I told her to find them, to do something!"

Leora took a deep breath before starting again, in a quieter, more somber tone. "She relayed my message to city guards, who investigated with local dock workers. There'd been no record of anyone with my surname arriving in any of Gravenport's docks for months."

Thessa sighed. "I'm so sorry. I wish there was something I could do or say."

Traveling by sea for trade, school, or leisure was common, but despite all forms of magic, the seas were beyond the control of their goddess. They were as formidable and unpredictable as their ruler and god, Poseidon.

Without access to her family or accounts, Leora had the same options as any other orphan once they completed secondary school. A work-and-board ticket. The program was established in Andera for any witch in need, like them.

Leora's chancellor had arranged for her private transport to the Central Divinity early this morning.

"I accepted the ticket because I wanted to escape, at least for a little while. I sent a letter to my aunt across the seas, and I've been praying." Leora placed a hand over her heart, "Praying my parent's vessel will find a dock ... and that they'll find me. And until then, here I am."

Thessa couldn't blame Leora for running or longing.

Despite the shadows of grief dancing under Leora's eyes, she said, "The goddess has helped. I'm working toward replacing my sorrow with hope. Hekate guided me to this very seat, next to you, to Mabelton." Leora patted the upholstered bench beside her hip. "I know the goddess has her purpose for me."

Hours into their ride, the horses whinnied as the carriage slowed. Thessa peered out her curtain to see soldiers, indicating they've arrived at the checkpoint between the northern and southern territories.

5

LECTURE NOTES FROM SPELLCASTING AND CURATION:

A pentagram must be drawn in one continuous stroke and contain the spellcaster's blood. For best results, apply the mixture directly to the skin above the heart.

Thessa blew out a sharp breath aimed for the stray hair tickling her eye. Her hands were preoccupied under the suds, as they had been for the past few weeks. Professor Shovak would've laughed had he known she traded her calloused, soot-coated fingers for pruned, supple things.

Kitchen duty was not what she'd envisioned as her future work placement, but it turned out there was a hierarchy for preferred positions in Mabelton's work-and-board program. The tradition was that newcomers received housekeeping roles.

The days had been monotonous, and the weeks had passed slowly. Work wasn't difficult, but it was laborious.

Leora had been assigned laundry duties so they hardly saw each other, despite being roommates. The house matron had taken easily to Leora, and the two witches roomed across the hall—Ivy and Beatrix—were always knocking for her. Thessa wasn't sure what life in the townhouse would've felt like without her; she'd been a beacon of good energy.

After turning off the faucet, Thessa was greeted with a familiar echo of silence. She walked to the closet for the mop and bucket.

The cooks were long gone by now. There'd been too much space and time to think in the kitchens. She preferred when the cooks were shuffling around her and howling at each other. At least their noise helped block out her own.

Every swipe of her mop was a little more aggressive than the last. When the checkered tiles finally shined, she tossed her soiled apron in the bin and left.

Opening her door revealed Leora, Beatrix, and Ivy seated on the floor, surrounded by a large circle of salt. Thessa, wide-eyed, could barely say hello before a bare-chested Leora beckoned her over.

"Tess! Come sit, we were just about to begin." Leora had created a nickname for almost everyone by now. She was patting the empty floorboard beside her.

Salt was generally used for protection, left on doorsteps and windowsills, but when used to form a circle, it provided more than that. It held and purified the energy within it, for spellcasting.

"What's this for?" Thessa asked, knowing very well what it was for.

"The Communication Spell, I've decided to do it." Leora glanced at Ivy and Beatrix. According to Leora, the two witches were the queens of the laundry room. "We were talking while folding, and they said they wanted to help. With their magic to support the spell, now I can really speak to my parents."

Thessa nodded and sat beside Leora.

She knew Leora was practicing her Communication Spell, but without magic, spells were just unique phrases. It was kind of the Celestial witches to offer their services.

In secondary school, studies focused on curating words and blending herbs, not the *after* part. *After* is what special training and tertiary schooling were for because magic only manifests when a witch turns eighteen. Without it, both their practices had been limited.

When a witch sought guidance or foresight, they'd seek out a Celestial service. Many Celestials go on to be energy readers, matchmakers, fortune tellers, astrologists, palm readers, and tarot card holders.

The four witches sat with four pillar candles between them: representing north, south, east, and west.

Ivy's hair was so straight and light, almost white in the candlelight. It was sheared short to frame her face, with violet dye added to her bangs. Her fair skin had a hint of peach to it, and her eyes were as light as Kellan's.

Where Ivy was like a bright sunrise, Beatrix was like a warm sunset. Her dark bronze complexion complimented her hazel eyes and long auburn hair, which was always in three pigtails—*one for each face of their goddess.*

Ivy added mugwort and clove to Leora's mortar, the herbs needed for a Communication Spell, before crushing them into a fine powder.

Flames flickered, reflecting off Leora's ritual dagger as she braced the hilt and sliced through her palm. She held her bloodied fist over the mortar while Beatrix cleaned her blade.

Once satisfied with her pool of blood, Leora wrapped a cloth around her hand.

Ivy took to mixing and mashing the contents into a paste.

Leora set the last letter she'd received from her parents before her, dipped her finger into the paste, and swiped a five-pointed star on the parchment. Then again across her chest.

Ivy met Leora's focused stare. "Ready?"

Leora replied with a single nod.

Ivy glanced at Beatrix, and the two Celestials began conjuring their magic. Their fingertips glimmered white as their magic readied to escape—concentrating. Heartbeats later, milky tendrils whirled around them all.

Everyone joined hands.

"We call upon our goddess with the help of our moon and stars, to guide our sister." Ivy eyed Leora, as if saying it was her turn.

Leora spoke, her voice fierce. *"Goddess be, you must tell me. Are my parents lost at sea? Take my blood and take this spice. Find them for this sacrifice."*

They all swayed in harmony while Leora repeated her spell.

Thessa couldn't help but stare at the opalescent magic, it was twinkling alive.

One moment Thessa thought the spell wouldn't take, and in the next, Leora's eyelids fluttered closed as her torso flew back. Everyone released their grasp and Beatrix expertly cupped Leora's head before it smacked the floor.

The Celestial magic receded. "She's in, it worked." Ivy confirmed.

"In where?" Thessa wondered, staring at the specks of stardust glittering Leora's bare skin.

"The In-Between." Beatrix stated.

"Right, that's where they say, but what really is it?"

"Hmm." Beatrix mumbled and gestured to Ivy, "You can explain it better."

Ivy cleared her throat before starting, "In school they teach us the In-Between is where souls exist, a medium of sorts, right?"

Thessa nodded.

"Well, it helps to think of it as an invisible layer to our world, one without physicality. A place where aura, spirits, emotions, and vibrations exist. Only souls, spells, and wishes can travel through the tangled mesh of energy."

"Where'd you learn all this?" Thessa asked.

Beatrix chimed back in. "Training workshops at the House of Hekate. They're held monthly without cost."

"But these spells don't always take," Thessa added, glancing back at Leora.

Ivy nodded. "Yes, but we've combined our powers, it's Friday the thirteenth, and I suspect this room is supercharged from the turnover of witches in here."

Beatrix agreed.

Thessa asked, "So she's here, but also in *there*, with souls?"

Ivy answered, "Precisely. Some spells work this way, entrap the soul for a bit rather than letting the spell weave through the framework alone. It all very much depends on the mechanism of the spell or wish. Right now, her soul is doing the work. A Communication Spell typically works like this."

"Will she see her parents there?"

"It depends."

"Depends on what? Wasn't that what this was for?"

Leora shrieked awake. Her eyes were big and *brighter*.

"Leora, are you okay?" Thessa asked, hovering over her.

"I ... I'm fine."

Ivy and Thessa helped Leora up. "Take this, it's sage water." Beatrix handed the glass to her.

"Thank you." Leora gulped it down, panting after it was gone.

Thessa looked directly at Ivy, asking, "Depends on what?"

"*What* decided to find her. Provide the spell, then the magic does the rest. Relics, like the letter, help."

Beatrix added, "The letter held a connection to her parents, so it helps with specificity."

Thessa turned back to Leora. "Leora, are you sure you're okay? Who did you see in there?"

Leora set her glass down. "I'm okay, I'm okay. I saw no one actually. You can't really see in there. Well, I could see everything, but everything this world isn't. It was like a void, of sorts, but it glistened with light." Leora glanced at all of them before saying, "Thank you so much."

"Of course," Beatrix replied.

Thessa was so confused. "So you didn't speak with anyone?"

Isn't that the purpose of a Communication Spell?

"We spoke, but there were no words. I felt it." Leora closed her eyes to breathe in. When she opened them, her tears fell. "My parents, their energy, they were there. It was soft, and so delicate. It was them. I know it. They shared the feeling of peace and certainty, as if this was the path that was set for me, and for them. There was no anger or fear, only rest." Leora looked downward, more tears falling. "They're at rest."

"Leora, I'm so sorry—" Thessa started.

"Don't be. I felt their touch ... their love. It was everything I could've asked for. Then, the goddess came to me."

"What?" Ivy cut in. "How do you know it was her?"

Leora wiped her eyes. "I just do. Her energy was pungent. Soothing all the same. She made me feel like my purpose is soon to come. But it was more like a push. A sensation to keep moving along this path."

Beatrix smiled as she reached for Ivy's hand. "I'm glad it helped, let us know if we can do anything else."

Leora eyed Thessa. "You *could* try too, if you wanted to."

After a brief pause Thessa replied, "Not tonight, thank you."

Ivy said, "Well, you know where to find us. In the meantime, I'm hungry. We could eat in town? You two must be tired of the food here …"

While Thessa was thankful Ivy swayed the conversation, she just wanted to be alone.

Leora responded first, "That'd be so nice."

As they all stood, Thessa said, "Sounds good but I'm going to rest for a bit, work was tiring."

"You sure?" Leora asked.

She forced a smile and pushed words out of her mouth. "I'm sure, I smell like garlic anyway. I'll pick something up from downstairs later."

Leora scanned Thessa. "Do you need anything before we go?"

"No, no, I'm fine."

Leora yielded.

Thessa sighed when the door shut, collapsing on the floor to cry.

Her breath hitched as a flurry of thoughts struck her. She was in a new place, surrounded by new witches, with relatively no time to herself, and too much time to think.

Using magic to communicate with the dead was something she'd thought about doing many times; daily. But she never had magic, funding, or friends to help her do it. She'd practiced the spell, her Communication Spell, over and over, except the thought of what would happen when she'd actually do it was nothing shy of terrifying. Her heart was pounding inside her chest—its cage. If she couldn't find the strength to fight this mental siege, it would win.

Thessa unscrewed the pendant around her neck and breathed. While her body trembled, she traced her fingers along the remnants of stardust on the floorboard. It felt like powdery sea sand. She crumpled some of the shimmering substance between her magic-less fingertips ... then some more.

A part of her wondered if maybe there was still some Celestial magic in the air, if her room was truly supercharged, and just how powerful Friday the thirteenth really was. In her next breath, she'd screwed the vial shut and was up, moving through her things with haste. She fetched her ceremonial dagger, her mortar, the pestle, clove, and mugwort.

Thessa sat inside the circle of salt, candles still aflame, grinding the herbs into a powder. Then she sliced the point of her dagger across her palm and hissed. With an angled fist, her blood dripped, mingling with the herbs. She blended it, not caring about her wounded hand.

Unbuttoning the top of her tunic, she swiped a finger into her bloodied herbs, then painted the five-pointed star on her chest. She had no family relic to add, only blood and her galloping heart.

"*Blood, herbs, heart, and soul. Take my gift, take this toll. Seek my mother, not another. Goddess be, please help me.*"

Nothing.

She repeated the spell, louder this time. "*Blood, herbs, heart, and soul. Take my gift, take this—*"

The room went black.

6

LECTURE NOTES FROM SPELLCASTING AND CURATION:

Never perform spellwork alone. There is a high risk of hemorrhage and head trauma.

Thessa stood frozen. She was in another realm, one cast in dark shadows and mist. The wind whipped past, blowing her hair violently across her face. There was no glimmer, no light, and nothing pretty in sight. The air was heavy and too thick to see anything.

"Thessa." Her name boomed from a feminine, majestic voice. "You've come."

She spun in place, looking for the owner of that voice. There was nothing but darkness. She blurted the first thing that came to mind. "I thought we couldn't talk in the In-Between?"

"This is not what they refer to as the In-Between." The response was snappy and short.

Thessa would've left if she could. Regret weighed on her shoulders like two boulders. "Then where am I?"

"This is your soul. Dark and lovely, isn't it?"

"What?"

"The English language, and other customs your realm adopted from the mortals are nonsensical, my translation may not be perfect, but it will do. The soul is best for direct communication, you can hear me, can you not?"

She kept looking for the owner of that curt voice, an exit ... anything. "We're inside my soul?"

"Well, technically ours. Our soul, yes."

"How?"

"Thessa. Too many questions. Our souls are connected, of course, otherwise this communication would not be possible."

She paused, then asked, "Are you, my mother?"

"That I am, but I am you, and you are me, well, soon to be."

A riddle.

Thessa shook her head, confusion taking over. "What?"

The voice spoke again, "On the Shadow Moon you will know."

"I don't follow the moons."

"You will understand soon."

It was too vague. "You're my mother, but you're me? You realize that doesn't add up."

The majestic voice continued, "You called for your mother, did you not? I did not birth you, but I am your mother. You are of my essence and my blood."

"Hekate?" Was this the goddess of witchcraft? This was far from soothing, as described by Leora. In fact, it felt like quite the opposite.

The feminine voice laughed, sending a rumble beneath Thessa's feet. "No, no. Not Hekate."

"Gaia then?" Could this be the goddess of all living things?

"Oh Thessa, so many questions. There is more to your world than Hekate, and her great grandmother, Gaia. Is that all they taught you in your history lessons? Why am I not surprised."

She wasn't sure the voice knew what she was saying, after all it was working off translations. "So you're not me, not quite my mother, and you're not our goddess, or *the* goddess. So, who are you then?"

"I am all of those things."

Thessa palmed her forehead, mumbling about tricks.

"You will understand soon, the Shadow Moon is coming," the voice continued.

This was not making sense, and Thessa was losing her grip. She sank down and sat on the cool substrate. "Just tell me who you are. Your name. I cast this spell to find my true mother," her voice shook. "And why do you keep talking about the moon?"

"Enough. We don't have the time for all this. I am your mother. I am the mother of thousands. The mother of the *forgotten*. The mother whose children were taken, murdered, tortured, and banished." The voice continued, urgently. "My bloodline has been shunned for two centuries, executed cowardly. What you see is not the darkness to fear, witchling. You cannot escape this."

She blinked, unsure what any of it meant.

"Our time is ending." The thunderous voice faded. "I'm sorry, there's nothing left to hold me here."

Thessa gasped. Air shot in her lungs at the same time her eyes popped open.

Perched over her like a crow, Leora screeched, "Tess!"

Thessa rubbed her temples. "Woah."

Leora wore the face of utter concern as she helped her up

to sit. "I almost lost my mind waiting for you to wake up. Are you okay? What happened?"

Thessa babbled while Leora fetched her a cup of water. "I have no idea what just happened. When did you get back? How long was I out for?"

Kneeling beside her, Leora passed her the glass. "Here, drink." Resting her hand atop Thessa's shoulder, Leora said, "I got back a few minutes ago. I ended up not going. I had a bad feeling about leaving, and now I know why."

Thessa looked down at her wrapped hand, then back to Leora. "Thank you."

"When I found you in the circle, I knew what you did. You know better than to perform spellwork alone, especially a spell like this." Leora's worry shifted to an impressed look. "I can't believe it worked, how'd you do that alone?"

"Ivy must've been right." Thessa scanned the room before continuing, "This room is possessed."

Leora laughed, "Is it?" Her face shifted back to a serious one. "Do you want to talk about what happened?"

Mustering an unfamiliar strength, the witch who'd held in too much, for too long, started to speak. Thessa's words poured out. They were muddled, and there were many, but they came to the surface. She had no home, no family, no love, and now no certainty or purpose.

But there was Leora, the witch full of light and hope despite the darkness she'd been served, listening to her every jumbled word.

7

LECTURE NOTES FROM IMMORTAL GENETICS:

Magic remains unexpressed and dormant until a witch's eighteenth birthday—their Summoning Day. A goddess-chosen object will act as a conduit between the physical and non-physical world, unlocking your power upon contact.

The chatter of witches sounded over the clinking of cutlery. The dining room smelled of cauldron-fried hog belly and something sweet.

The aroma woke Thessa and Leora from their slumber not too long ago. Thessa was on the other side of the kitchen today—her one day off each week, Saturdays.

The shared dining rooms between the two townhouses were filled with witches in the midst of their morning meals. Leora was beside Thessa; Ivy and Beatrix found their seats across from them. She waved to Rhetter and Noam seated at the far end, before pouring herself some tea.

The two long tables were filled with pitchers of sage

water, woven baskets of bread, several sizzling plates of meat, and heaps of fresh berries scattered about.

Her evening with Leora had been late, so late they'd missed dinner and were stuck with the bread and cheese Thessa had scrounged up from the kitchen. So there they were, eating pig like pigs, with berry juice lining their lips.

Ivy and Beatrix were discussing their evening out, but Thessa's mind moved elsewhere. She couldn't stop hearing the voice from the spell.

Leora gave her a look, as if reading her mind. "You okay?"

The witches quieted around her.

Thessa asked, "Do any of you know about the Shadow Moon?"

Ivy eyed Beatrix before answering, "We're Celestials, we study every moon."

Beatrix started, "The Shadow Moon is the darkest of all full moons. It rises once every few months. Its purpose is to cloak the realm in darkness, so it can be born anew."

"Like putting the world in a deep slumber to awake refreshed," Ivy added.

Leora chimed in, "I believe it rises on my birthday this year."

Thessa looked to Leora, wondering why they had yet to discuss this. "And when exactly is your birthday?"

Leora smiled bright, "One week from today. When's yours?"

Thessa's eyes widened, "My birthday is next Saturday, too."

"Twins!" Leora exclaimed.

"A pair of Cancers," Beatrix proclaimed, eyeing Ivy who was nodding. "No wonder we liked you two."

Thessa was more confused than excited.

After their meal, she spent the rest of the morning by

herself. With no desire to perform any more spells, and after promising Leora she wouldn't, Thessa went for a walk into town.

Other than spending the evening watching the sun fade at Crescent Moon Bay, she hadn't explored much of Mabelton since arriving. When her boots met the cobblestone streets, brisk air from the sea brushed her cheeks. There were no belligerent fishermen, shouting guards, or ship horns sounding off here. There were only seabirds, calm water, and a small, private dock. It was nothing like Gravenport, and that she loved.

Thessa walked past the water.

The elm trees grew sparse as the center of town neared. She passed an apothecary, several vendors, a slew of taverns, and gasped at what came next. She pressed her nose against the glass window. The male inside was splattering molten chocolate all over his creation. Drool threatened to fall down her parted lips. Without any Cheltz to spend, she spun around and ran across the street.

The signage overhead read, *The Brew Leaf*. Peeking inside revealed row after row of tea-lined shelves, nestled behind a wooden bar. The side walls were stuffed with books, while the space between offered wingback chairs and small tables.

There'd been nothing charming about Gravenport's smelly fish markets, filthy gravel pits, and suffocating army base. These streets were the opposite. The sounds of cackling, conversation, and music only confirmed it.

Thessa noticed the same signs posted everywhere. "Summer Solstice Festival, the twenty-first of June. Join us on the greens behind the Mabelton Library. Event sponsored by the Mabelton Society."

Also next Saturday.

A solar event and a rare moon; the longest day followed by the darkest night.

Of all the days to turn eighteen ... Thessa's skin prickled as her thoughts twirled. She was still unsure of what to make of everything, especially the riddle.

I am you, and you are me, well, soon to be.

❧ 8 ☙

MENTAL NOTES FROM CHANCELLOR DULAMEER'S COMMENCEMENT SPEECH:

*The phases of our moon represent the eternal cycle
of impermanence and growth.*

The stone was grounding beneath her bare skin, so Thessa laid there, staring at the beamed ceiling of her washroom until her panic subsided.

When she stood to prepare her bath, she couldn't add enough salt. She added some for protection and more for her invisible wounds.

Stepping in, she let the water wrap around her like a silk shawl, before plunging beneath it.

The past week had bled away.

Each day that passed had been a reminder of what was coming. Her quiet hysteria brewed all night—the evening before her Summoning Day. Instead of sleeping, she'd tossed in her bedsheets, trying to tune out her thoughts, and that riddle, until surrendering to the panic.

Thessa gasped, breaking the surface of the water.

When she left the washroom, Leora was making her bed. Thessa asked, "Morning, when'd you wake?"

"Not too long ago."

She exhaled, relieved that Leora had slept through her misery. "Washroom is all yours."

"Are you feeling alright?"

Thessa opened the doors of her wardrobe, trying to focus on anything but her feelings—but it was useless.

"Tess?"

Thessa groaned, turning to face her. "I'm not sure, honestly. I didn't sleep well thinking about all this."

"I'm sorry, I'm nervous too, but I'm especially excited to share this day with you."

"I know, me too."

Leora held her chin high and said, "After I clean up, we're going out for some tea, so get dressed."

"Oh?" And before she could counter, Leora shut the washroom door.

❦

Leora tapped Thessa's teacup. "*May the beams of our sun light our path for years to come.*"

"Happy Summoning Day to us," Thessa added, as light yellow liquid splashed over the side of her rim.

The two witches enjoyed their tea while cackling over the mess they were making. Thessa knew what was coming, Leora too, so they bided their time.

Witches had been taught about their eighteenth birthday since primary school. It was considered one of the most important days of their life. In order to find their goddess-given gift, they must first be called to it.

The gift pulses with anticipation for one witch only. The

invisible presence is similar to a guide in the right direction. Once found, the transfer of energy is instantaneous, unlocking a witch's magic.

"You were right by the way; this place is adorable. I love these." Leora stroked the velour wingback loveseat they shared. "I want one just like it."

"We should save up for one."

The witches smiled, trying to let small talk color over what's to come. They were both excited for their magic, but it'd been unnerving. A tea break was just what Thessa needed, and Leora too, it seemed.

Thessa rolled her eyes. "What if our gifts are back in Gravenport?"

"Not even a curse a witch could cast, Thessa. Of course they won't be, the goddess is with us everywhere we go. You know that."

"Let's hope you're right. Not even magic could drag me back there."

Leora laughed. "You should really come to the House of Hekate sometime. A little faith would do you some good."

Thessa sipped her tea, unsure of how she even felt about the goddess. Which reminded her of something very important. "Leora, I'm so sorry I've not asked. How are you feeling with everything? Everything else, I mean."

"Thank you." Leora took a breath before continuing, "It's difficult, yes, I always expected to spend this day with my parents. But they're at peace, so I'm allowing myself to be too. The routine at the townhouse, going to prayer sessions, having you, Vy, and Bea, has all been so helpful. I feel blessed." Leora paused. "But it's you I worry about, Tess."

Thessa's smile faded. "Please don't, you've got enough to worry about. I'm fine, promise."

Leora raised her eyebrow.

The lie had slipped off Thessa's tongue. She tried to remedy it. "Well, I wish I didn't battle with my own thoughts, but I think everyone does that."

"To an extent, yes, but staying up all night in the washroom is no easy battle to fight alone."

Leora had known then ... the whole time. Thessa dipped her chin in embarrassment.

"I don't want you to hide how you feel from me. *Not me.* I'm not sure if you've realized it, but you're about all I have in Andera, and I care about you. *A lot.* Promise me, you'll come to me next time?"

When Thessa looked up, silver lined her eyes.

"Now drink your lemon balm tea, the tender said it's calming," Leora winked and took another sip. "Because we've got a busy day ... and night," she added with a wicked grin.

"I cannot believe I agreed to this," Thessa mumbled.

"Oh but you did. The festival will be fun, and we'll both need to unwind after today."

The door to *The Brew Leaf* whooshed open, bells jingling. Thessa looked, but no one was there.

Leora squealed, "Tess. Something is tickling my feet."

She looked at Leora, then down at her legs. "Nothing is there."

"Oh, it's something." Leora's smile was glittering. "It's bending around my ankles like shackles, it wants me to stand."

Thessa smiled. "What? Is this really happening?"

"Yes! Let's go."

They stood and dropped the coins they'd received during yesterday's wage distribution. The tender nodded from behind his bar, and the two witches rushed out the door.

They walked together down the cobblestone street, twinning in white muslin dresses and leather clogs. They'd ditched their cloaks today; it was so hot.

Leora squeaked ever so often as the wind pressed her onward, nipping her ankles like a young canine.

Thessa asked Leora, "What else do you feel? I can't believe this."

"My blood feels just as excited as I am, it's bounding, but I'm not sure if my nerves are helping."

Thessa reminded Leora, "Don't worry, we're doing this together." For once, she could offer some support.

They dashed past taverns, eateries, live music, and laughter. The vendors were ahead. Potions, daggers, jewelry, cauldrons, treats, fortune tellers, herbs, flowers, and anything Thessa could ever want was here.

"Come on." Leora grabbed Thessa's hand and started running. "We're close. I can feel it." Thessa sprinted to keep up. There were about six inches between them height-wise, and Leora was all legs. The soldiers in Gravenport would have stopped them three times by now.

Leora halted and Thessa crashed into her; they collapsed in a heap of laughter.

"Excuse me, are you trying to damage my property?" A female witch bent down and assessed, trying to help untangle their mess of limbs.

Beyond the female vendor was a table of shimmering stones. Thessa's eyes could hardly focus on one as she rose to her feet.

"Easy does it, you two, you almost took my table down."

Leora stood and stilled. Her warm eyes were locked on the vendor's crystals. "Sorry about that," she managed, as if in some trance.

Thessa nudged Leora. "Are you okay?"

"You don't see that?" Leora whispered.

"Which one?" There were hundreds of stones.

"Any interest?" The vendor cut in. With Leora's eyes preoccupied, the vendor flashed a dark blue gem in front of Thessa. "Hmm. How about this one, to match those darling eyes of yours?"

Thessa waved her off. "Oh, no thank you."

Closing her palm, the vendor gave Thessa a flat-lipped smile.

"Neither of you see that?" Leora repeated her question. "It's glowing."

"Your gift is glowing?" Thessa questioned her. Sure, gems sparkled in the sunlight, but glowing—no.

The vendor cut in and said, "That explains the ruckus. Summoning Day, is it then? What do you've got your eye on, hmm?"

"There," Leora pointed to a hollowed rock lined with lilac-colored crystals. "That one."

"Ah, my amethyst geode."

Leora eyed the vendor. "Tell me more."

"Amethyst is a gem of high vibration, sincerely, it must be bursting with energy to be chosen for the occasion. Go on then, take your gift."

"How much for it?"

The vendor shooed Leora. "Now, now, the goddess would send me straight to the underworld. I can't accept payment for what's rightfully yours. Go on." She gestured toward the rock with her hands, insisting.

Leora accepted, picking up her gift. Her eyes were as big as her smile. "My whole body feels like it's shaking."

"Yes, yes, that's it," the vendor said.

"I'm right here," Thessa added.

Leora closed her eyes just as her fingertips began to glow. Her power emanated from each like little white halos.

"Leora, open your eyes!"

She did, and then burst into tears, collapsing back to the ground. Her crystal was still cupped in her hands.

Thessa took a seat beside her.

The vendor cleared her throat. "Congratulations, witch. Be sure to tell your friends where you found your gift."

Leora peered up, weeping, and thanking the vendor.

Thessa asked, "Is this what you wanted?"

Leora nodded. "My mother was a Celestial. This was always my wish."

"The stars did well then."

Leora wiped her tears. "That, they certainly did."

"Let's go share the good news with Ivy and Beatrix."

Leora's white-tipped fingers faded the moment she dropped the geode into her satchel. Without her gift's contact, conjuring her power would take practice and training.

On the walk back to the townhouses, Thessa asked, "Have you thought about where you'll train?"

"I've thought about it all my life. But things are different now."

Thessa quieted, listening.

"I dreamed of going to Trinity Tertiary in Captiva, the school my mother attended. I've never pictured going elsewhere."

Uncertain of what to say, Thessa apologized.

"Don't be sorry. I'm not sorry ... not anymore. This is where I'm meant to be. I'm excited for what's to come, and what the goddess has planned for me. I'll start my training at the House of Hekate. I quite like it there."

"And I like the sound of free workshops," Thessa added.

"Indeed. It'll be your turn before we know it."

Thessa's mood withered at the thought.

Leora must've sensed it because she said, "I'm with you, Tess. We're doing this together, remember?"

Thessa nodded, afraid to look at Leora—afraid she'll see her uncertainty. So as they headed back to the townhouses, Thessa looked at the shops, their displays, then the bay, and all the trees instead.

9

LECTURE NOTES FROM SPELLCASTING
AND CURATION:

Spells performed without care are ineffective. A witch must believe in the words delivered.

Thessa stared over the basin, watching the water ripple as she blew out her breath.

She would not retch. She would not.

Any moment now, the goddess would present her gift.

There was a light knock at the door. "Tess, are you alright?"

Thessa's knuckles were white from clenching the sides of the washroom table. She released her grip and masked her tone. "Yes, be right out."

Get on with it.

Ivy and Beatrix had swarmed her and Leora with birthday wishes when they'd returned. Thessa took the opportunity to slip into the washroom, letting Leora fill them in.

Smiling blankly, attempting to hide her disarray, Thessa opened the door.

Ivy and Beatrix were enthralled by Leora's shift. Their excitement was thick in the air while Leora beamed as bright as ever.

Beatrix was commenting, "This is amazing."

"I know." Leora placed a hand over her heart before outstretching the other. "Tess, come, I'd like to say a prayer to the goddess. I want to thank her, but I want to pray for you too, for your gift."

Thessa gestured to decline, but Leora gave her a *don't be stubborn* look.

"Let's pray then," Thessa said with reluctance, and stepped over to the Celestials.

They formed a circle and interlaced their fingers before Leora started. "We join hands to thank the goddess for her offering. Her endless offerings. For our blood, and for our magic. The essence of her being is forever mine, and forever ours." Leora looked them all in the eyes, landing on Thessa's gaze last. "Now we ask the goddess to guide our sister to her destiny. May the strength of our stars light her path into eternity." Nodding in conclusion, Leora asked, "Vy, will you send the prayer up for us?"

"Of course."

The witches released their grasp, but Thessa watched Ivy closely. She held a white-tipped finger out, twirling it in tight circles. Her magic escaped in a tiny wisp, now spinning in the space between them. Thessa noted Leora's whirling finger beside her waist, as if studying Ivy's movements.

Ivy kept her finger working until the Celestial energy froze between them. But it wasn't frozen at all, rather buzzing with momentum while condensing into the tiniest sphere of starlight. Then, she flicked her finger to the sky, and the Celestial Messenger shot through the roof, as if it were air itself.

Leora's prayer would reach the stars soon, and maybe the goddess herself. For what it'd be worth, Thessa was not certain.

Ivy broke up the silence. "Shall we eat while we wait for Thessa's kick in the leg?"

Thessa grinned, the humor easing her nervousness. "I'm in."

"I could eat," Beatrix added.

Leora patted her stomach. "Oh, I'm so hungry after all this."

༄

THE SMELL OF SWEET SPICES SWEPT THROUGH THE DINING room.

Thessa was relieved to be away from the kitchens today, the midday meal was cauldron boiled apples and oats—incredibly crusty and a nightmare to clean.

Waiting for her Summoning was agonizing. Unable to focus on much of anything, let alone converse, Thessa dug into her cinnamon-dusted meal.

The two long tables were full of witches, consumed with chatter about the Summer Solstice Festival this evening. Thessa wondered how she'd get out of that commitment.

She could develop a mysterious illness, or something that would require her bedridden.

Hmm.

It wasn't long before there was a swift thump to her knee —Leora had nudged her. Thessa made eye contact and Leora silently asked if she was okay, but Thessa shrugged. Leora's next look softened Thessa's heart: *I am with you.*

Ivy finished a swig of sage water, then asked no one in particular, "So, who's excited for the festival tonight?"

"There'll be honey mead from Wilcrest. I can't wait!" Beatrix chimed in, nearly lifting off of her seat.

"Is there something special about the mead?" Leora wondered.

Ivy's face lit up, "Oh it's the bees—"

"And the flower fields," Beatrix added.

"The mead is made with their honey. It's so divine," Ivy finished.

Leora smiled. "I can't wait to try it."

Back in her room, Thessa worked up the courage to tell Leora she wouldn't be going to the festival tonight. The panic inside her had been simmering under her skin all week, waiting to boil over. If time between her own breaths was hard, casual talk and laughter would be impossible.

Leora spoke first. "Tess, you're too quiet."

Thessa walked to her bed and curled under her sheets before saying, "It's because I don't know what to say." Leora sat on the edge of her bed, giving her space, but the silence encouraged Thessa to continue. "I didn't think waiting for my magic would be this difficult. Adding the festival on top of today is going to be too much, but I'm happy for you and I want you to go. It's just ... I've barely slept, and I'm so tired. Would you be mad if I didn't?"

"I don't think I could ever be mad at you, especially when you're that honest. Would *you* be mad if I skipped the festival too?"

Thessa objected. "You can't. I want you to play with your magic and have fun. You deserve to celebrate." She pointed toward the room across the hall before burying her head into the pillow. "And they're going to be so upset if you don't go."

"Well, you and I both know Vy and Bea would forget about me the moment their lips touch that mead, and besides they'll miss you much the same."

Thessa rolled back over, facing Leora. "Well that last bit is simply not true."

Leora shoved Thessa's leg over her blanket. "Don't be ridiculous."

Leora's good energy pierced through Thessa's walls, and a grin escaped her. "You're still not staying back."

"Yes, I am. Why are you so stubborn?"

"I thought this was about making me feel better."

Leora pushed her leg again, laughing.

Thessa sat up, asking, "You'd really stay? What about the mead?"

"It's just mead."

"Okay then ... I have an idea."

Leora cocked her head, listening.

10

LECTURE NOTES FROM THE ART OF BLACKSMITHING III:

Tires, rims, or anything round require a block for molding. One end is fixed to your anvil while you strike the other with your hammer.

Sea water caressed the soles of her feet.

Thessa was seated beside Leora on the ledge overlooking Crescent Moon Bay. It was the same boulder she'd sat atop many times before. The warm stone beneath her seat and salt air whipping through her hair were just as calming as Leora's presence.

Thessa looked toward her. "Thanks for coming. You really didn't have to—"

"But I like your spot." Leora cut in. "Thank you for sharing it. You don't have to do everything alone ... You know that, right?"

Thessa shrugged. As the sun grew larger, and the tide higher, she wondered if her gift was somewhere past the horizon, perhaps too far to find her.

Her thoughts were interrupted by the sound of horseshoes clopping on cobblestones. One male hopped off a wagon as it rolled to a stop. He was tall and lean with ivory skin and wine-red hair, long enough to tuck behind his ears. He inspected the wagon, crouching down by the hind wheel before shouting, "It's the rear; the spokes are broken."

A loud curse cracked from the other side of the carriage.

A different male, bronzed from the sun, hopped off next. His ink-black hair was sheared shorter than his companion's but still long enough to catch the light. The shining blue hues reminded her of starling feathers.

Thessa and Leora had already slipped their clogs back on and climbed over the iron barrier between the sea and land. They were approaching the wagon like two curious felines.

The first male continued, "Axel looks in good shape, but the rim is warped. Would need a proper forge."

Thessa's ears perked up while the other male kicked the wagon and grumbled something coarse about cobblestone streets.

What a shame, she thought. Not the broken wheel. It was a shame there was no forge at the townhouses. That's what she needed right now. Thessa missed the workshop. She missed the soot on her brows and the hammering, all of it.

Her trade had been deemed useless in the townhouse. The house matron secured the town blacksmith for all repairs, and for things that weren't even broken—*things* that needed tending to inside her private room, it seemed.

Thessa would huff while scrubbing when he'd waltz into the kitchen after one of his *repairs,* schmoozing the cooks for a free meal.

Thessa and Leora were a few feet away from the wagon when Leora asked, "Everything alright?"

Thessa gestured at the bent iron and broken spokes. "Their wheel is mangled."

Leora made an "O" shape with her mouth, before restarting, "Well, our townhouse is a short walk away, our matron can request the smith, if you'd like."

Thessa grunted.

Leora elbowed her.

The red-haired male replied, "Thank you, but we're expected at the festival before it begins. We'll have to make the rest of the way by foot."

"But what about your wheel?" Thessa asked, eager to fix it even though she had no tools.

"We'll figure it out," the dark-haired one answered before turning back to his companion. "The greens aren't far, grab a barrel, we're walking."

"What's in the barrels?" Leora asked. She'd never been one to mind her own, so why start now.

The red-haired one replied, "Sack mead, my dad brews it. I'm Emiel by the way." He smiled briefly, but long enough to reveal two dimples and lively green eyes.

Leora and Thessa eyed each other in silent agreement— these males were delightful to look at.

"This is my friend Soren, please ignore him," Emiel added before turning toward him. "I can run back for the last barrel while you set up and serve? I'm faster than you—"

"And leave me to fend off the murder of witches?" Soren pointed toward her and Leora.

"Did you just refer to us as a flock of crows?" Thessa asked sharply.

"Vultures, better? These barrels will last this festival an hour, two tops."

Thessa ignored him, her nose high.

Unloading the barrels, Emiel repeated his question, "So I'll run back for the last barrel?"

Soren rolled his eyes. "Fine."

Thessa and Leora jostled their heads in silent conversation and then Leora spoke for the pair—one of Thessa's favorite parts about their friendship. "We could help carry the last barrel."

"No, you can't—" Soren started.

Emiel objected, "Yes, they can. They're quarter barrels, together they'll be fine."

Soren pursed his lips, shaking his head at Emiel. They were having a silent conversation of their own, it seemed.

Leora interrupted, "Listen to Emiel. You have little time before the festival begins, and we can help. I'm Leora by the way." She tilted her head to the right before saying, "And this is my friend, Thessa."

Emiel shouted at him, "Load 'em up."

Soren's nostrils flared as a barrel rolled and landed perfectly beside Thessa, as if it were magicked to.

Thessa peered down at the oak cylinder, bulging slightly at its center. She may not be strong enough to carry this alone, but she could manage it with Leora.

Soren stepped closer, hoisting the barrel up for them. When his gaze locked on hers, she couldn't help but see what was missing. His eyes were as dark as a moonless night, like any light that'd been there, was stolen away.

"Are you sure?" he asked. "Those arms look quite small."

Thessa furrowed her brows. "Hand it over," she ordered, then looked over to Leora and said, "Keep it low for me."

Leora nodded, each of them gripping their end of the barrel before Soren let go. Thessa's knees buckled at the shift of weight.

"Commanding little witch you are," Soren noted.

His arrogance was slithering under her skin. "Shall I drop it on your foot, or should we get on with it?"

"Thessa!" Leora objected, "She doesn't mean it, it's been a long day."

Soren grinned. "For us as well." He yelled back to Emiel, "Roll me the last one, tie my horses, and let's get out of here."

Thessa mumbled under her breath, "And I'm the commanding one?"

As the four witches lugged their barrels on the path toward town, Leora asked, "Where were you two coming from?"

"Wilcrest," Emiel answered. "I take it you're both from Mabelton?"

"We are now. We left Gravenport about a month ago."

Soren muttered something unpleasant before Emiel shushed him and asked Leora, "How do you like it?"

"It's been wonderful, I like it very much, but it's nothing like Sanabria." Leora's smile was serene.

"You're from Sanabria?"

She nodded. "Captiva, it's in the south."

"I hope to make it there one day."

"I'd be happy to help with travel suggestions." Leora paused before adding, "If you'd like."

Emiel's eyes lingered on Leora's; her burgundy lips curled in response. His questions about the eastern continent flowed from there, occupying Leora, and filling Thessa's head with mindless words.

"That's it, right up there," Soren shifted his barrel to one arm, pointing toward the expanse just beyond the library.

Between the bay, the males, and this strenuous walk, she'd been successfully distracted. She hadn't thought about her gift, not until the library greens neared.

The festivities were in the midst of creation.

Mabelton Library was modest, made of brick like the path leading up to it. Stained-glass windows flanked the garland-decorated entryway. Its greens were vast, and full of marquee tents draped with gray linen canopies, braziers blazing, and witches scurrying around.

She hadn't paid much mind to the Elemental soldiers on guard, not until they started lighting the lamps. As the sun drew closer, and the sky cast a golden hue, Thessa remembered it was called Summoning Day for a reason—it was supposed to happen during the day.

Leora may have come to the same realization; she eyed Thessa warily as they stepped onto the greens. They were quickly consumed by festival hosts, the Mabelton Society members, and were shuffled toward the food and beverage vendors.

Familiar smells of smoke and herbs filled her nose. Pigs and goats were roasting while cauldrons were boiling. One food tent was full of breads and cheese wheels, while another was packed with berry-topped cakes and chocolates.

Her mouth was watering.

She noted the next tent, stacked with elixirs and mood-benders, before getting distracted by the massive willow tree across the field, and the stage beside it. Musicians were tinkering with their flutes, fiddles, and enchanted amplifiers.

Slicing through her daze, Emiel wrapped his arms around their barrel, relieving her and Leora from duty. "Thank you. I'd like to offer you both some mead once everything is set up. On me, of course."

Leora declined, "Thank you but we'll be leaving." She moved some of her chestnut curls out of her eyes; the longing in them was not lost on Thessa.

Thessa looked toward Emiel. "Mead sounds perfect, thank you."

He smiled but looked confused.

Leora met her stare with a brow raised high. "Are you sure?"

Thessa nodded. She needed this. She hadn't known that before, but she knew it now. Maybe her gift would call for her soon, but probably not. Jerking her head toward the weeping willow tree, she asked Leora, "Can we talk for a moment?"

"Sounds settled then. I'll see you both soon." Emiel winked at Leora before taking his exit.

Thessa watched the rosy color bloom on Leora's cheeks as she watched him go. She gave it all of a moment before clearing her throat. "Shall we?"

Leora snapped out of her love spell and grabbed Thessa's hand. "I was hoping you'd ask, let's go."

As they walked toward the old tree, witches holding trays of tulip-shaped glassware and buckets of ice hurried past them. Ice in Andera was harvested from the mountains in Greenshire, kept cool magically by the Elementals who transported their supply across Andera. After release from the army, work for Elementals varied. There were artistic avenues like fire dancers, glassblowers, and ice carvers, then the more practical applications, like cooking, lamp lighting, sailing, and blacksmithing. Others were hired by the most fortunate, contracted for heating and cooling their homes.

Thessa rested her shoulder against the furrowed bark and began. "I think we both know my gift isn't coming, there's barely any daylight left." She gestured to the dimming sky between the swaying branches. "I feel somewhat relieved, in a way. I've been orphaned my whole life. I've always suspected my birthday may have been some placeholder, and now I know. So, I want to stay. I want to drink Emiel's mead, and those mood-benders we saw, then I want to forget about my gift." She shook her head, before adding, "At least for tonight."

Leora forwent words and embraced Thessa.

The long, wispy tree branches swept around them as cooler, night air blew past. Their breath synchronized on an exhale before releasing their grasp.

Leora's round eyes met Thessa's with sincerity. "Thank you for talking to me, I can't imagine how you feel. But when your day does come, I'm going to be right here. And I think enjoying the festival is a good idea, but when you're ready to leave, you'll let me know, okay?"

Thessa nodded, but she was certain of her decision: to stay and forget.

Leora continued, "Let's go see about that Emiel—I mean mead." She grinned wickedly.

❧ 11 ❧

LECTURE NOTES FROM HERBOLOGY 101:

Elixirs are herbal only, whereas potions are both herbal and charmed. Charms are a temporary form of magic, diminishing with a set time. They require a carrier, so an herbal liquid is common.

Today was not her birthday. How old was she? Who was she? Those were not questions Thessa needed to worry about this evening. She'd spent enough years doing that.

This night was for feeling less, or more, or something else—anything but her thoughts.

The sun faded, leaving skinny ribbons of gold weaving through the dark sky. She could barely make out the two males serving mead beyond the crowd of witches. Soren had been right, they were flocked. She even spied Noam and Rhetter waiting in their line.

Thessa and Leora eyed each other, agreeing to flee. They skirted right, towards the food.

The Elemental in the tent before them was finger-searing meat sticks. He held a wooden skewer in one hand and used a flaming-finger from the other to crisp the edges.

A few Cheltz later, they were eating goat thigh on sticks and headed toward the next tent. The one full of botanicals.

Waiting in line, Thessa engulfed her meat. The bitter char on her tongue tasted heavenly as she glanced around the tent. The elixirs and potions were arranged by color, in different vials and pitchers. The lighter the color, the milder, according to the signage.

Many Botanical witches were masters of chemistry. If not healing, they were often found gardening, tea-tending and brewing concoctions for various purposes.

Thessa stared at the specials listed on a hanging chalk-board with Leora. For the mood-bending effect she desired, Thessa would need a potion.

Leora had left the choice up to her, not encouraging, nor discouraging.

The vendor eyed Thessa now, awaiting her order.

"One Violet Dream, please."

"Make that two," Leora added.

"That'll be five Cheltz each." The Botanical witch with silver hair but a face of youth, drummed her bone-thin fingers along the make-shift bar top.

As Thessa reached into her satchel, Leora dropped ten coins in the vendor's open palm. The witch closed her fist and spun around. "This one's on me," Leora said, smiling.

"You didn't have to—"

"I know but I wanted to, and I secretly wanted the same thing. Good choice."

"Thank you." Thessa half-smiled as she read the description again.

Violet Dream: butterfly pea flower tea with added euphoric and energy boosting effects.

When bony fingers flashed before her, they were holding two vials that contained no more than a gulp. Snatching their mood-benders, Thessa and Leora ditched the tent.

Witches were everywhere now, some in groups and others coupled.

Standing there with lush grass under their clogs, Leora questioned her, "Are you sure you want to take this?"

If Leora was searching for hesitation, she wouldn't find any. Thessa tipped her head back and gulped the potion down.

"To the music?" Thessa asked, tossing her vial and stick in the nearby bin.

"That answers that." Leora followed suit.

Hand in hand they walked across the field, toward the sounds of flutes and fiddles. Some witches were sitting for the show, but most were dancing. Thessa moved along with the music, entering the crowd.

With the potion setting in, her body felt lighter, and her mind buzzed with—nothing. Nothing at all. She and Leora danced together for a while, before parting into their own moves.

The bottom of Thessa's white dress muddied as she twirled. She didn't care about the dirt. She didn't care about anything other than the music and the handsome fiddler who kept eyeing her. His mahogany eyes and hair were so beautiful. So was Leora, and everyone else around her.

A male voice cut across her ecstasy. "Think you could get away without your fair wages, did you?"

Thessa and Leora whirled to see Emiel standing under a string of lamplight. Soren stood behind him, like a shadow.

Leora launched with her arms outspread. "Emiel!" She hugged him as if he were her long-lost friend.

"Someone found the potions tent, I see." Emiel smirked as Leora squeezed. His cheeks turned as bright as his hair. "Go on, take your mead," Emiel pleaded, working desperately not to spill the glasses in his hands.

Leora pulled back and flashed a smile, swiping it from him.

Emiel eyed Soren—who was holding two glasses of mead —and jerked his head towards Thessa. She went to take one, but Soren's grip was too strong. It splashed over the rim at her attempt.

"Are you sure you didn't want both?" She asked, brows scrunching.

"You don't need any mead, you're—"

Thessa rebutted, "It was one potion. And we earned this. Hand it over." She really wanted to taste it after all the jabber about wildflowers and honey.

Soren spoke through his teeth. "Vulture."

"Enough." Emiel eyed Soren, shushing him.

Soren—now sour-faced—gave her the mead. "Fine."

Thessa retrieved it with a spiteful smile.

"Well, we must say a toast," Leora said. Nothing would break her spirit.

"That we must," Emiel countered, tipping his glass to meet Leora's.

Thessa's glass followed next, and Soren's last—as if he was forced against his will.

Leora laced her voice with elegance. "*A wise witch once said, leave strife for yesterday and bestow what's ahead; forever we are blessed, so let's raise a glass instead.*"

After their rims clinked, Thessa took a *big* sip.

Delectable wasn't the word, it was realm-shattering good.

As mead fell down her parted lips, she wondered how long Soren had watched her. Long enough to see her wipe it away, she supposed.

Soren snapped his focus to Emiel. "We need to get back."

Leora pressed Soren. "But Emiel just told me all the mead's gone, what for? Can't we dance?"

"The hosts would like us to *clean*," Soren pressed back, flashing his teeth. There was something different about them, or maybe Thessa was envisioning sharp things. Years of forging would do that to a smith.

Emiel shook his head. "We can *clean it* later, let's enjoy the music first. Come on we never get to—"

Soren ignored him and walked away.

Thessa didn't care, she was back to dancing.

"He's not always this angry." Emiel spoke over the music. "Well, that's not entirely true, but he doesn't mean any harm."

Leora shook her head, sipping her mead and dancing too.

"Emiel, he can call me whatever he wants, your mead is amazing," Thessa slurred.

Leora cackled and Emiel joined their dance, joined Leora really. It wasn't long until Ivy and Beatrix found them, squealing over Thessa's change of heart.

Soon, the greens turned into a blur of lamplight and music. Ivy and Beatrix were nose-to-nose, Emiel and Leora too. Thessa danced and danced, letting the bright sounds of flutes and fiddles consume her thoughts—other than wishing that warm-eyed fiddler would come twirl his fingers through her hair instead of that instrument.

That was until her euphoria was overshadowed by screams of terror. Witches were running about. Some were fleeing, others poised their daggers, but many were jumping as hundreds of juvenile serpents coiled through the field. The grass did nothing to mask their black and blue iridescent scales.

Many scurried between limbs and wrapped around ankles. Thessa saw a cook take a butcher knife to one, only for it to grow a new body from pure remnants. There were daggers swinging all around her now, and the serpents kept multiplying. Some witches must've thought continuous chops would yield less serpents. That it did not. Slice after slice; more and more. The field was consumed in minutes.

Thessa stood frozen as Emiel mouthed an apology to Leora before running back toward the tents. Ivy and Beatrix must've run for the streets. The crowd moved around her, Leora too.

She'd not purposely stood still. She'd never witnessed a Multiplicity Spell. They were forbidden. It didn't change the fact that the serpents seemed harmless. There'd been enough to overrun a town in hours—with the wrong kind of retaliation.

They were slithering up her legs now.

The Elemental soldiers were shouting in unison, "Exit the field! Everyone off!"

Most townsfolk had already fled. Many bolted down the cobblestones, while others gathered at the edges of the greens to watch. Though, some were still in the field, in a state of shock, like Thessa was.

The ground was a rippling heap of blackness.

"Get back! No one is permitted on the field!" The soldier before her repeatedly shouted.

Thanks to his piping hot fingers, Thessa woke up. He was flinging the snakes off of her before pushing her chest back and back.

When her clogs clinked with stone, she blinked, taking in the chaos.

Soldiers rallied. Two split off to incinerate the border of the greens, creating a shallow wall of fire. Any serpents that managed to escape were flamed by other Elementals patrolling the area.

With flame, there were no remnants for reformation.

Before Thessa took her next breath, the soldiers set the entire field ablaze. She winced at the onslaught of heat. All the tents, the stringed lights, the potions, the food, the instruments, the chairs, the beautiful green grass, and the sweet old willow tree, were bathing in fire.

A fiery solstice, indeed.

Her upper lip curled as ash feathered on her hair and atop her bare shoulders. She'd never felt more at home in her life. *This* was what it'd been like living in Gravenport. To think she'd almost forgotten about Andera's Army of Egomentals while living in Mabelton.

Incinerate and forget, should be their slogan.

Thessa preferred using fire to create, not destroy. How could a power be so beautiful, and yet so ugly?

"Tess! I lost you, are you okay?" Leora was in front of her, panting.

Ivy and Beatrix trailed close behind.

Leora peered at the scorching field behind her. "I'm so glad I found you. This is madness, we have to go home. We shouldn't be here."

Home.

The word ripped through Thessa's chest. She hadn't known the meaning of it since she was born. She didn't know who her parents were or where she belonged, and never would.

She walked back to the townhouses with the others. While there was talk about magical serpents and fire, she had no words to share. Leora eyed her when they passed the bay, and the tree where the two horses were no longer tied. Only a wagon with a mangled wheel remained.

LECTURE NOTES FROM PRINCIPLES OF WITCHHOOD:

Neglecting your Summoning will lead to death by asphyxiation. The air serves one purpose—to guide you to your powers. Similar to a serpent, it will wrap itself around you and pull. If you do not abide, you die.

Thessa's blood was thrumming, urging her to wake. The pang of panic had been a familiar echo in her body, however tonight felt different. The feeling of serpents encircling her limbs accompanied the buzzing in her veins.

Thessa jerked upright and whipped her linens off. Instead of shimmering scales, or hissing creatures, darkness swirled around her lower legs. It was an opaque, yet airy substance, and black as the pinpoints of her eyes.

As she covered her mouth to silently scream, it crept higher, trying to push her out of bed.

Thessa dropped her hands and whispered, "You can't be serious."

Inky tendrils followed her as she tiptoed across the moonlit room.

Leora was still in the midst of her mead and mood-bending slumber. Thessa thought about waking her, but it didn't feel right. None of it had felt right. Her Summoning was happening in the middle of the night.

She pulled open the massive doors to the wardrobe, grabbed her boots, and slid them on. Peering down at her sleeping tunic, she tugged at the fabric. It outlined the shape of her breasts and exposed her upper thighs. She'd worn the same one when Kellan had come to her chamber back at CSA, begging for a *goodbye*. Ridding the thought of his searing gaze upon her skin, she swung her cloak around her shoulders and buttoned it up.

The air was circling her hips now, like a belt. She watched a thread escape, latching onto her windowsill. A moment later, it began tugging.

"Hades," she swore under her breath.

Mustering some slack from her tether, Thessa managed to reach for her satchel, looping it across her chest.

At the windowsill, she cursed up at the Shadow Moon before ducking out. Thessa descended the wooden trellis of the townhouse, freeing her cloak from catching vines along the way.

On land, the black air churned, encouraging her onward.

Thessa put on her hood and moved. "A Night Summoning?" she mumbled to herself.

Witches were called upon by the goddess during the day, so this had to be some full moon nonsense.

On the Shadow Moon you will know.

What she *knew* was Summonings shouldn't happen at night, and there'd never been any mention of this color.

Thessa was led beyond the residential area and into the heart of town. Most taverns in Mabelton remained open until the sun returned, which seemed to bother her guide. As the noise set in and the streets came alive, it was as if her ink ran dry; the black sheen disappeared.

She let out a breath, relieved a bit, though glad it was still pulling her along.

Approaching a strip of shops and taverns, Thessa kept her head down and hood covering her features. Other than warmth in the winter, privacy was the one thing she liked about her cloak. She ignored the late-night festivities and pressed on.

It wasn't much longer until the smell of ash struck her. She wished to turn back, but the thrumming in her veins intensified, as if to say, *you're almost there.*

A few steps later, it stopped her. She looked up to see the Mabelton Library, seated among a sea of soot. Nothing remained of the library greens, but char.

Her escorting wind swirled away from her, and toward the entry. It may be translucent now, but it left a flurry of ash in its wake. When the doors to the library groaned open, Thessa grinned.

❧❦❧

GRIMACING, SHE STRUCK HER FLINT ONCE, TWICE, THREE times ...

Forget it, too complicated.

Shoving the tinderbox back in her satchel, she squinted for a better view. Moonlight streamed into the library, casting eerie shadows through the stained-glass windows. Thanks to the tin roof, the interior had been unscathed by flames, saving loads of books. There were about a dozen shelves, a long desk spanning the back wall, and several round tables set in the middle of the space.

Thessa breathed in the stale, musty air and pivoted left, strolling down the first aisle. She thought about Leora's gift, glowing for her. Thessa hadn't been so lucky. She paced up one dark aisle of books and down another.

It wasn't until she reached the final shelf that the thrumming in her veins reignited. She swept her fingertips along the roughened spines, desperate for a clue. Every touch felt like she was getting closer. Then, like the force of a lodestone, her fingers halted.

Thessa pulled the black, leather-bound tome free, coughing as dust bloomed around her. It was *very* old. She swiped some grime away, observing what she could. There was a golden triple moon inked on the cover, surrounded by intricately carved borders.

As the buzzing in her veins reached a crescendo, her magic burst to life.

"No, no, no."

Her fingertips didn't shift into Celestial white, Botanical green, or Elemental blue. They were pitch black.

Thessa wasn't a witch at all; she was a demon.

LECTURE NOTES FROM REALM RULES & METHODOLOGY:

Hexes and curses are strictly forbidden in Andera. The mortals burned our kind on stakes for such reckless acts of magic.

Thessa watched the sunrise from the ledge overlooking the bay. Once the birds sang their morning tune, she dragged her feet back to the townhouse.

She pushed through the entryway doors, strode across the checkered tile, up the winding staircase, and into her shared bedroom.

After closing the door, her mouth fell open. Small bursts of air escaped her lungs as the room spun in circles. She sank to her knees, falling victim to the panic clawing its way up her throat.

Soon there were strong, smooth arms wrapping around her. Leora's hushed voice begged her to breathe slower.

Thessa couldn't, she sat crumpled.

Leora's arms helped lower her down until she was lying on her back. Through her tears, Thessa could barely make out the thick beams of wood cutting across the ceiling.

"I want to tell you a fairytale my mother would tell me before bed, especially on hard days."

Thessa's breath and mind were both ragged; she was unable to speak.

So, Leora shared her story.

"There once was the happiest little witch, skipping through a field full of flowers. She was on her way to the forest for a tea party when a toad leaped in her path.

He asked, 'If I could grant you one wish, what wish would it be?'

The witchling twirled in her pink ruffled dress, then wished for her woodland friends to come to life, and for a true tea party.

'Granted,' croaked the toad.

That's when she invited the sweet toad to join her, and so, they crossed the small river leading to the forest together. He even taught her how to hop across the lily pads, keeping her shoes clean and dry.

Entering the forest, the witchling was greeted by a creature shaped like a mushroom, wearing a small, yellow hat. Another creature, made of twine, curtsied and offered her a flower crown. There were rabbits tending to the tea, and foxes dusting the tableware with their tails.

As the guest of honor at a true tea party, she was as happy as a little witch could be. When it was time for her to return home for supper, she hugged her woodland friends goodbye, and offered the toad a kiss on the cheek. 'For the happiest day of my life.'

The toad replied, 'Anything for you, princess.'

She smiled, feeling like a princess.

Back at home, the little witch told her parents about her tea party over supper, which happened to be the same story her parents listened to her share every night.

You see ... a long time ago, when the little witch was even littler, she fell. One rainy afternoon, on her way to the forest she tumbled down the riverbed and crashed into a boulder. She didn't know it, but that toad watched it happen. He couldn't help the sleeping girl, but she was breathing, and beautiful. He croaked as loud as he could, trying to signal for help. When no one came, he sat with her for hours, watching her chest rise and fall. He felt horrible and most of all, useless. But, when the sun began to set, a large male with identical white curls as the witchling came and scooped her up.

Guilt and worry consumed the toad, so he followed them, leaping as fast as he could. When she was carried into a house, the toad hopped from windowsill to windowsill until he found her. It was there where her mother wept, and her father prayed. It was there he watched the healers come and go, shaking their heads.

Days like that turned into weeks.

But one day, the toad yawned awake on the witchling's dewy windowsill ... and so did she. He leaped for joy, as did her parents.

But not all was well. She never remembered her fall and she couldn't store new memories. She woke up each day reliving the day of her fall.

So, every afternoon the little witch would skip through the field of flowers. Amidst the multi-colored blooms, a toad would leap into her path. He'd ask her, 'If I could grant you one wish, what wish would it be?' She would twirl in the same pink dress she picked out every day. Side note: my mother said her parents would terrorize the tailors until they made the same exact dress for her every year. Anyways, she'd wish for her woodland friends to come to life, and for a true tea party every time.

'Granted,' the toad replied, today and every day. Because while the witchling's wish was to have a true tea party, it was the toad's wish for his true love to live happily. So he waited for her every day, making sure of just that.

But what the little witch didn't know, nor did her parents, was that a long time ago, in a kingdom not so far away, a wicked queen cursed a magical princeling. She cursed him to a lifetime as a toad, until true love kissed his lips. The princeling didn't know he would fall for a girl who woke up each day without a memory of who she was, but he spent the rest of his life as a toad, granting her wishes, and getting kissed on the cheek, so long as she remained happy."

Thessa whispered, "Only you would have me feeling sorry for a toad trying to kiss a child. At least tell me he got his true kiss eventually?"

Leora laughed. "My mother said they went on to live *happily ever after in the afterlife.* Then, she would kiss me goodnight and say, *"You must seek happiness every day my little Ora. Sadness will come in waves, some are small and others are larger, but there's always a break. Just remember what's inside,"* then she'd wiggle her finger on my chest until I giggled before adding, *"That's your heart in there and you must feed it with love."*

"Quite the lesson for a child."

"Indeed."

Thessa sighed, unaware of when her pulse and breath had calmed down. "Thank you, Leora, I—"

"You don't have to talk."

"No." Thessa sat up, unlaced her boots, and slipped them off. "I *need* to talk to you."

The two witches curled up together in Thessa's bed. Facing Leora, Thessa asked, "Promise you won't tell anyone?"

"Tess, don't be ridiculous."

"I'm serious, promise me."

"I swear across the stars. Now out with it, where were you?"

Thessa swallowed before answering. "My Summoning."

Leora shot straight up and screeched, "What?"

"Shh."

"What happened Tess? Tell me everything."

Thessa whispered, "It happened around witching hour. I was called back to the library. My gift is an old tome."

"A Night Summoning," Leora said the words slowly.

Thessa sat up. "You've heard of it?"

"No, I just like the sound of it. How peculiar."

She shook her head, refocusing Leora. "You don't understand, I can't conjure my magic."

"I can barely either, that's normal in the beginning."

"No, I mean I can't *show* anyone."

Leora's puzzled face flashed with clarity. "Oh, no. Tess, I'm so sorry."

All those nights ago, Thessa had shared with Leora her biggest fear—to become one of *them*, an Elemental. She knew the last place Thessa wanted to go was back to the capital for training.

"No, it's not even *that*." Worse she wanted to say, but couldn't bear it.

Leora's gaze narrowed. "Show me."

Thessa spoke through her teeth. "*I can't.*"

Leora cocked her head in confusion. "I'm going to tell you this again, Thessa Skiafer. You're about all I have in Andera and I care about you, a lot. Now out with it."

"You're stubborn too, you know that right?"

Leora grinned.

Thessa threw her covers off and crept across the room, to the space where she'd collapsed earlier. As she pulled the tome from her satchel, her magic sparked to life. Her heart thumped in her chest, but she turned back to face Leora— whose mouth fell open.

Thessa's words came out in a rush. "No one can know. Tell me it's a curse, tell me I'm hexed, tell me we'll figure it out. Tell me it's not what I think it is."

Leora's mouth was still resting in that "O" shape.

"Say something," Thessa pressed.

"I—I—"

Thessa groaned and dropped the dust-ridden book. She was done with her magic, done with her gift, and done with everything.

But the impact caused the book to fly open. The pages flipped frantically while Thessa's hair blew in their frenzy. The inked parchment shifted back and forth, until settling.

Nervousness edged Thessa's voice as she said, "I know gifts are magical and all, but *that* was not something we learned about in school."

Leora agreed.

Thessa peered down at an otherworldly, dark feminine figure with raven-like wings drawn across both pages. "Who, or *what* is that?"

Leora scurried over to her. "I'm not sure, but we'll figure this out together. Hex, curse, or—" Leora paused before adding, "We'll undo it."

Thessa bent down to slam the old book shut, unbothered by its delicate structure. Her demonic magic sparked at the touch. Shaking it *all* away, she stomped to her wardrobe, opened the doors, and stripped from her sleeping tunic at last.

She changed into a linen dress and glanced over her shoulder. "Get changed then, we're leaving."

⚜ 14 ⚜

LECTURE NOTES FROM REALM RULES & METHODOLOGY:

Charms, enchantments, and glamour spells must degrade with time, otherwise they are forbidden.

Starlings warbled in the distance. The smell of ash was just as potent as last night when they neared the Mabelton Library. Thessa forced herself to take a deep breath after Leora asked, "Are you going to tell the book-keeper it's your goddess-given gift?"

She exhaled audibly. "No, I can't risk him asking about my magic." Standing before the soot-stained path, the two witches made eye contact, signaling their plan intact.

Act casual.

Thessa rejected the threatening déjà vu and slipped inside.

She'd worn gloves today. It was not unusual to wear gloves in the warmer months because magic was considered sacred. The privacy they offered was a tradition passed down after inhabiting the Mortal Realm. In her case, they'd hide any trace of her corrupt magic.

Thessa and Leora strolled up and down the aisles of books, side by side.

After tabbing through the one she'd found the book in last night, the pair aimed for the large desk spanning the back wall. Its thick, red wood was full of knots and imperfections; a cut only found in Greenshire forest.

Behind piles and piles of books, some stacked taller than Leora, stood the bookkeeper.

Thessa cleared her throat before speaking. "Hi."

The bookkeeper had kept his back turned toward them and replied with a surly tone. "Can I help you?"

Leora eyed Thessa, encouraging her. Thessa ignored the magic thrumming beneath her gloved hand and placed the book on the counter. "I have a question about this book."

He turned, meeting her eyes briefly before peering down.

"This one, please." She pressed it toward him.

The bookkeeper quirked a wiry brow as silence filled the stale air between them. He swept a finger across the worn leather before opening it. His hands moved with grace, before frowning with distaste. "Are you here to play tricks, witch? Where did you get this?"

Thessa tilted her head, unsure of his meaning. "I found it right over there." She pointed to the aisle of dusty books, as if she'd just picked it up.

"It's not even a book." He pressed it back toward Thessa, tapping the parchment and flipping through. "Look, empty pages."

He was right, there was nothing to see.

"What?" Thessa replied in disbelief. She tried to suppress the urgency in her tone when she asked, "Can you tell me anything about it?"

"I can't tell you anything about what's not written. I've worked in this library for over one hundred years, I've never seen this. Take this *nothingness* elsewhere, witch." The book-keeper turned, mumbling about tricks, and resumed stacking books.

Thessa scowled at his back while slapping the book shut.

Defeat washed over her as they saw themselves out.

"Well, that didn't go well," Leora mentioned as if it weren't obvious.

Thessa was trying not to panic. "Leora, this is too much. My gift is cursed. Blank pages? You saw it earlier ... it wasn't blank. I give up. I just won't use my magic. I've gone eighteen years without it, I'm good without it."

"Tess! You can't give up."

"Blank. Leora."

Leora shook her head. "Let me have it."

Thessa handed over the tome without hesitation.

Leora flipped through blank pages furiously.

Thessa narrowed her eyes. "See. It's cursed."

Leora shook her head, handing it back. Upon transfer, language and bits of art immediately inked across the worn parchment. Leora's eyes widened as she said, "That's magic Tess! It's just a charm, no curse at all. It must be a protection charm, one that responds to touch ... specific touch."

Thessa slapped the book shut, coming to the same realization.

Leora went on, "The bookkeeper opened it, not you. And earlier, I only stood over it after *you* opened it, I didn't. I think you've got yourself a charmed gift."

"Charms are supposed to diminish with time; this book is ancient. And it doesn't explain why my fingertips turned—" Thessa didn't finish that thought, then whispered, "If it's not a curse, then you and I both know what *this* is."

Leora stared blankly. After all, it's not every day one learns they're roommates with a demon.

Thessa grumbled, "I've had enough," and started moving. Her pace was as strong as her heartbeats.

"I'll pray for guidance," Leora offered, hurrying beside her.

They were both about to be late for their shifts.

15

LECTURE NOTES FROM REALM RULES &
METHODOLOGY:

Definitions from Courtly Affairs
Seized—taken into custody, typically due to a
crime.
Dismissed—released from custody, typically due
to innocence.

Thessa's supple, sudsy hands did nothing for her mood. The chef, Katerine, had the nerve to scold her for being late this morning.

She couldn't scrub hard enough.

Tap, tap, tap, tap.

The sound of steel framed boots on the tile floors sounded. She turned to the sight of an Elemental soldier standing beside Katerine. The chef was pointing toward Thessa while the soldier stared at her, smugly.

He ordered, "Thessa Skiafer, you are to be seized and escorted to the Central Divinity, at once." His tone was sharper than the useless knife she was washing.

"What," she seethed.

The soldier flashed his fire-magic in warning.

Her thoughts whirled. This had to be about her magic. How could they have learned about it so soon?

"You are to be trialed in front of the Supremes. Come willingly, or I will take you."

Rage brewed inside her. She eyed Katerine with venom as she chucked her apron on the floor. Arms crossed, Thessa marched right past the wicked chef.

The soldier was on her tail, continuing his orders. "Get your cloak. Leave all your belongings and bring nothing else with you."

Thessa almost laughed on her way upstairs, if only he knew she had nothing.

He'd waited by her door while she retrieved her cloak then followed her back downstairs. A slew of witches happened to find work to do in the foyer. Emberly pretended to dust the molding, Hyacinth was sweeping non-existent dirt on the floors, and Magdalene was wiping a rag against thin air.

Thessa hissed at them.

The soldier grunted, pushed her out of the town-house and into the carriage before slamming the door shut.

"Leora! What are you doing in here?"

"Tess! What's happening, what's going to happen to us? They just took me. I didn't have a choice."

The horses whinnied, likely from the whipping they'd received to move the carriage onward.

Thessa whispered, "Did you say anything about my magic?"

"Of course not. What's happening?"

Thessa shook her head. "Listen to me. If you submit,

they're harmless enough. It's the Supremes who make the decisions, the soldiers are just their pawns."

A thump sounded through the carriage wall, "Quiet, that's an order!"

Thessa stuck her tongue out, managing a laugh from Leora. "Only you would find amusement right now."

"It's just that, this is reminiscent. You stuck your tongue out on the way here, you're sticking it out on the way back." Leora's smile faded quickly. "Do you really think this is about your—"

Thessa just shook her head and mouthed the words, "stop talking." It was best they didn't say anything else.

Seated side by side, they rested their heads on each other. Thessa didn't remember her eyes closing, but at some point between Mabelton and Gravenport, she'd drifted to sleep.

In her dream, she was sitting on a cliff, overlooking the sea.

That majestic voice boomed across the shoreline. "They mustn't take you, my child."

Thessa spoke toward the horizon as a delicate wind swept across her cheekbones. "So it's true then, you're my mother?"

"Not quite, but also yes."

Thessa sighed. She wasn't in the mood for riddles. "How'd you find me in *here*?"

"I'm always with you, and all those who share my blood. I'm sorry to come to you like this, but our time before was cut short. More blood next time, dear. I thought you'd cast the spell again, and I wanted to give you time, but now there are things you *must* understand."

Thessa remained quiet, listening.

The voice went on, "My remaining bloodline was diluted after the so-called UnResting. Eighteen years ago I conjured enough strength to plant a new seed—a kernel of my darkest energy—to restrengthen our line. It's the type of power to end the culling, once and for all."

"What are you talking about?"

"Conception by possession, my Thessa. *You*."

Thessa shot awake.

The sound of rain beating down on the carriage reminded her of one thing—Gravenport. The capital should've been named after its perpetual precipitation instead of the little rocks and ports it offered. Even the sky hated it here. Thessa looked out the window, recognizing the gravel streets leading up to the massive iron gates.

Poking Leora awake, she whispered, "I just had the strangest dream, but we can't talk here. Please, whatever you do, just do as the soldiers say."

Leora blinked her eyes open as Thessa mouthed three words, "deny, deny, deny."

Leora nodded in understanding as the clang of the iron gates indicated their arrival.

When the carriage rolled to a stop the door whooshed open—air-magic.

"Out," their escort shouted, before shuffling them inside the Central Divinity. Upon entering, they were flanked by more soldiers.

Thessa and Leora eyed each other warily before they were taken through a smooth marble hallway. Aside from fire-sconces along each wall, it was empty. No windows. No rugs.

From there they were led down a wide staircase, across a corridor, and down another dark stone stairwell.

The *tap, tap, tap* of metal boots echoed all the way down to the stone-lined dungeons.

Thessa wondered how the Supremes had already learned of her magic. She knew Leora, *her sympathizer*, didn't deserve this, and she regretted telling her. It wasn't her fault.

When the soldier halted, fiddling with a ring of keys, Thessa toyed with the idea of belonging down there.

As the door creaked open, fear washed over Leora's face. In some miserable attempt to help, Thessa went in first.

When the guard barked, "Not you," she turned to see an arm outstretched across Leora's chest.

Thessa's mouth fell open to protest, but the solid, steel door slapped shut before she could say anything.

16

LECTURE NOTES FROM THEOLOGY, OUR GODS AND GODDESSES I:

Gaia emerged from the void with her three siblings: Nyx, Erebus and Tartarus. Gaia is the mother of many gods and goddesses, and grandmother to Hekate, our goddess of witchcraft.

Only a flicker of lamplight shined through the small, barred window of her mucky cell. The stone floor was cruel on her back, despite the thin pad provided for the floor. It smelt of fear and isolation in here—things Thessa had been accustomed to over the years. But she worried for Leora, for that light that shined within her.

Thessa wouldn't let it dull.

Knocking on the stone wall proved to be useless, bloodletting included. She watched the black-flecked blood trickle down her knuckles, cursing it under her breath.

She didn't want this.

After wiping her hand on the inside of her cloak, she shouted through the small window, "Leora! Are you okay?"

A bang rang through the corridor, startling her. "No talking unless you're told."

Thessa's nostrils flared.

She sank to the floor, resting her head against the uneven wall. She unscrewed the pendant around her neck, letting the lavender scent fill her senses. Closing her eyes, she breathed in through her nose and out through her mouth, slowly, just as the school healer had taught her. Again and again.

As she opened her eyes to screw the pendant back together, her breath hitched. She'd conjured her magic. Thick, black tendrils had escaped her fingertips, swirling around her.

"Well I am glad someone feels free," she whispered. "What makes you so wicked anyway?"

As if commanded, several tiny wisps floated away from her. Thessa's mouth fell open, not understanding what she'd done.

No, no, come back.

They flew up and out the minuscule window. And a moment later, everything went dark. Her eyes roamed the shadows of her cell for a clue.

What just happened?

Steel-lined boots scuffed across the stone floor just before the dim lighting returned.

Nothing, apparently.

Losing focus, her magic disappeared.

Thessa blew out a breath, thinking. She knew witches used their breath to control their magic, but she didn't know how excitable it could be. Nothing seemed to go wrong, but she wondered what her magic had done. She needed to learn how to control it before ever attempting to use it again.

A soldier started fiddling with keys beyond her cell. "Back up from the door."

When the door creaked open, Thessa panicked.

Then, a plate of steaming food with a cup of water slid inside her cell before they slammed the door shut.

She sighed in relief while her stomach had the nerve to moan, hunger gripping her. It looked like cauldron oats, but smelt like minerals and dust, as if it were prepared on this very floor. Though, unsure when her next meal would be, she finished it all.

As her bladder expanded, she quickly realized what the bucket in the corner of her cell was for.

So be it.

Thessa relieved herself like a caged canine.

Afterwards, she paced around her cell. She'd completed the shape of a square 291 times until the dungeon went dark and the guard shouted it was time to sleep.

She couldn't sleep. Not yet. She thought about praying but didn't even know who to pray to. She didn't know who to curse to, or who her mother even was. She knew nothing.

Your mother was a descendant of my line, the voice had said.

Thessa wished she'd paid more attention in all those theology courses.

Think, think, think, Thessa.

298.

17

THESSA'S PRIVATE NOTES:

Thessa and Kellan, forever.

Thessa awoke to the jostling of keys.

When her cell door creaked open, she wondered if this was all a continuation of one bad dream. Amidst the darkness of her cell, she had no idea what time it was, or *who* had stepped inside.

A hand cupped over her mouth.

She tried to pry it off, until the familiar scent of cedar and smoke overcame her.

Kellan whispered, "Shh, they don't know I'm in here."

After a silent promise she wouldn't scream, he removed his hand.

Kellan's touch sent memories coursing through her, ones she'd happily relive in this depressing cell.

She sat up, observing the shadowed outline of the male she knew all too well. "All uniformed up, I see."

He was one of *them* now, undergoing his mandatory

training.

Kellan shook his head. "We don't have much time, shift change is in thirty minutes."

She didn't know what he must think about her on this mucky floor, or that bucket of her urine in the far corner.

"How'd you get down here?" she asked.

"It's my duty as a first-year to make sure the night guard stays awake. Incredibly low, I know, but because of it, I slipped a sedative in his tea." He smiled brightly.

"Why would you do that?"

"I read your name on the seized list yesterday. I had to see you. You can't tell anyone, or that I came in here ... the cadets share information for rank."

She wondered if he would share her information for rank. "So, you're not helping me escape?"

"Thessa ..."

"What's going to happen?"

"The charges are serious, you know that. But you're innocent, so the trial will be done soon and you'll be dismissed." He sounded so confident. But if he didn't believe her charges, then good.

"I'm scared," was all she managed to say.

Kellan brushed her face with the back of his hand. "I'm sorry they've treated you like this."

Thessa leaned into his touch, craving some sort of connection in this lonely place. "It's not *your* fault."

His eyes trapped hers before she could look away. Lifting her chin with a single finger, he said, "Let me back in."

She shook her head no, but the movement was slow and reluctant.

"Thessa." Her name slipped off his tongue like a plea.

"You still have my heart Kellan, you've always had it." She

paused to breathe, changing her tone. "But you can't expect—"

His lips plunged into hers.

The satisfaction of his touch overshadowed her will to stop. She felt his longing in every press of his kiss. She'd missed how soft, yet needy his lips were.

When his fingertips trailed down her torso, a small sound escaped her. For a moment, she thought he was warming his hand magically. The heat was palpable enough to cut through her lust.

He's an Elemental guard, and you're a prisoner.

Thessa pulled away. "I'm not doing this."

"I shouldn't have," he countered, and stood. His outline was more regal than usual in uniform. "I came to say I'm sorry. I should've said it before you left, and I didn't."

She was at a loss for words.

Thessa had needed an apology months ago, not now. What did he want from her? She had so many questions yet couldn't seem to ask one.

He broke the silence. "Your trial is scheduled at first light. I wish you the luck of a thousand suns."

And then he left.

The sound of the lock clicking into place pierced right through her heart.

Thessa touched her lips, now cold and full of hatred. How dare he kiss her, wish her luck, and then lock her back up. Not even the luck of a thousand suns could help her out of this.

A thousand suns.

Thessa wondered why that sounded so familiar.

A thousand suns.

She repeated it to herself, over and over, until it hit her. It reminded her of that damned voice.

I am the mother of thousands.

Her mind reeled in pieces from her past, remembering the dark deities from stories told to scare witchlings into behaving.

She wondered if the voice meant she was the mother of a thousand *sons*, as in the Oneiroi, and daughters, as in the Keres? The Oneiroi were keepers of nightmares, and the Keres were takers of life.

The same goddess mothered Thanatos, the god of death, and his brother Hypnos, the god of sleep ... which would have made communicating through her dream a possibility.

I am always with you, and all those who share my blood.

The dark energy in her veins was no curse. The magic was not from Hekate's bloodline, rather another.

Thessa gasped in realization.

Her *mother* was the goddess of night—*Nyx.*

Why the bloodline had diminished to demon status wasn't at all surprising, given the stories of nightmares and death. Perhaps the magic had been so spoiled over the centuries, they'd all turned evil.

Then what did that make me?

Her dark thoughts were relieved as dim lighting returned in the corridor. It wasn't long before a tray holding juice and a heel of bread made its way into her cell. It was better than oats, she supposed, and dug in.

After her meal, Thessa gathered her necklace. She wanted to breathe before the trial. She kept her eyes open this time, managing to settle her magic down when it begged to rise. It was the same method she'd used to steady her thoughts— when she didn't have her blacksmith hammer.

However, learning to conjure and retract her magic didn't mean she understood what it did. It wasn't doing anything, and she certainly wasn't going to ask it anymore questions.

The sounds of guards stomping through the corridor sent her skittering to her feet. Her magic dissipated the moment she'd lost focus.

Thessa patted her dress down, as if it would help press out the indentations, but her finger snagged on some fabric. She peered down to find five little holes along her waistline.

Her eyes popped in realization. Kellan had burned right through her dress. Embarrassed over her moment of weakness, she threw her cloak on and buttoned it up.

When the escort of soldiers retrieved her, Leora wasn't in sight. Thessa was led out of the dungeons and through a maze of hallways until they approached a set of double doors.

She took a deep breath as they crossed the threshold of the Trial Room.

18

LECTURE NOTES FROM REALM RULES & METHODOLOGY:

The Troika was formed upon creation of our realm. It consists of our three Supremes, and it is their consolidated belief that will weave your fate. If you ever find yourself before them, I'd suggest you pray to the goddess for grace.

The Trial Room was cast in tawny marble, lit with hundreds of candles, enchanted to float. Guards lined the oval-shaped space where several pews were set before a small podium. The far wall held three golden thrones, one for each Supreme.

Thessa noticed Leora seated on the opposite side she was being led to and shouted, "Leora!"

"Silence! Face forward!"

Thessa scrunched her upper lip.

As a soldier shoved her into her seat, she noticed two other prisoners, all the way in front. She couldn't help but shift her eyes back and forth between them. She knew them.

A bell chimed, snapping her attention back.

A soldier took to the podium and raised his arms. "Rise for your Supremes."

As Thessa stood, she supposed she was in an In-Between of her own, stumbling between what was really happening, and what had to be a long-standing nightmare.

There was a domed door behind the thrones with a wheel-shaped handle. A blast of air-magic from a nearby guard had it spinning. When it opened, the purest of all the realm strode through. The Supremes walked as if the floor shifted beneath their feet. Their thick, long gowns were bound by cords, wrapping around their breasts and knotting along each shoulder.

As they found their seats, Thessa examined each.

The Botanical Supreme's tight, brown curls were trying to escape her hood, bouncing just above her shoulders. Her warm skin and emerald eyes were like mirrors of the land.

The Celestial Supreme's long, silver hair billowed down atop her opalescent gown. Her almond eyes were lined in stardust, complimenting her silver jewelry.

The Elemental Supreme, General Valstrom, had beady eyes and thin lips. Her short, copper hair was hiding beneath her hood, while her expression remained cruel.

Moments later, a guard ordered everyone to be seated as the Botanical Supreme rose, moving toward the podium. She removed her hood, releasing her hair with a shake, and dismissed her escort with a flick of her hand.

She reviewed the pages of parchment before her while humming like a bird. The sweet sound resonated off the walls, until she spoke. "Mr. Soren Whitfield, Mr. Emiel McPorter, Ms. Thessa Skiafer, and Ms. Leora Saint Jamith."

Hearing her name roll off the Supreme's tongue made her skin prickle. The males hadn't known about her magic. She had no magic when she met them. She didn't understand why they were here.

The Supreme looked Thessa in the eye, as if silencing her thoughts before continuing, "The charges are as follows: One, unorderly conduct at a public event. Two, reckless use of magic, including but not limited to forbidden charms and spells. Three, endangerment of townsfolk. And four, the cause of mass extinguishment."

She shuffled the papers before saying, "The case is presented as follows: Several members of the Mabelton Society stated they witnessed Mr. Soren Whitfield, Mr. Emiel McPorter, Ms. Leora Saint Jamith, and Ms. Thessa Skiafer arrive together on festival grounds in Mabelton the evening of June twenty-first. Each male was carrying their own barrel, and the females shared one. Mr. Julian Athel, a Mabelton Society member, said he witnessed Mr. Soren Whitfield opening a barrel just after sundown, and out with it came a tangle of small serpents. Mr. Athel thought it was for amusement, initially, he stated here. But it goes on to say that was until Soren bolted." She peered up and raised a brow at him before drifting her eyes back down to the parchment.

"The power of multiplicity is repeated here, ad nauseam, by the Mabelton Society members, as well as several townsfolk who were questioned after the event. To conclude, serpents were spelled illegally and released with the intention to bring harm, leading to public chaos and grounds incineration, resulting in the four charges today."

This wasn't about her—Thessa fumed in realization.

The Botanical Supreme looked up again, tightening the pile of papers. "Please rise when you're addressed by the Troika." She gestured briefly to her fellow Supremes. "Then you will state your status: at fault, or not at fault. We will begin with Ms. Leora Saint Jamith."

Thessa's heart dropped.

Leora stood with certainty in her stare. Neither of them had to lie. This was the males' fault, let them have the blame. Thessa didn't even want to think about what barrel she'd carried into that festival. She gagged at the thought of her mead being serpent-infused.

"Not at fault," Leora said with spark.

"You may be seated. And Ms. Thessa Skiafer, please rise and state your status."

Thessa stood and cleared her throat. "Not at fault."

The Botanical Supreme nodded once, signaling her to sit. "Mr. Emiel McPorter, you're next. Stand and state your stance."

Emiel rose. "Not at fault, Madame Hearthling."

The Supreme's features hardened as she said, "And Mr. Soren Whitfield, what is your stance?"

Soren stood, slowly. "Not. At. Fault." He'd sounded out each syllable.

Thessa was confused, this *was* his fault. There were witnesses.

The Botanical Supreme lifted her nose and said, "Then let the trial begin."

19

LECTURE NOTES FROM REALM HISTORY:

The UnResting occurred one century after the Immortal Realm was forged. The demons infiltrated our world and tried to seek control of it. The Elemental regime at the time was small, but victorious in battle. Demons were exiled thereafter.

The three Supremes sat atop their golden thrones, frozen like impassive statues.

A soldier called Leora up for questioning first.

Thessa tensed, but Leora's graceful stride and smile were there.

A soldier turned the podium around to face the Supremes and stepped aside, gesturing Leora to stand before them.

The Botanical Supreme asked, "Ms. Leora Saint Jamith, where were you at approximately six in the evening on June twenty-first?"

Leora spoke eloquently, "I was walking toward the Mabelton Library."

"And with whom were you walking with?"

Leora turned, eyeing Thessa, and then the males, before turning back to the thrones. "The witches behind me."

"Please point for the Troika," one guard barked.

Leora turned to point to each of them. Guilt laced her eyes when her finger landed on Thessa.

"Now clarify your purpose in walking toward the library."

"The purpose was to get to the festival before it began."

Leora had never been short for words before. She had to be protecting them the only way she could. The Elemental Supreme was visibly agitated, rolling her hand for Leora to elaborate.

She did. "The males, their wagon broke down near the bay. Thessa and I offered to help carry a barrel, that's all."

The Botanical Supreme asked, "And did you know what was in the barrel you offered to help carry?"

"Honey mead, it's a sort-of wine made of—."

"Enough," General Valstrom snapped. "Did you know about the serpents? The spell?"

"Of course not. If I'd known, or if they were in the barrel I was carrying, I would've screamed and ran the opposite way, just like I did when I saw them at the festival."

The Botanical Supreme exchanged glances with General Valstrom before she spoke again. "You may be seated. The Troika will take a momentary pause for discussion."

The three thrones swiveled, facing away from the court.

A soldier escorted Leora back to her seat.

The room was so quiet, Thessa wondered if anyone could hear her heart galloping.

When the thrones turned back, the Supremes stood in unison.

General Valstrom spoke for the trio. "Ms. Leora Saint Jamith and Ms. Thessa Skiafer, you are hereby dismissed from the court. Mr. Emiel McPorter and Mr. Soren Whitfield, you are hereby seized by the court for a later trial to discuss your sentencing." She eyed the soldiers lining the room and said, "Take the seized back to the dungeons."

Without another word, the Supremes left the room.

That can't be it?

Soldiers were caving in, though Soren growled loud enough to shake the space. "You'll have to kill me first."

In the next instant blue magic was pulsing from every soldier in the room.

The soldier nearest him retorted, "Don't tempt us," as flames streamlined toward the males, wrapping perfectly around their wrists—fire-cuffs.

These were the kind of shackles that burned when you struggled, and Soren was not holding still. He launched his flaming fist into the soldier's nose, then kicked his leg back like a horse, fending off the one behind him. Outstretching both his arms, with a force Thessa had never seen before, he took out the two soldiers barreling towards him.

Every soldier collapsed on impact, but it wasn't enough.

A dozen guards closed in.

Emiel watched in horror, they all did, while the soldiers beat Soren with their air-magic until he collapsed. Despite being cuffed and pummeled from every direction, he kept trying to stand.

A pair of soldiers sent more flames toward him—wrapping around his neck and ankles. They'd cuffed him entirely. Soren's body finally curled on the marble floor, surrendering to each volatile strike after the next.

Thessa cringed, having never seen this use of force before. Air-magic couldn't cut skin like fists or daggers, and perhaps that'd be Soren's only mercy today, because they were going to kill him.

A soldier hauled Thessa back and she turned to see Leora being taken by another. She was pulled through the double doors just as Emiel's head struck the marble floor. Air-magic had taken him out in one swift blow.

Thessa's anger sparked. "Get your fire-paws off me and tell me where you're taking us." Seeing the soldiers abuse their magic fueled something monstrous inside her.

The hand clamped on Thessa's shoulder dug in. "To the Records Department for sign out. Keep walking." The soldier wasn't much taller than her, but the female had arms meant for lumber.

Leora turned her head, trying to face the soldier shoving her along. "What's going to happen to the males?"

"You heard the orders. Back to the dungeons."

A moment later, tears fell down Leora's cheeks.

Her guard snarled, "Now be silent, both of you."

After passing through an endless hallway, they were escorted past a quartet of guards, and into the city services wing. Thessa spied the only bit of peace inside this entire marble fortress—the Solarium. Other than the Blood Moon Rituals performed there, it was left as an observatory for the witches of Andera. The room was magically warmed to support trees shipped in from the eastern continent, Sanabria.

Leora gasped when she saw them, mouthing the word, "palmae."

The wide, light-green leaves were a far contrast from the stubby ones growing in Gravenport. Apart from the trees were florals, surrounding streams of water coursing through the entire room.

But the soldiers shoved them past it, under an archway, and into the Records Department. The space looked much like a library. The marble walls blended with wooden beams and shelving, extending beyond view with too many aisles to count.

Thessa had been here before, many times. It was where she'd collected all her boarding assignments. Every witch in Andera had their own personal file as well; some were more useful than others. Hers had contained nothing but a birth scroll, her boarding assignments, and her Scroll of Achievement. Now, she was about to top off that list with a Seized & Dismissal Note.

The soldier behind Thessa reached around her and rang the bell aggressively, as if she had somewhere else to be.

A voice shouted from a distance, "Be right up!"

The records clerk was just another soldier.

After exchanging salutes, the guard on Leora's back said, "Sign these two out, they've been dismissed from the court. There are no outstanding charges for their record."

"Very well." Retrieving a quill and parchment, the clerk reviewed their names, birth dates, and charges, then began to write.

Thessa's mind shifted to the males. Emiel had done nothing. He'd submitted and still been struck down. And Soren ... had he wanted to die? None of it made sense.

When the seized & dismissal notices were turned around, Thessa and Leora signed in agreement. Afterwards, the clerk retrieved their files.

"Skiafer and Saint Jamith." The clerk smiled. "Thankfully your last names start with the same letter, otherwise I would've been running all over this place."

Thessa wondered why one was so thick while he turned to emphasize the size of his department. Opening Thessa's file first, the slim one, he tucked the notice inside.

As the clerk unstrung Leora's file, letters flooded out. He picked one up, reviewing the markings inked along the top corner. "This one came in from Chrisnol Academy two weeks ago, and Sanabria before that." He gripped another. "This one came from Chrisnol Academy three weeks ago, and Sanabria before that." He repeated similar details for the last and said, "Looks like these hit a dead end and have been stored here ever since."

Leora eyed Thessa. "I never told my chancellor which carriage I planned to take. I didn't decide on Mabelton or Greenshire until the very last minute, well, everything was last minute." Leora's warm eyes held surprise as the clerk passed the stack of letters towards her.

Thessa was relieved to see a glimmer of hope restored in her friend. She squeezed her hand and said, "I can take us out from here."

"Ah, just one moment, here are your carriage tickets." The clerk slid them over.

Leora grabbed both.

After leaving the Records Department, Thessa escorted Leora through the main doors. Townsfolk usually come through this entrance to purchase a carriage ticket, visit the Solarium, visit a cadet, or for other city services.

Thessa almost cried when gravel crunched beneath her boots, but the sky cried for her.

Throwing her hood on, Leora asked, "But what of the males?"

"What do you mean, what of the males?"

"We can't just leave them."

Thessa wondered if Leora had gone mad. "Come on, we have a couple hours until the carriages depart."

"Where are we going?" Leora asked.

"Somewhere we can talk."

20

LECTURE NOTES FROM THE ART OF BLACKSMITHING III:

A dagger must undergo the "true test." Professor Shovak will stab the blade into a wooden surface and expect it to stand. If it doesn't, that's an <u>automatic fail</u>. "A useless blade is a useless fight."

The rain let up, giving way to mist as she and Leora approached the gates of Central Secondary Academy. The school stood on a field bordered by trees the size of mountains, which was a welcomed contrast to the gravel-ridden streets behind her.

Thessa recognized the two CSA guards, who halted them.

She lied, sort of. "I'm here to pick up my final project. Professor Shovak said he left it in the workshop."

And just like that, the gates opened.

School grounds were open year-round for boarding students. Thessa had spent the last four summers strolling through this campus. Most days she preferred the library, but only because the forge was fireless between terms.

Instead of taking the gravel path towards the school's main entrance, she led Leora around the back of the building. "We can talk now, there's no guards this way."

"Tess, that was horrific. Are you okay?"

Thessa shook her head. "I know. I'm not sure, honestly. I'm really sorry."

"But none of what happened is your fault. Well, all last night I kept thinking it had to be about your magic, but this morning everything changed. I don't care about the serpents anymore. I want to know if the Supremes know how violent their guards are." Leora paused, exhaling. "What are they going to do to them? To Emiel?"

Thessa wasn't sure how to say they would likely never be released. She wasn't sure if Soren had been hoping for incineration over imprisonment, but it'd seemed like it.

She said, "I wish I could say I was surprised. Emiel should be okay if he continues to cooperate. He seems to understand the ways here better than Soren does."

Leora went quiet.

Thessa lowered her head and apologized again.

"Stop apologizing for this continent and their sense-lessness."

She still didn't feel good about it.

Leora asked, "Where are we going?"

She pointed to the stone-clad workshop with a long metal pipe jutting out the top. The door was painted green, with the lettering CSA chiseled into the wood. Thessa's smile was small, but it was there. "My favorite place in Gravenport."

As they approached, Leora cocked a brow. "Are you taking me to another dungeon?"

Thessa swung the door open. "Not funny."

The space was quiet and empty. Rays of natural light shining through the windows illuminated her workbench, as if to say, *this seat is open.* Thessa walked toward it. Her eyes moved to the silent forge in the center of the room, and then softened at the memories it evoked. Those were the only flames worthy of her admiration.

"Welcome to the workshop." Thessa pulled an extra stool across her workbench then plopped atop hers. "We can rest here for a little while. No one comes in during the summer."

Leora looked around the room before settling into her stool, perhaps unimpressed with the soot-stained floorboards. "This ... is your favorite place?"

"This place showed me how to turn my misery into something useful."

Thessa tapped her oak workbench then turned in her seat, scanning the familiar space. Something shiny caught her eye on Professor Shovak's desk.

Leora was talking about Emiel, but Thessa's attention was locked. She shot up and paced over, plucking her dagger free. She grinned, wondering how long it had stood upright like that?

Back at her workbench Thessa went on about daggers, and Professor Shovak's theatrics, until Leora cut her off.

"As much as I want to hear more," Leora said politely, "I should open these." She placed the three letters atop the table.

Thessa agreed, sliding the dagger in her boot.

After sorting them by date, Leora used her sharp fingernail—painted Celestial white with shimmering stardust—to flick away each wax seal.

Leora opened the first one and read aloud. "It's from my aunt. *Our sweet Leora, we've sent messages to all the docks up the western coast of Sanabria to stay alert for a missing vessel. We are so sorry this has happened, say the word and we will travel to meet you, we'll bring you home."*

Leora skimmed the rest before trading it for the next one. As she read the words to herself, her eyes widened with shock. When she set the letter down, her tears fell with it.

Her parents' vessel had never returned.

Thessa slid her hand atop Leora's to say, *I am with you.*

The final letter was thick. With tears streaming down her face, Leora breathed in before opening it. After a moment, she dropped the letter and its contents. One of the smaller pieces fell to the floor, like a feather.

Thessa retrieved it, unable to unsee the numbers and signatures. She placed the inked parchment on the table. "Looks like you won't be needing to work at the townhouse any longer." It was funding unlike Thessa had ever seen, well off didn't describe Leora, she was *extremely* wealthy.

Leora explained how the funding department had closed her parents' account and signed over the value to their next of kin. Her parents' fortune was now hers, and her aunt was overseeing her estate until told otherwise.

Estate?

"I'll write the moment I can." Leora pressed, "I can't believe I hadn't thought to update my chancellor, I'll write to her as well. Thessa, you realize what this means?"

"You're moving back home?"

"Sort of," Leora smirked as she said it. "We're going to find somewhere to live together and you're moving in with me."

Now Thessa was crying. She objected, "Don't think for a moment I'll let you stay in Andera when your heart is in Sanabria. What about Trinity Tertiary, your aunt, the palmae?"

"Tess, I have no desire to travel by sea. I am where I am

supposed to be." She paused, wiping her eyes. "I prayed for hours in that dungeon; the goddess showed me the way."

"You can't stay," Thessa urged her.

Leora pushed right back. "Of course I can. But first I need your help."

"Right, we need to get back to Mabelton."

"Before that."

Thessa raised an eyebrow. "Anything."

21

LECTURE NOTES FROM THE HABITS OF MORTALS:

As much as the mortals feared our existence, a small subset chose to mock us. There was a single night of each year—called Halloween—where they would dress up as anything they wanted, including us. The results were disturbing, though some disguised themselves so well it would fool a witch.

The trunks stored behind the Auditorium stage were made of oak, held together by steel bolts.

Thessa smiled in relief. The last two trunks had contained nothing useful. She reached in, her body was halfway inside, and dug through.

Soon, scarlet fabric flew. One set, then two.

"Start folding, neatly," Thessa called over her shoulder to Leora, who was standing behind her collecting the red projectiles. "I knew we had them, the Theater Department reenacts the UnResting every Winter Solstice, it's barbaric."

Thessa hopped out of the trunk and closed it. When both sets were folded, they each tucked one inside of their cloak.

Thessa eyed Leora and said, "Let's get out of here," and headed toward the Auditorium exit.

After crossing the greens and nearing the front gates, Thessa unsheathed the dagger from her boot.

A gate guard shouted, "Point that dagger down and slow your approach."

Thessa slowed, tucking the dagger by her side. "It's from the workshop. My project, remember? I was trying to show you." She made a face as if it were glaringly obvious.

"Sheathe your blade at once. You're still on school grounds," the other guard demanded.

Although soldiers don't take kindly to waving daggers, they're not forbidden. Blades were permitted across Andera. Daggers were as much ceremonial, as they were useful, but the rules on school grounds differed. Here, all blades must remain sheathed when carried, unless in a faculty-supervised setting.

Thessa slipped it back in her boot and lifted both hands. The guards parted and opened the gates with a small whoosh of their air-magic.

When the gates clinked behind them, Leora whispered to Thessa, "Why'd you do that?"

Thessa whispered back, "To distract them from the stolen uniforms bundled in our cloaks. We look like smugglers."

Leora grinned.

They paced away from CSA, and towards their next stop, Gravenport's Funding Corporation. Leora had to make a very large deposit.

After stating their purpose to the guards perched along the entrance, Thessa and Leora entered unfamiliar territory.

Inside, they were greeted by a clerk with mint-dyed hair and a narrow chin. Leora discussed opening an account, then followed him into the back of the building. Thessa waited there, examining the small steel boxes lining the entire space. She drummed her fingers on the iron railing separating her from all the locked-up possessions of Andera.

When Leora returned, she was flipping through a small booklet of slips.

The clerk's presence was warmer than their initial exchange as he said, "We're here if you need us, be well."

Leora muttered her goodbyes, and they were off.

Thessa led Leora through the mist-ridden city before yanking her arm. "Down this way."

"Where are we going now?"

Thessa pulled Leora into a narrow, brick-lined alleyway, and said, "Back here," before slipping behind a row of rubbish bins.

"Tess, why?" Leora's nose scrunched; the smell of fish and rot permeated around them.

"This is the only place we'll find privacy around here."

The trash bins behind the fish market were buzzing with insects. Thessa held back her bile while removing her cloak and dress. Leora was shaking her head when her cloak hit the floor. Thessa wasn't sure if it was because of the uniforms they were changing into, the critters scurrying around before the next dousing of rain, or the filth, but it was likely a combination of all three.

Thessa rolled the bottoms of her sleeves, then pants. Her limbs were shorter than most witches. She flattened down both lapels, fastened the six steel buttons along the front of the double-breasted jacket, then slid her boots back on.

Leora asked, "Do I look alright?"

Thessa nearly lost her footing at the sight of Leora in uniform. "Hardly, it's vile."

Leora countered, "Scarlet is really your color, you know."

"Don't you dare."

Leora laughed while burying her paperwork deep inside her new coat.

"Are you ready?"

"Yes," Leora said. "Just finishing up these buttons."

They ditched their old clothes in the bin and walked out of the alleyway—on guard—like the rest of the soldiers in Gravenport. The feeling of marching irked her bones, but Thessa kept her footsteps intentional and face stern. As long as the rain held off, they'd blend right in. After all, Elemental soldiers were as numerous on Gravenport's streets as the insects were in their alleyways.

She could recite this role by memory alone. She'd observed exchanges between guards since she was born. Even townsfolk had to cross them if they wanted access to the Solarium, carriages, or other city services.

Bending the final corner revealed sky-high gates, glistening with moisture. Thessa reminded Leora, "I'll do the talking, follow my lead." And *only for Leora,* Thessa reminded herself.

She hadn't understood the full effect Emiel had on Leora ... not until she'd spewed her heart out in the workshop after reading her letters.

Thessa's workbench had that effect, it seemed.

When Leora had insisted it was part of her *divine purpose* to save him, Thessa had objected, coldly, insisting not even Hekate would send a witch on a sacrificial mission.

Nothing had worked. Leora would've done this alone, and that was not happening.

Leora's so-called purpose had overshadowed all logic, yet there they stood, before the gates of the Central Divinity. This plan would likely end with fire-cuffs around both their wrists—or worse—but Thessa shook off her lingering doubts.

She'd never let Leora do this alone. Helping Leora, who'd been the one light flickering in her darkest corner, was an easy choice to make.

Approaching the gate guards, Thessa placed her right palm on her left shoulder and lifted the elbow—the proper salute of the Elemental Army.

Leora copied her movements.

A female soldier called out, "Guards, stand to attention."

The guards stood taller, pressing their feet together and saluting.

Thessa could hear Leora's boots crunch gravel as she toe-heeled them closer. She regretted not reviewing some basic commands with her first, but there wasn't time for that.

Thessa spoke in a tone not of her own. "Guard K. Phillips and Guard S. Blooning, reporting for duty."

In unison, the gate guards relaxed their salute. "Orders?"

"Resource Department: Record Keeping." Thessa knew they'd never confirm details of such insignificant work. *First-years*, they'd think. Record Keeping was low priority, nor desired, and considering Elemental soldiers saturated the city, recognizing them wouldn't be an issue.

The guards turned, pushing the gates open with their air-magic.

The clang of iron sent shivers down Thessa's spine. She inhaled what may be her last breath outside the gates before walking through.

Get in. Get out.

THESSA'S PRIVATE NOTES:

~~Thessa and Kellan, forever.~~
Does he even love me?

Blending in with the interwoven guards, Thessa and Leora stepped inside the marble fortress.

The Solarium straight ahead was tempting Leora, however, they had to stay on task. Instead of turning toward city services, Thessa tugged Leora the opposite way. The metal lettering overhead read, *Restricted Access*, and there was a quartet of guards blocking the long hallway.

Thessa tapped her shoulder before speaking, "Guard K. Phillips, escorting Guard S. Blooning to her quarters. She seems to have gotten lost." The respect for new cadets was minimal, and Thessa had used that to their advantage.

The quartet stood to attention, mumbling something brash about first-years before parting.

They marched down the never-ending hallway until it came to fork. Right looked familiar—the dungeons were that way. Turning left, they entered another hallway cast in sleek marble.

It was eerily silent until a group of guards burst through a door, laughing with relaxed shoulders.

Thessa kept her eyes from bulging and her pulse steady as the group crossed their path with nothing to say but brief hellos.

Off-duty soldiers.

Leora whispered, "Do you think we're close?"

She nodded.

When the guards turned the corner, Thessa jerked her head toward the door they'd exited from. She pressed her ear against it, encouraging Leora to do the same.

Thessa listened and asked, "That's jabber. Right?"

Leora nodded.

"This has to be it. If anyone greets you, just remember your name. And don't salute off duty, that's only at posts." She opened the door and stepped one boot in front of the other.

The room was vast with cots assembled in rows. Hundreds of cadets were stationed here. She paced forward, unsuccessfully holding back a smile knowing she'd just infiltrated the residential quarters.

Fire-spewing fools.

Thankfully, the guards in here were not paying them any mind. The ones that weren't sleeping were reading, eating, or flirting with each other. About a third were asleep, the ones on night duty, she supposed. She scanned the mounds of bodies, but it wasn't hard to spot the soldier who'd taken bites from her heart. He was lying on his side, and that chiseled jaw was prominent from across the room.

She spoke out of the side of her mouth. "That's him."

Leora pivoted for the water table beside the door; Thessa's pulse quickened as she made her approach.

She used the empty cot across from Kellan to sit, and for a moment, she watched him, wondering how his lips maintained that puckered shape while he slept. Then, she poked him.

When he blinked awake, she returned the favor and cupped a hand over his mouth. "Shh."

Kellan's eyes shifted from dazed to furious as he forced her hand off.

"Ouch."

He pressed up, looking left and right, then spoke through his teeth. "What are you doing here?"

"Oh, but *I just had to see you*," she mocked his words.

His eyes trailed along her uniform. "How'd you, are you—?"

He started but Thessa shushed him again, there was no time to explain. She leaned closer, whispering, "Give me your keys."

"What? Absolutely not."

"Kellan, I need the keys."

"Thess—"

She cut him off. "Don't say my name here. The keys."

He threw an arm up. "What's gotten into you?"

"Not your concern, just like my heart has *never* been your concern. You won't ask me another question unless you prefer to be implicated, right? Give me the keys and report them stolen when you wake up."

Kellan scrunched his face in disagreement.

Thessa held firm. "You owe me."

He rolled his eyes and mumbled, "My boot," before slamming his head into the pillow.

23

LECTURE NOTES FROM ANIMAL HUSBANDRY:

Knots —

Horses require slip knots. If they startle, all it will take is a quick pull and they're free. They're far too large to panic safely. Canines require the opposite. The stronger the breed, the stronger the knot.

Thessa turned to Leora, smiling wider than she had in months. "We did it."

They marched from the residential quarters and toward the dungeons, not paying any mind to the guards they passed along the way. Walking with purpose was what kept them from being stopped. Soldiers were always confident—despite being pawns—that she knew. Moving past each guard with the keys inside her pocket kept her heart thumping and feet moving.

When they reached the wide, marble staircase, Thessa

made eye contact with Leora. There were no guards at the bottom, just a hall leading to a single iron door.

They stepped down.

Thessa reached for the keys and sifted through them. The lock was circular with four indents, so it wasn't difficult to match. She pushed it in, and the satisfying click had her smirking. They slipped inside, shut the door, and wound down the dark stairwell.

When the smell of rock and moisture hit her, it sent a familiar prickle down her arms. Landing at the bottom she overlooked the dungeons, lit by a single flame, watched over by a single guard.

Her smile faltered.

The guard was larger than most. He stood to attention. "Orders?"

Thessa and Leora stopped, tapping their shoulders in salute. Thessa recited their names. "Guard K. Phillips and Guard S. Blooning, reporting for duty."

"Your orders," the guard repeated, viciously.

She pursed her lips, thinking. Thessa hadn't thought this far, her lies were running thin. "Relieve you of duty, you've been called upstairs," she said blindly.

The guard scoffed. "On whose order?"

When Thessa hesitated, Leora answered, "General Valstrom's. You've been called to review records on the Greenier family, on her behalf."

The guard relaxed his stance and stood. "I see." As he walked past them, he said, "Thank you for the message." There was nothing about his tone that made Thessa feel like he'd believed them.

And he hadn't. The soldier whirled around with a cold expression on his face. "The general doesn't call on fifth-years for record review."

Thessa had known that, Leora ... had not. She swore under her breath as Elemental magic, the same color as the guard's ice-blue eyes, pulsed to his fingertips.

He'd trapped them down here; his massive body blocked the only exit.

Leora stepped in front of Thessa and said, "This is *my fault*. Take me, I'm the imposter." She dropped both hands, spreading her fingers wide. Thessa watched Leora's opalescent magic flourish, giving away their lie.

"Leora!" Thessa gasped, part in shock by her actions, part not surprised, and part impressed.

Leora looked over her shoulder. "Other than praying, I had time to practice last night. I'm so sorry, Tess. The goddess will help us. I promise."

"She better."

The guard laughed, as if enjoying his preys' panic. "What will you *soldiers* do now? Especially with *that* pitiful magic."

Elementals held little respect for any magic other than their own, of course.

If she was going back in that cell, she'd do it on her terms. Thessa drew in a breath before stepping beside Leora. "There's a wall behind us, you know. Must you play with your meals first?"

The guard snarled, Thessa's words awakening an animal within him.

What he hadn't known was that there was an animal inside her too, desperate for escape. "Move." Thessa shoved Leora behind her, taking the witch off her feet. "Let's have it then, me first."

The look on his face turned wicked as he drew both arms towards her. Thessa stood tall as he sent flames spiraling around each of her wrists.

The guard sneered, "Too easy," then looked to Leora,

sending fire-cuffs around her wrists too. "You should've thrown some stardust out for good luck," he chided.

Leora whimpered in pain.

"No!" Thessa called out, trying to shield Leora from him. Searing pain coursed through her arms; pain so awful she collapsed. She panted through her teeth, refusing to scream.

"Now that I have you both cuffed up," he drawled, "what fun shall I have? I've been wanting to practice some new methods of interrogation."

His magic continued to glow; his personal supply of cruelty illuminating the dimly lit hall. He stepped closer and laughed again. "Looks like I get to do whatever I want."

Thessa glared. "Hades wouldn't have you, you know. That's likely why you've been assigned to dungeon duty. I can't imagine anyone wants to be around *you*."

He crouched down before her, flashing his teeth.

Thessa jerked back in response, pain coursing through her again.

His flaming fingers wrapped around her neck and squeezed. "Shut up, witch," was all he said.

Thessa was trapped between her last breath and scorching heat. She closed her eyes remembering what she'd practiced, even blocking out Leora's cries.

When she opened them, her fingertips were as black as soot. One pulse of her magic and the fire-cuffs around her wrists vanished. She eyed Leora in wonderment, but her cuffs were still intact.

The guard stopped sneering and released his grip. "What in the—"

Thessa spat, "As I was saying, even Hades would find you rather unpleasant."

He stood, taking his hands into the shape of a ball and conjuring a sphere of flame so hot that Thessa began to sweat. "Looks like today is my lucky day. I get my very own demon to play with."

The flaming ball hovered atop his hand, looking strong enough to sear a hole through her abdomen. Thessa rested a few feet away from death, and she had no idea how to use her magic.

"Tell me who sent you?" he asked.

She wouldn't tell this flaming puppet anything. An inhale for strength sent her magic free, but the silky, black ribbons only twirled around her.

Help.

As if listening, her magic hovered before her, like a shield. A speck of fear shone in her predator's eyes, but it was gone in a blink. "Last chance."

Thessa pursed her lips.

His face shifted into disgust as he hurled the flaming sphere towards her.

Leora screamed.

Thessa curled, bracing for impact, but the fireball was consumed by her magic. Sizzling smoke remained in its wake.

The guard's eyes widened as he roared, "Demon filth." He conjured another fireball, this time as big as his oversized head.

Thessa snapped, "You'll kill us both with that thing."

He grinned. "I should've known you're untrained. This is fun." The guard drew both arms up, the flames swirling with fury between his palms. "If you won't speak, consider your deaths my honor, it's always been my honor to loyally serve Ander—"

His words were cut off by thick tendrils of black magic entwining his neck. He began choking for air. Without control of his breath, he couldn't control his magic. The strength of the fireball in his trembling arms weakened, but he fought to steady it.

Thessa wasn't sure how her magic got there, especially when it was weaving through her lower legs like a stray feline.

The guard's eyes bulged as he fought to breathe, his fireball was fading as much as Leora's fire-cuffs were ... until it all fizzled out. Fear washed over the guard's features as the dark magic morphed from murky to shimmery smooth, and hissing. He reached for his neck, clawing apart the serpent strangling him.

The slimy thing did not budge, and the guard had no air left.

Leora squeezed Thessa's arm as they watched him go down. He fell to his knees before toppling forward. The thud of skull on stone made them both shriek, and her magic retreat. When the serpent dissolved into nothing, Thessa squinted, unsure of what had just happened.

On cue, Leora stuttered, "W-what just happened? Did you do that?"

"She did not," a low voice grumbled, popping Thessa's eyes wide open.

Another voice, lighter, called out, "What exactly are you two doing back here?"

"Emiel!" Leora was on her feet, running toward his voice. Thessa watched her rise to her toes, reaching through a barred window. "I know, it was foolish, but I had—"

She'd stopped talking because Emiel had kissed her. Thessa never thought a smile would bloom on her face in a dungeon, but there it was.

She fumbled for the keys in her unfamiliar pockets and paced through the corridor. "I should've known it was you."

He grumbled, "Leave before they change shifts."

Following the sound, she spoke through the door. "Easier

said than done, your friend is currently latched onto mine." Shoving key after key into the lock mechanism, which proved to be more complicated than the first one, she finally got it.

The door creaked open.

"They've tied you," she said.

Soren's hands and neck were bound, leashing him to a hook. He was curled on his side, lying half-naked on the floor.

His body looked like it was carved from the stone he'd surrendered to. A mass of muscle rested along each rib line, while his arms and abdomen held strips she'd not known could exist.

Despite being riddled with bruises, she made out a black serpent tattooed along each arm. They traveled to his chest, where the two heads met. Even in the dim light they shined blue, just like the ones from the festival.

Kneeling beside him, Thessa unsheathed her blade and sliced through the ropes between his wrists.

He cleared his throat. "Why is it you keep appearing and insisting on helping?" His tone was spiteful.

She ignored him and kept sawing until it severed.

Next, with a single swoop, she sliced through the rope tethering him to the wall.

"Don't move," she said, moving the edge of her blade against his neck. They'd wrapped the rope three times before knotting it.

The first layer sawed off easily, and the second unraveled well enough, but the third gave her trouble. It was adhered to his smoldered flesh.

When her blade got too close, he let out a low growl.

"Hold still," she said, "it's really stuck," and started nicking the threads with the tip of her blade instead. She got too greedy and her hand slipped, cutting him.

As black-flecked blood dripped, Thessa recoiled. "You're a demon."

He huffed, pressing up to sit. "Don't call me that."

"It's what you are, is it not?"

He ignored her, wiping his neck clean.

Her eyes betrayed her, moving to his waist. She didn't know what that V-shaped area was called, but it was very distracting. It tapered down like the tip of her blade.

"Tess!"

She blinked, breaking her stare.

Leora shouted again, "Come get Emiel! Let's get out of here."

Thessa sheathed her blade and stood. "I thought you were dead, by the way. And to answer your original question ... I owed you this time, but I'll have you know, *serpent-wielder*, you were not part of the plan. Grab your cloak and put your hood on, we're leaving."

There wasn't time for a rebuttal, she jiggled the key free and took off.

Once Emiel was out and cloaked, Thessa and Leora refitted their uniforms and hoods. The flame-retardant material had kept them intact and concealed their burns well enough.

A loud thump snatched her attention. "That should hold them off a little longer," Emiel noted after locking the guard in his cell and patting the door for good measure.

The other prisoners wanted nothing to do with them.

Thessa and Leora escorted Emiel and Soren out of the dungeons, up the wide marble staircase, and toward the long, infinite hallway leading towards city services.

This role Leora enjoyed a bit too much, it seemed. She ordered Emiel to stay silent while whispering something in his ear that made him blush brighter than his cloak.

Thessa was almost half the size of Soren, but pretended not to be. She held her head high and marched, pressing him onward. Touching him reminded her of how he looked curled on the floor, first in the Trial Room, and then in the dungeon.

Had he truly wanted to die?

They'd lost time, but if her calculations were correct, they'd be traveling toward Mabelton in less than five minutes. There was only one more barrier—passing the same guards at the Restricted Access border.

When the infinite hallway came to an end, Thessa's group slowed their steps. Twenty paces away from the guards, another set of four approached. The groups of guards stood to attention, greeting each other. It was a quick exchange before the original four split off, marching right toward her.

Thessa's heart pounded.

She whispered, "Heads down," then extended her voice, "Keep moving and keep quiet!" There was still a role to be played. She knew they couldn't stop now, not without suspicion. Nudging Leora, she encouraged her to keep up her ruse too.

A few feet away from the guards, Thessa's hope shriveled. She peeled her mouth open to spill some lies, but the guards parted, letting them pass.

Soren muttered, "Shift change," under his breath.

The new group of guards were still flattening their lapels when Thessa and Leora saluted. They were paid little mind as the guards were still adjusting to their shift. There was a collective sigh from Thessa's group after they rounded the final corner. A few more strides and they pushed the males through the main doors.

As the clock tower rang, a jolt of energy shot through her. *Noon.*

The driver in the first carriage called out departure to

Greenshire, and the one in back shouted the last call for Mabelton. Thessa moved with determination, swinging open the door to the rear carriage. They all trampled inside. And they weren't alone. A lone female sat in the far corner.

"Tickets, tickets." The driver popped his head into the wood-paneled cabin.

Thessa eyed Leora, who then handed the driver their tickets.

"Two tickets and four passengers, two of you are out," the driver grunted, throwing his thumb back.

Leora pulled out the booklet of payment slips she'd received from Gravenport's Funding Corporation and infused every word with Elemental ego as she said, "Get us to Mabelton without a word about missing tickets, or my companions, and you'll be compensated well enough to leave this dreary city forever."

The driver examined Leora's booklet, mentioned something about having a quill, then spun around and slammed the door shut.

24

LECTURE NOTES FROM HERBOLOGY 101:

The strongest of Botanical magic can grow an herb from dirt, cultivating life itself. The mortal serfs and their green thumbs were never magicless. Take our Botanical Supreme for example, with the power of Earth Rendering.

Thessa awoke to the smell of salt air and fresh moss. She sprang upright, unsure when her head had landed against Soren's shoulder. Her cheeks flooded with heat, but thankfully, he'd been fast asleep.

Thessa rubbed her eyes, coming to terms with the three possibilities that existed by now. Honorable Kellan had reported the keys stolen, the guard had been found locked in a cell, and messengers had been sent with warnings about rogue guards and prisoners escaping.

"You're up," noted the lone witch, Quinnley, while peeking out her window covering. "We're at the border now."

Thessa looked to see border guards directing them towards the river.

Quinnley was a freckled brunette who'd remained mute during their carriage ride south—they all had. Hours in, Leora had broken the silence. One question had been all it took to keep Quinnley talking until Thessa had fallen asleep. She'd been going on about her Botanical magic, her love of potions, the salves she'd been working on, and all the flowers she'd hoped to collect in the southern territory. There'd not been one question raised about their unseemly carriage entrance. There was only uninterrupted information about bee balm and sea lavender before Thessa had slapped her eyes shut.

When the driver halted the horses, he came around to open the carriage door and shouted, "Ten-minute rest."

Leora lifted her head off Emiel's shoulder as both males groaned awake. Quinnley squealed before jumping out.

Thessa left next, embracing the late afternoon sun with a smile. She scratched the horses' chins on her way upstream, nestling her knees into the riverbed. She didn't have to look up to see the cloudless sky, the water reflected that for her, as well as the fatigue under her eyes, and the way the sun made her onyx hair shine with violet streaks.

Cupping her hands beneath the surface, she drank, then scrubbed her face.

When her reflection eclipsed, she turned to see Soren settling on his knees beside her. He hadn't greeted her—nor thanked her for untethering him—instead, he gargled and spit water.

She rolled her eyes and stood to leave when he spoke under his breath. "The outfit suits you well."

She paused, wondering if that was some sort of compliment. They were about the same height as he knelt there. "Excuse me?"

He eyed her, clearing his throat and said, "It suits you."

Thessa knitted her brows. "And what's that supposed to mean?"

"Since we've met, all you've done is give orders. You're just like *them*."

"You don't know a thing about me."

He stood, towering over her.

Thessa didn't cower, she lifted her chin. "Your reckless use of magic is exactly why we're in this mess."

Venom brewed in his obsidian eyes. "*Reckless?* Have you seen the burn marks on your neck?"

"Have you seen yours? We could've all been killed because of you."

Soren lunged down, leaving an inch between their noses. "*Me?*"

Every second that passed without giving him an answer had another muscle in his jaw twitching. Thessa delighted in it for another moment before stomping back to the carriage.

While still within earshot, she glanced back to say, "You're welcome, by the way."

She made sure to sit beside Emiel and Leora for the last leg of the trip. They'd collected about a dozen apples for the ride and she helped herself to their stash.

Quinnley, seated across, was whistling while sorting through what looked like freshly picked hemlock flowers.

Soren made his way back into the carriage last, not bothering to look at anyone. The tension rolling off his cloak was thick enough to quiet them all, including Quinnley—his new bench mate.

As the carriage rolled on, Thessa bit into her apple and stewed. Her long-awaited plans for normalcy were diverted thanks to her forsaken magic, a lovestruck female, and the brute sitting across from her. If she wasn't caught for impersonation and releasing prisoners, it'd only be a matter of time before her magic was discovered. She wasn't sure what that meant for tomorrow. Leora's plans aside, living as a solitary witch was starting to feel like a real possibility.

After dropping the core of her apple into the small bin, she leaned her head against the window. She grazed her fingertips over the burns along her neck before gathering the delicate chain beneath her uniform.

Thessa pulled her necklace free, unscrewed the top, and breathed.

❧

THE SUN WAS LOWERING, SHINING BIG AND BRIGHT AS DUSK neared. The golden hues glimmered through the tall grasses and mature trees flanking the cobblestone road.

The townhouses were a mile south from the carriage drop-off point, and the center of town was a half-mile from there.

Leora was borrowing the driver's quill to fill out his payment slip. Thessa didn't want to ask how much she'd offered to keep him quiet.

Soren had taken off already, and Quinnley was strapping her belongings across her back.

When Leora parted ways with the driver, she took Emiel's hand and looked back to Thessa. "Are you coming?"

"Right behind you." Thessa waved her off while mouthing the word "go."

Leora smirked before turning her attention back to Emiel.

"Let's go." Thessa hurried Quinnley, unsure why she was even waiting for the witch.

The first few minutes of their walk had been quiet, but Quinnley's fidgeting was hard to ignore.

"Such a useless thing to gather."

Quinnley twirled the plant with fern-like branches between her fingers and said, "Oh but they're beautiful, one would not disagree, would you?"

Thessa glared at the clusters of tiny white flowers before saying, "What does it matter how pretty they are, they're deadly."

"Not all deadly things deserve dislike. And tell the witchlings who cough until their lungs bark how useless it is. In the smallest of doses, of course."

"Is that why you've picked it then, for settling coughs?" Thessa's tone was skeptical.

Quinnley's emerald-green eyes met her stare for a heartbeat before darting back to the path ahead. "I gather many plants. The purpose of some yet to be studied, and others to collect for times of uncertainty. Do you collect things?"

Now was not the time to discuss the collection of handmade daggers she'd left behind in Gravenport. "Uncertain enough not to ask questions about our arrival *and* pick a plant that you and I both know is as useful as a weapon?"

Quinnley's berry-colored lips parted briefly before speaking. "I don't ask questions I don't seek the answers to. I travel alone, most days. And I don't have companions, *unlike yourself.* Plants serve many purposes, yes, but it's them whom I trust. Some may be more poisonous than others, is all. I'll be journeying farther south anyway. No need to worry about my uncertainties, or my plants any longer."

Quinnley picked up her pace before Thessa could reply. She wasn't sure what to make of the witch who skipped past everyone and out of sight. All she wanted was to remove each layer of this repugnant uniform, take a long bath, and eat a hot meal.

With hardly any guards existing in Mabelton, the walk

back to the townhouse had been uneventful. A goodnight warbling of starlings sounded when Thessa stepped up to the front doors. She'd interrupted Emiel and Leora's smooch session and pushed herself inside. The smell of baked bread and clean linens filled her nose as the matron's feline hissed by way of greeting.

"Tess! Wait." Leora said her farewells to Emiel and shut the door behind her.

"You're not inviting him up? I can find somewhere to be …"

Leora was blushing bright. "He's meeting Soren at the wagon."

"Fine. I'm bathing first. You can sit in your filth." Thessa winked and ran up the staircase.

"Absolutely not."

Leora was faster despite Thessa's best effort, and swung their door open first.

As she tumbled inside behind her, they were greeted by two identical witches with skin and hair as white as jasmine flowers; it was a crisp contrast to their rose-red eyes.

"Leora! Thessa!" Ivy called out from behind before bursting through the threshold. "I thought I heard you two." Ivy apologized to Mina and Mora, or Mira and Mona, for the disruption, before yanking her and Leora out of the room.

Thessa huffed.

Leora held her arms up in question.

Ivy shut the door and jerked her head across the hall. "Why are you both wearing—never mind. Come in my room and we can talk."

Thessa followed and her eyes immediately darted to the far corner of the room. She walked over and crouched down, opening her duffle bag. It was meticulously organized. Even the wicked tome was tucked in there.

Thessa could hear Ivy behind her saying, "We had to pack all your things."

Leora asked, "But why?"

"You both didn't have much, I hope you don't mind, but we had to. Beatrix and I did it."

"What happened, is it a short-term stay?" Leora questioned her.

Ivy shook her head. "After you left, the matron came upstairs with Novia. I peeked at the commotion, and they were clearing out your room! We wanted to help, but more importantly do it nicely—Novia's folding skills are atrocious, just ask Leora."

Thessa stood, pivoting around to see Leora nodding. Her legs were weak, but not from her journey south. "But we never said we were leaving."

"You were both seized," Ivy reminded her.

"And dismissed," Thessa added, leaving out the bit about helping prisoners escape.

"You know what, I'm not even going to ask about the uniforms," Ivy declared, throwing her arms up. "Either way, the matron isn't pleased. Fuming, in fact. She kept repeating, *my townhouse, my rules*, while emptying your wardrobes. Beatrix and I told her to go back downstairs, that we would collect your things, and help Novia clean the rest."

"So the matron is replacing us? Is that what you mean to say?" Thessa asked.

Ivy's expression was solemn. "I think the twins' arrival was a coincidence, *but* yes."

Leora exhaled before speaking to Thessa, "If Mina and Mora need a place to stay, then that doesn't make them much different than us, now does it?"

Thessa frowned. "But what about us? I'm desperate for a bath."

"Please, use ours," Ivy offered. "Beatrix won't be back from her shift for a couple of hours. You could sleep here tonight too, share my bed." Ivy was stripping her sheets before adding, "I'll run down and get you some food, apparently the chef isn't happy with Thessa." Ivy eyed her. "So mind your distance."

Thessa took her head between her palms and squeezed.

Leora moved beside Thessa, patting her back. "Thanks Vy."

Ivy smiled, offering them each clean bath linens. "Thessa, go take a bath."

She didn't object, she couldn't hear beyond the noise in her head.

25

LECTURE NOTES FROM REALM HISTORY:

In the aftermath of the UnResting, there were a series of necessary changes. The Elemental Supreme bolstered her regime by enlisting every Elemental in the land for mandatory service.

Thessa hadn't slept. Not one wink. Thoughts of evading Elemental guards and her forbidden magic left her wide awake.

She'd crept out of Ivy's bed, certain she'd spend the night conversing with Hades in the washroom, but the god of the underworld had canceled their plans. Instead, the urge to escape had coursed through her.

Everything she owned was strapped across her back, with the exception of the dagger in her boot. Her duffle bag didn't weigh her down as much as leaving had, but it was the right thing to do.

Her friends didn't need her burden.

As she passed Crescent Moon Bay, and that damned

wagon with the mangled wheel, she cursed about serpent-infused mead.

Signage painted on the trunk of an elm tree read, "Wilcrest, twenty-one miles." It'd take her about seven hours by foot, or more like eight with breaks, but she'd arrive by mid-morning. The soldiers couldn't have what they couldn't find, and Leora would be safer without her.

As Mabelton disappeared, a small part of her hoped she'd run into Quinnley. She wanted to apologize for being accusatory. What she'd meant to say was that she understood what it felt like to be alone. And right now felt no different than living in Gravenport for eighteen years.

Each mile-marker she passed, Thessa grew more anxious. Even her fingertips itched, like her magic was just as tense as she was. When the sun finally graced the sky with its presence, she plopped down to rest. To her relief, the birds were louder, and more distracting than the night insects had been.

She breathed, conjuring her restless magic. Thick, black tendrils flowed from her fingertips, soon shielding her in a plume of smoke. Its dark veil shimmered in the early light.

"Happy now?" she wondered.

They'd never taught her about demon magic in school. Studies of demons had focused on the days leading up to the UnResting, and the exiles that followed.

"Go on then, show me how evil you are."

There was no answer. Her magic hovered around her, rippling like the surface of a quiet sea. She remembered in the dungeon it had never attacked the guard, instead it protected her. The idea contradicted everything she'd thought about demon magic. It was supposed to be lethal, not twirling around her like it wanted to braid her hair.

Thessa exhaled with irritation, effectively ridding her

magic. She got to her feet, adjusted her bag, and continued south.

She'd been traveling alone, on the same dirt road, all night and into the morning, so suddenly hearing footsteps behind her made her heart race. She worried that a soldier had tracked her down, or worse, they'd seen her magic.

Thessa peeked over her shoulder for a clue.

A large, cloaked figure was walking with determined footsteps. It wasn't a soldier's uniform, but their hood covered their features.

She whipped her head forward and walked faster, finding solace in the feel of steel sheathed inside her boot. She may be small, but that meant she was eye-level to some serious organs. Tacking on her vivid memory of Immortal Anatomy lessons, she could figure out where to jab. But before she could recount the major arteries, Thessa was on the ground, taking in a mouthful of dirt.

"Hades," she swore, spitting.

She tried to stand but failed as something tugged at her feet. She looked to see a slimy, juvenile serpent strung around her ankles. Its slitted tongue flicked in and out, as if it was pleased with itself. A binding didn't mean she couldn't defend herself; she wouldn't remain trapped like prey.

Not again.

She pressed her weight into both hands and jumped to her feet, unsheathing her dagger in the same motion. The serpent hissed, tightening around her ankles. She bent down and slashed right through the slimy thing.

When one turned into a dozen, she stopped furiously slicing and looked up to see Soren sneering. There was no way she could move without falling again.

Thessa spoke through her teeth. "I should've sliced your throat in that dungeon."

He removed his hood and dropped his ear toward his shoulder, revealing a fresh cut across his burns. "You already did that."

"How are you even here? Why are you doing this?" She tried to mask the panic in her tone.

He didn't answer.

Thessa just had to lure him a little closer to take her shot. "You're no better than *them*, tying me up like this," she said, glancing at her legs.

He snarled, but not before lunging at her.

Thessa made her move, launching the tip of her dagger toward the center of his abdomen—a large vessel lived there, feeding the entire lower body with blood.

A serpent seized her wrist faster than the blade could puncture the fibers of his cloak. The slithering beast squeezed so tight, refusing to let her hand move.

Thessa kept trying to pierce Soren's gut, shaking with effort while her lip curled. As her fingers blanched and all sensation was lost, she was forced to drop the blade. Unable to stop her momentum, she crashed into his chest.

Soren didn't stumble; he felt like a sheet of steel.

"Pathetic," he muttered, shoving her off.

She collapsed by his feet, next to her useless dagger. Still bound by his serpents, she stared up at him. "Retract your beasts, or just kill me already." She knew death would mean no more tomorrows to fear anyway. "What are you waiting for?"

His magic slithered away from her, shifting into black dust before disappearing into nothing. Thessa wondered how he'd done that, despite worrying she was about to die.

26

LECTURE NOTES FROM REALM RULES & METHODOLOGY:

Multiplicity Spells are forbidden for their ability to impose exponential damage, risking both immortal lives and the land itself.

Soren hunched over her, "I'm not trying to kill you."

Spitting out remnants of dirt, she replied, "I'd argue otherwise."

He picked up her dagger and offered it back, pommel forward. "Then your argument would be as useless as your fighting skills."

She ignored the glimpse of the serpent tattoo looping around his forearm muscles and snatched it.

"You could at least aim for open flesh next time."

She angled her blade toward his face. "Shall I try again?"

He disregarded the gesture with a wave of his hand. "Put that thing away."

Thessa glared at him before sheathing it. She was

outmatched, and he knew it. "At least tell me why you restrained me, that can't be how you greet everyone."

"You flashed your magic. I was curious if you were prepared to fight for it."

Her heart sank. "What magic?"

He stood. "Don't play tricks with me—*demon*." Irony leached from his tone.

"Don't call me that."

"Why not?"

That name made it real. Her magic *was* different; she *was* different.

A small, satirical laugh escaped him as if he'd heard her thoughts. "Denial doesn't suit you as well as that uniform did."

The insult hit her like a stone. She growled and got to her feet. "How'd you even find me?"

"I was resting in the wagon but couldn't sleep, so I left. When morning broke and you—what's the word I'm looking for —ah yes, *recklessly* displayed your magic, I took it upon myself to find out exactly who I was sharing this road with all night. I wasn't expecting the mouthy, small-armed female I just met."

Her eyes bulged with rage. "You've been following me *all night*?"

"You should work on your awareness, and learn how to defend yourself."

She spat, "Excuse me?"

He tapped a finger to his chin. "There's still dirt on your face."

She grimaced, wiping it off with the back of her hand.

"Our magic shouldn't be displayed. Don't show it off unless you're prepared to die for it. Didn't you learn anything in history class?"

Thessa knew very well her magic was a death wish, that's why she was leaving in the first place. She said, "Right. Well, if you're not going to kill me, I'll be going now. I hope you acquired all the information you needed regarding my *skill set.*"

As she walked away, he hissed and yanked her arm. One swift pull from him and they were face to face. "Not before you tell me why you're here."

Thessa recoiled at the sight of his hand on her. It took up her entire upper arm, all he had to do was twist and her shoulder would be sprained for weeks. She spoke through gritted teeth. "I'm leaving." Her eyes floated to his. "I have no place to live, barely enough Cheltz for food, and soldiers to hide from."

He released his grip, and she pulled her arm back, shaking it out.

"Leora deserves a better friend than me anyway." She fanned her demonic fingers, conjuring just enough magic for emphasis. "If you care to stop me, summon your beasts again."

Thessa spun around and kept walking.

Ten footsteps later there were still no serpents. She let out the breath she'd been holding, only to zip it back in when Soren appeared by her side.

"Why are you still following me?" she begged to know, not slowing her pace. Not that it mattered, his strides were twice that of hers. She wondered if he'd intentionally slowed his pace to match hers.

He huffed a laugh. "Following you? I'm going home. The wagon is useless without a wheel."

She forgot he was from Wilcrest. "What about Emiel, where's he?"

"Emiel's fine."

Thessa couldn't help but wonder if Leora would be. She was afraid to ask, but it had to be done. "So, does this mean my friend is smitten with a demon?"

Soren barked a laugh loud enough to silence the birds.

She raised a brow. "What is it?"

"He's an Elemental."

Her jaw unhinged. "What!" It wasn't a question; she was in shock. How was it possible for a demon and Elemental to be friends? Lovers? She had too many questions, unsure where to begin. "So he was a soldier?"

Soren shook his head. "Not exactly."

Thessa didn't understand. "What do you mean?"

His eyes churned like liquid night as he spoke. "Is the female who infiltrated the Central Divinity asking me what *I mean?*"

❧

ACCORDING TO THE LATEST ELM TREE, THERE WERE ONLY A few more miles until they reached Wilcrest. The barren path eventually shifted to a forest, and the foliage provided much needed reprieve from the morning sun.

She hadn't been anticipating company on her journey south. Soren wasn't very pleasant, or talkative. She broke the silence that stretched between them. "You never told me why you did it?"

He sighed. "I already told you. You flashed magic you weren't prepared to fight for."

"While I appreciate the reminder, your methods of interrogation were not what I meant. I'm talking about the festival. The serpents. All of it."

He went silent.

"Go on," She rolled her hand, gesturing for an explanation. He'd have to fly away if he wanted to avoid her.

"It was meant to be a small distraction."

"Small? Multiplicity Spells are forbidden for a reason."

"I didn't expect the *entire* town to be dense enough to keep chopping. I expected witches to flee and distract the guards. I was thinking there'd be minor incinerations ... not setting the entire field ablaze. I shouldn't be surprised actually."

Thessa countered, "No, you shouldn't be."

"You know them well, then?"

She exhaled, knowing who he was referring to. "I was raised in Gravenport. My entire existence has been consumed by Elementals." Including her heart but she didn't feel like getting into that. Thessa tilted her head before asking, "What do you mean a distraction? For what?"

"I needed to search the library."

Thessa scrunched her face. "You risked exposing your magic and using a forbidden spell to search a public library?"

Soren's jaw was working. "It's not a *spell*. That's just the way my magic works. It's a long story. And the book I seek is charmed to be unseen. Another long story, but it's an ancient charm," he explained. "Rather than fading, it requires *our* magic to unlock it, so a diversion is needed. Emiel usually helps with a small fire here and there, but the event was too—"

She cut him off. "How could a book be so important?"

"It's not just a book. It's the Hidden Grimoire of Eiliana."

Quirking a brow, she asked, "Who is Eiliana?"

He paused before speaking. "A fierce warrior who died in the war. Her spellwork was unmatched, which is why I need the book."

"Let me guess ... you didn't find it?"

"I barely had time to skim the shelves. Soldiers surrounded the greens too fast. Emiel and I sprinted to the horses and galloped home. Capital guards seized us the next morning, and you know the rest." Soren shook his head.

"And it only trusts *our* magic?"

"According to the stories told, yes."

She looked up at the sunlight spattering through the leaves and swore to the goddess of night herself. Halting without a word, she dropped her duffle bag.

Soren turned and asked, "Are you alright?"

Rummaging through her neatly folded clothes, she searched until her hands met the smooth leather of her Summoning gift. Her fingertips sparked with magic as she pulled it free. "Here's your grimoire. Please, take it." She wanted nothing to do with it.

Soren chuffed. "I highly doubt you have the book I've spent a century searching for. And stop flashing your magic, haven't you learned anything today?"

Only to appease him, she reeled it in. "It's my Summoning gift, I can't help it. You said your book has trust issues and this book has trust issues, *trust me*." She outstretched her arms farther. "Take it and see for yourself."

He snatched it from her, feverishly flipping through some pages.

Frowning, he said, "They're all blank."

"Go on." She wiggled her fingertips before him. "Introduce yourself."

Soren had conjured his magic faster than she could finish her sentence. "I don't believe it ... this is her handwriting."

"You can keep it, I don't plan on using my magic."

"Then why did I spy you using it earlier?"

She threw her duffle bag back over her shoulder. "I wasn't. We should be going."

As they continued their trek south, he flipped through the old book, utterly fixated. The road forked and Thessa followed him through another wooded path. He'd said the sea was close to his property, so better him lead the way, than her getting lost. It sounded like a perfect place to start over.

"Does a horse sound fair?" he asked.

He must need water, she thought, but amused him anyway. "A horse would be convenient right now, yes."

"No." Soren shook his head. "In exchange for the grimoire. If you truly don't want it."

She choked on her saliva. "You can't be serious." Only the wealthy children in primary school were offered riding lessons. She'd been stuck mucking stalls, although that turned into a task she enjoyed—not the manure part, the horses. They were peaceful creatures.

"You're right. That doesn't sound fair," he said.

"More than fair," she blurted. Transportation aside, a horse would make good company.

He slapped the book shut. "We're talking about a century old quest and your Summoning gift."

"A horse will do just fine. But if you've been searching for it for so long, how'd you know it'd be in the Mabelton Library?"

"I didn't. That library has been searched, along with all the others in Andera. It's not easy finding something charmed to be unseen. Many who've searched for the book never make it home. You saw where we ended up." He shook his head before adding, "Only the goddess could manage to gift it safely."

Thessa's legs were wobbly. It was a twist of fate or cursed luck.

When the trees grew sparse, thick fields remained. The roads may have been full of dirt, but this land was sprinkled with wildflowers. It was no wonder Quinnley had skipped south; it was paradise for a Botanical witch. If Mabelton was charming, Wilcrest was beautiful.

Soren cleared his throat, "My property is around this bend."

Thessa swallowed, remembering to breathe as she followed the demon into his den.

Oak trees lined his driveway, ending in a two-story, weathered wood home, fixed with white shutters. The front porch extended around the house, which was something she'd never seen before. A porch swing, stuffed with fluffy pillows, had a vibrant view of the southern sea. Waves tumbled into the jagged cliffs lining one side of his property, while a pasture filled with horses lined the other.

The barn was twice the size of his home. She could count at least two dozen horses in sight. "You have so many."

"It's the family business, to breed."

As they neared the end of his driveway, the front door swung open. A robed female shuffled outside barefoot. She lunged toward Soren, wrapping her arms around him. Her body was shaking as she spoke. "My son. How'd you escape them?"

Soren pulled away, eyeing Thessa in answer.

His mother followed his stare. She reached her arms around Thessa next and said, "Thank you, thank you, you must come inside, let's get you both something to eat."

Thessa looked up to see a male that looked a lot like Soren standing in the doorframe. Regaining her focus, she said, "I'd love to."

"I'm Soren's mother, Maradine. That's his father, Jussal. Welcome to our home. Come, come." She wiped her eyes free of tears and led Thessa up the steps.

Thessa was inhaling the steam from hibiscus tea in a

matter of minutes. Her first sip was as divine as her last. Maradine refilled her cup while encouraging everyone to eat the pumpernickel bread she'd baked. Thessa didn't need encouragement, she took two pieces.

Sitting around the table, Soren explained every detail to his parents, from meeting Thessa, to setting her grimoire down on their dining table. Explaining the book was her goddess-given gift had done nothing to dull his parents' curiosity. They'd kept eyeing her like she wore three faces. Although, she supposed it was not every day a demon returned from the capital, carrying a spellbook they'd hunted for centuries.

"I've no need for it." She insisted.

Soren glanced at his parents, who were still examining Thessa. "We're giving her a horse in return, we've already agreed to it."

"Ridiculous," his father retorted before looking at Maradine. "Honey, count fifty thousand Cheltz for Ms. Thessa." His father's black eyes bounced back to Soren's. "Any horse she wants, fitted with leathers."

Thessa's breath hitched just before her vision faded to black.

When she came to, there was a cool cloth resting atop her forehead. Opening her eyes revealed Maradine perched over her like a bird, "You're alright dear, you're alright."

Soren helped her sit up. "You fainted off the chair," he noted, as if she wasn't aware.

Her cheeks flushed, nonetheless.

"Stay as long as you need," Maradine offered. "I tucked the envelope of Cheltz in your bag, keep it safe." His mother smiled and spun around, clearing the mugs and plates off the table.

Jussal wasn't in sight, nor was her gift.

She asked Soren, "Can we look at the horses now?"

۞

WARM SUN SPLASHED ON THESSA'S FACE.

Walking into the pasture Soren asked, "When's the last time you rode?"

"I've never ridden."

"You're joking."

"Should I lie next time? Go on, ask again."

He grunted. "Fine. One horse, leathers, *and* a lesson."

Her lips curved up.

Passing a few bay horses with bright white socks, she continued through the pasture.

Soren was on her tail, wasting no time on beginning her lesson. "Horses sense fear, remain confident and the horse will too. Don't stand behind them either, their hind legs can't tell the difference between a friend and enemy, and speaking of enemies, pinned ears mean back off."

She looked over her shoulder to say, "I know those things, I've worked with horses, just not *ridden* them." Thessa turned back and smiled, pointing to a horse she spotted on the way in. "There. How about the black and white patchy one?" Its coloring reminded her of a cow.

"No."

She whirled around, her long hair following suit. "What?"

"No," he repeated, this time crossing his arms.

She scrunched her brows in confusion. "But your father said I could have *any* horse."

"As much as my father would be pleased to get Hades off our property, I won't allow it. That horse is trouble."

"I'd argue the same of you." Thessa lifted her nose, and turned back around, walking toward the horse anyway.

"Your arguments are pitiful."

She rolled her eyes. Stopping about ten paces before Hades, she looked back to ask, "Why would you name him that?"

"It's not a male."

"You named *her* Hades? That's awful."

"Awful? See for yourself."

Thessa approached the mare with her hand outstretched, laying atop it was the carrot she'd carried with her.

Hades' nostrils flared in silent inspection, before bobbing her head in horse-like approval. Her thick, top lip found the carrot and chomped the thing to pieces.

Thessa looked back at Soren. "She's just hungry."

Soren tipped his head back and laughed.

❧ 27 ❧

LECTURE NOTES FROM GEOGRAPHICAL
DISTRIBUTIONS:

There are sea caves in the south-western tip of Andera. Some are quite large, and others too small to explore. Typical creatures that reside in those waters are serpents, slugs, crustaceans and several fish species, well tolerant of dark conditions.

Thessa forgot all about Elemental soldiers when death flashed before eyes.

The moment she'd mounted Hades, the horse reared. Gripping the part of the saddle that reminded her of a hilt, she held on with desperation. "W-woah, woah."

"I tried telling you." The amusement was alive in Soren's tone. Thessa didn't have to look to see him grinning, she could feel it.

When Hades stomped her hooves back down, she exclaimed, "You never mentioned she was unrideable."

His smirk lingered. "Oh, she's fully trained, just dramatic. I suggest you hold on tight."

Before Thessa could scold him, Soren took the back of his hand to Hades' rear and smacked. The horse bucked, sending her forward, before launching out the barn door.

Screaming would require her to breathe and that she could not do. Hades was all might. Thessa couldn't do anything other than hold on tight.

Seconds later, Soren rode past her. Despite the striking pace, he remained tall in his saddle. Thessa tried to mirror his posture, but hunched in fear was how she remained. His all-white quarter horse, Ares, was one of the larger ones on his property. Despite his enormous size, the stallion was docile and had nuzzled Soren during harnessing.

The leather reins in her hands felt as unfamiliar to her as her first day swinging a hammer. Soren had taught her how to hold them; use a relaxed grip and give the horse enough lead, but not too much.

She pulled in her first breath as they rode into the seemingly infinite flower fields behind his home. The ground was a heaping mess of pink, purple and blue. The smell of freshly bloomed wildflowers was as pungent as the salty sea to her left.

He looked over his shoulder, shouting, "Press into your feet, you need to sit up."

Sending her weight down and into her stirrups, she found herself seated taller.

"Good," he relayed, and faced forward.

Gaining confidence in her seat, she shouted, "What kind of lesson is this?"

Soren glanced over his shoulder. "The one where you learn to squeeze with your legs, or you fall off."

Thessa hadn't realized the grip of her inner thighs until he'd said that.

"Next, lean forward a little."

"What?"

There was no reply, only a whistle and kick to Ares as his horse flew into a full gallop. Thessa swore under her breath, Hades was about to—

The speed took her breath away. Hades was as fast as lightning. Her horse caught up with Ares, dashing alongside him.

Soren's eyes flashed with approval before he looked ahead and roared. Thessa joined in his song. This feeling of freedom was unmatched, and something she'd never felt before.

Soon they veered left, galloping toward the sea.

When they approached the giant cliffs, Soren drew back on his reins, easing Ares into a walk. Thessa didn't have to do anything, Hades copied Ares.

Soren looked her way. "You're a decent rider for someone who's never ridden."

"No thanks to you." She spoke, trying to catch her breath. "What will I do when Hades doesn't have a leader?"

He tilted his head. "Are you reconsidering your selection?"

Thessa glanced sidelong at Ares. "Well, if you're offering the stallion—"

He cut her off. "Ares is mine."

Looks as though she found the demon's soft spot. She weaved fingers through her horse's black mane and vowed, "I quite like Hades, I'm just inexperienced."

"If you managed to hold on through her rearing, bucking, and galloping, it's fair to say you can handle her."

"Is this how you teach all your riding lessons?"

"Depends on what type of riding lesson." His tone matched his wicked grin.

Thessa's skin flushed.

Soren halted Ares, dismounting in one swift swoop. "Get off."

"Where are we going?"

"You'll see." His expression gave nothing away as he removed ropes from his saddlebag and tied both their horses to a boulder.

He led her down the rocky ledge and toward the sea.

The afternoon sun was blistering hot, but the breeze was refreshing as they paced the shoreline.

Soren stopped at a cave's mouth.

She asked, "Have you been in there?"

"Emiel and I grew up playing in this one. Come on." Soren didn't wait for her answer before he ducked inside.

"Why would I follow you in there?" He was a demon, and the sheer size of him made her bones sweat.

No answer.

She rolled her eyes, grumbling, "Fine," before dipping inside. The entrance was small, but the cavern was vast. "Why are we here?"

He spun to face her. "I understand you're on a mission of solitude, but you've no idea where you're going, correct?" He'd gathered that much on their journey south and she couldn't say he was wrong.

"Does it matter?" she rebutted, taking in the moss-coated walls, dripping with sea water. The scent in here smelled familiar.

"This place is safe, if you need it, just don't wander too far back." He pointed to a tight corridor in the distance.

"What's back there?"

"Nothing. When the tide rolls in, you won't be able to get out," he warned.

"And how long before the tide rolls in?"

"Depends. You'll have about twelve hours each day."

Thessa scrunched her brows. "Why are you doing all this for me?"

"Why'd you untether me in that cell?"

Her gaze steadied on his. His gleaming black eyes reflected the sea beyond the cave's mouth to perfection. "Because it was the right thing to do."

"Likewise."

"And what about my magic?" she asked.

"What of it?"

"Will you teach me about it? It does nothing."

He scoffed. "What do you mean, *nothing*?"

"Well I *asked*, and it's yet to show me."

He laughed so loud it echoed through the chamber. "Oh yes, because a quick conversation is the best way to get your magic to cooperate."

"Well, it worked before," she snapped.

He crossed his arms. "Explain."

"I prayed for its help in the dungeon, and it managed to block the guard's fireball."

"Blocked a fireball? That's impossible. Shadows yield to flame like kindling to fire. How do you think we lost the war?"

We.

Thessa was still coming to terms with *herself*, let alone befriending a demon—if that's what this was called. "Then enlighten me, what does demon magic do?"

"Stop calling it that. You're a shadow-wielder, Thessa."

He took her name and attached it to an unfamiliar title. She swallowed, digesting the words he'd strung together. "Just tell me what it does. I was taught it's like a blanket of death, not much else."

"Not entirely inaccurate. Shadow-magic can drain the life from someone, yes, but that's not always a bad thing."

"What do you mean?"

"Offering the end to those who suffer has always been a neglected fact of our kind. Death can be peaceful."

Our kind.

"Explain the multiplying serpents then." She began tapping her foot.

"Explain how you blocked a fireball, and maybe I will." He mirrored her tone.

Her nostrils flared at the mockery. "I don't know! That's what I'm trying to find out."

"Fine. I'll go first." He started pacing the width of the cavern. "My magic is different for a reason. There was an experiment performed on my mother ... one that was successful. It's not a story I wish to share." He shook his shoulders as if bugs were crawling on him before continuing, "But what resulted were my shadows shifting into serpents."

"An experiment?" What in the world was he talking about?

"My father was adamant about restrengthening our line, it's a long story."

She leaned against the damp wall while memories of that voice coursed through her like a furious storm.

I conjured enough strength to plant a new seed, a kernel of my darkest energy, to restrengthen our line of magic. A power to end the culling, once and for all.

Thoughts reeling, she asked, "I thought demons were wiped out after the war."

"Shadow-wielders." His tone was sharp, slicing through her.

She never heard the term used so casually, as if it weren't

just another way of saying demon. "How many *shadow-wielders* remained after the UnResting?"

"After the war, groups of us scattered north and south. As far from Gravenport as possible."

It sounded familiar. She had the urge to escape Gravenport her entire life, and an undeniable disdain toward Elementals—as if her blood had known. A pit started forming in her stomach.

"Are you alright?" Soren asked over the silence.

She wasn't. Crumpling to her knees, she lost her wit and wept.

Why, why, why.

Soren knelt by her. "How long have you had your magic?"

She couldn't answer. The room was spinning, and her mind was about to burst. Curling on the floor, Thessa trembled atop the damp sediment in desperate search for air.

She couldn't seem to find any.

Soren hovered over her as she fumbled for her necklace. "Answer me," he said.

She ignored him. Every inhale was as short and sharp as her exhales, and the lavender wasn't helping.

"Thessa," he barked.

"I just got it," she managed to say.

His sigh rumbled through the cave. He tapped the bony center of her chest. "Put your hand here."

Without the energy to protest, she dropped the vial fixed to her nose and placed her hand atop her heart.

"Good. Now tell me, what do you feel?" His voice was softer than usual; nicer.

There was bounding beneath her palm. "My heart ... it's beating too fast."

"Can you shut your eyes?"

She swallowed, fluttering her eyelids closed.

"What do you see?" he asked.

"Darkness," she whispered.

"And are you afraid of it?"

She felt the warmth of her tears now. "Yes. I-I don't want this."

"If you want the truth, neither did I. But I've spent too many years consumed by fear. I promise it's not all bad. There are good things in dark places, if you care to look for them."

Her chest heaved at his truth. Cool air swirled inside her lungs. Why was he helping her out of this spiral?

"Slower on the exhale," he noted.

As she blew the air through her parted lips, slowly, she felt her heartbeats ease beneath her palm. Opening her eyes revealed Soren still hunched over her.

"Now breathe properly or I'll toss you in the sea," he said in jest, which was exactly what she needed right now. He stood, offering her his hand. "Just remember, we're only as demonic as we let them make us."

Thessa accepted the offer and got to her feet. "How can you be so sure?"

Soren sniffed, diverting his attention toward the cave's mouth.

"What is it?" she asked, rubbing her eyes dry.

He didn't answer, he ran.

"Where are you going?" she called, chasing after him.

Then, the smell of smoke hit her. Soren was already halfway up the cliff by the time she made it out. As she neared the top of the rocks, she watched him dart for Ares, mounting the stallion in one swift swing.

Impressive.

Climbing over the edge of rocks, Thessa shouted uselessly,

"Soren!" but he was already galloping toward the thick plumes of smoke—in the direction they'd come from.

She had to figure out how to mount Hades without him.

Thessa led Hades closer to the boulder, climbed up, and hopped on the saddle.

"That wasn't so bad."

Hades stomped her hooves down, grunting.

Thessa took her heel to the horse's side and kicked. A quick buck in retaliation and they were off. Hades thundered through the field of flowers to catch up. Ares was in the distance, moving like the wind with his fearless rider.

"Faster," she shouted.

As she reached the top of the hill, where Soren had halted, her mouth fell open.

Soren's entire property was engulfed in flames. His home, the barn, the pasture. All of it. Just like the library greens. Her fingertips darkened at the sight.

When she reached him, the unmistakable expression of horror filled his features. They were too late. This was the work of Elemental soldiers, and they both knew it. They are the epitome of destruction, leaving nothing but fire and ash in their wake.

Thessa's focus shifted to the horses that remained in his paddocks, whinnying with despair—being eaten by flames.

This was her fault. Had she not broken down, Soren would've been back there, he could've helped. She could've helped. Instead, she'd been a distraction.

Thessa couldn't allow anymore suffering at the hands of those fire-brewing monsters. She wouldn't. With no warning to Soren, she dismounted, sprinting toward the fire-struck land with her black fingers spread wide.

You've protected me, now help me protect them.

Willing the magic away from her fingertips, it danced around her.

More, she demanded with a fierce breath, and magic poured from her fingertips, encircling her body like a capsule.

And without another thought, Thessa ran directly into the flames.

❧ 28 ❧

LECTURE NOTES FROM THEOLOGY, OUR
GODS AND GODDESSES I:

Hades may be the god of the underworld, governing over the dead, but Thanatos is the god of death itself, carrying souls to the underworld.

Flames smothered under her every footstep.

Cinder from burning wood flew, and what landed atop her sphere of shadow-magic, fizzled into ash. Her magic hated fire, that's all she knew.

Bolting toward Soren's home, she searched for a clearing. Nothing remained, only flame and collapsing, burning wood. Snapping in the distance stole her attention as his barn crumpled next.

This land is fit for the god of the underworld himself.

She sprinted for the paddocks and burst through the burning fence. One grassy patch remained, and within it only three horses were left. Sparks flew across the clearing, star-tling them, while the fire reflected the panic in their big, round eyes.

Thessa called her magic to bloom around her, larger—wider. She had to learn how to control the flow of energy. The current within her felt endless, like a sea. She just needed to anchor down and pull. And she'd need a strong anchor, like something made of steel.

Closing her eyes she breathed her plan into action. Visualizing herself as the anchor, and unfaltering like her final dagger, she plunged into the sea. It was dark and soft, like satin.

A heartbeat later, her magic shot from her fingertips. The dark sphere she'd created grew large enough to add one horse.

Catching her breath, she stepped toward the one nearest and begged, "Let's go."

Gripping it by the halter, she sprinted toward the property line. Soren was waiting there with Hades in tow; his face was frozen. It had to be a combination of shock and grief.

Breath staggered, she could only manage to say, "I'm so sorry," before turning back.

The clearing in the pasture was smaller now. The two horses were rearing in fear, and she'd only conjured enough magic for one. They held doom in their eyes—a feeling she knew well, and one she refused to let another innocent soul feel.

Thessa roared, like her freedom call atop Hades, digging into her sea of magic. She pulled from its darkest depths, expelling enough energy to cover a dozen horses.

Flames died where her shadows bloomed.

Running between the two horses, she led them out to safety.

Soren's face had shifted to a ghostly expression as she drew her magic back in. She wouldn't ask if his family had fled, died, or been taken. She couldn't.

"I need your help," was all Soren said, his tone was weak.

She nodded once in agreement.

Curling Ares around, Soren galloped back across the field.

Again, he left her alone to mount Hades. Without a boulder, Thessa stood beside her, bracing the saddle. "You're going to let me mount you from down here, *right?*"

Hades chuffed, one hoof stomping in answer. Hoping that was a yes, Thessa shoved one foot in the stirrup, hurling herself up with the other. Nope. That was harder than she'd ever imagined.

Hades bobbed her long head in what had to be amusement.

Thessa tried again. She was close, but before landing in the saddle, Hades took off. Wrapping her arms around the horse's neck for purchase, she held on and screamed. Falling wasn't an option. The three remaining horses from Soren's property were herding around Hades, and being trampled to death was not the way she'd like to die.

Think Thessa, think.

Grunting, she remembered what Soren had said about her lesson earlier. Squeezing with her thighs, she made several, small hopping motions until she made it upright.

Huffing, she exclaimed, "Hades, you've officially earned your name."

The mare pricked her ears back, still pounding the earth beneath her hooves.

What felt like two miles had passed when Soren, who'd not been far ahead thanks to Hades' speed, threw his arm up —a signal. Ares slowed, and all the horses followed suit.

With their horses side by side, Soren said, "Emiel's property is across these woods. We need to get there before—" He looked up, scanning the sky.

She followed his gaze. He was right. If the soldiers had

come for Soren, then they'd hunt Emiel down too. Thessa whispered, "No smoke."

"Not yet," he added, kicking Ares into a canter.

Entering a birch tree forest, Thessa and Soren kept to the trail. The three other horses banded together, weaving gracefully through the thin, silver trunks.

About a mile passed when Soren threw up his arm again.

He jumped off first, tying Ares to a nearby tree. "We'll make the rest of the way by foot. The horses will draw too much attention."

Thessa understood. She dismounted and tied Hades beside Ares, who'd already started munching on tree bark.

After pacing the trail ahead, she started hearing muffled voices. Thessa and Soren crouched behind a row of mulberry bushes near the edge of the thick forest.

The voices came in sharper. "In the carriage, now!"

The bushes were dense enough to conceal them from sight, while still giving her a good look at Emiel's property. Peering through the leaves revealed a two-story brick home with black shutters and three chimneys. Two Central Divinity marked carriages sat in the driveway, along with six Elemental soldiers

A male with red and silver hair was on his knees, pleading up at them. Standing beside him was a weeping female with fire-cuffs encasing her wrists. Three other males stood behind them; two were very young.

Soren whispered. "That's Emiel's father Francis, on his knees, and his mother."

Thessa sighed, "The other three?"

"His brothers."

One soldier shouted, "We're losing daylight, everyone in the carriage."

The eldest among the brothers shoved the younger ones behind him and whispered something.

Every guard outstretched a sizzling hand in warning.

"That's Wayland," Soren said under his breath.

Wayland stepped aside and opened his arms in a plea of innocence, allowing his brothers to step inside the carriage.

"Neremiah and Brinkley," Soren noted.

Thessa exhaled. "We have to help them."

"Wait," he snapped.

"For what?" she snapped back. "They can't take them. You know what they'll—"

"Haste is useless. Wayland can take two, maybe three of them, but the youngest are defenseless and his mother is shackled. They'll kill them all or use the younger two for bait if we move too quickly. I'm thinking."

He was right—again.

Emiel's father boarded next. He was weeping with his arm outstretched toward his wife, who couldn't return the gesture without scorching her wrists. She paced toward the carriage last, about to step inside when two guards cut her off. They shoved her back before hopping inside with the others, and slamming the door shut.

A moment later, the driver whipped the horses and left.

As it disappeared down their driveway, Thessa asked, "Why would they leave her? Why are we still waiting?"

"Start conjuring your magic and listen for my whistle. Do the same thing you did at my house, and I'll take care of the rest." Without another word he dipped out of the bushes.

The four remaining soldiers stretched their arms, aiming for Emiel's mother. Just as Soren approached, fire rushed from their fingertips, incinerating her in one blink.

Thessa gasped. They were too late, again. Steadying her breath, she reigned in her focus.

The soldiers whirled around to find Soren standing with predatory stillness ... until serpents poured from his fingertips.

Flames were cast, killing them on impact. "Where have you been hiding? Soldiers, it looks as though our prisoner—or should I say *demon*—has come to his senses and turned himself in."

Soren snarled.

He'd lost everything and yet there he was, tossing more serpents at the soldiers. As one was incinerated, another leapt. One even found its target's neck, spinning around and squeezing. The soldier turned purple and crashed to his knees.

Retaliating swiftly, a shallow line of fire appeared between the Elementals and Soren—a barrier his magic could not cross.

Soren hissed.

Why had he not whistled yet? She could extinguish that fire.

Between leaves and flickering flames, Thessa winced when the soldier who'd been choking for air caught the blade tossed at him. He slashed the serpent, again and again, until his body was entombed with them.

The three remaining soldiers watched in horror. One shot a look across the flames and questioned Soren, "What are you?"

Soren growled, "Your worst nightmare," as he let his magic erupt. Tendrils of liquid night shifted to serpents around his feet like a rippling mound of death.

His magic was not like any other magic, and she was fascinated.

"Now," the soldier called, and flames streaked across the sky. Fireballs crashed into his pit of serpents. "Again."

More fire.

Soren's whistle rang through the air.

Thessa bolted from the mulberry bush and treaded through his bed of beasts. Stepping beside him, her magic stood as tall as he, encasing them both.

"Looks as though our prisoner has brought along a demon companion. The general will be awarding our unit that bonus after all," he sneered at his fellow soldiers. "Well, first, she'll be disappointed, had she known the prisoner was a demon from the start we could've had more fun with it in the dungeon." He paused, eyeing the pile of ash that was once Emiel's mother, and then back to Soren before continuing, "So tell me, *demons*, where's your friend, Emiel? Does he wield flames like his father or shadows like his mother?"

Thessa looked to Soren for silent confirmation. Indeed, Emiel's mother was not an Elemental.

Laughter echoed behind the barrier of fire. Elementals no longer feared shadow-wielders, not with their numbers being so vast, and the power to overcome them. But Soren was something else entirely, something to fear.

She was something to fear.

"Fine, have it your way," the talkative soldier called out before more fireballs shot across the sky.

Except this time, they fizzled into ash.

She could feel Soren grinning. He whispered down to her, "Not bad for someone who doesn't plan on using her magic."

The approval tugged at her lips. Maybe her heart.

Closing her eyes, plunging into her well within, Thessa became darkness. The sphere she'd conjured encased the soldiers easily.

Without access to their strongest power, she watched them fumble for their air-magic. Air pressed into her shadows, only to be sucked up and away, reinforcing her own shield.

It was not what she was expecting, nor the soldiers.

"How in the—" one called out before taking off.

A smile formed on her lips as she spoke softly to Soren. "Go on, then."

The soldiers' screams had not lasted long.

❧

CARVING THROUGH THE TREES, ARES AND HADES HEADED north—toward the carriage holding the McPorters.

She'd released the horses from the other carriage at the McPorters, and without ties, Soren's remaining horses had scattered by the time they'd returned.

As the trees broke, Hades and Ares continued their gallop down the familiar path to Mabelton. Their speed had been an advantage. She caught sight of the carriage just as Soren signaled the horses to slow.

He spoke in a hushed voice. "We attack from behind. The serpents will startle the horses, and the driver will halt at their distress. My shadows will do the rest. The trickier part will be the soldiers inside the carriage."

A smile appeared on the edge of her lips. "Speak for yourself serpent-wielder."

For a moment, a flash of joy sparked in Soren's eyes, but when he blinked, it was gone. What remained looked hollow, like two depthless craters.

As a pair of Soren's beasts slithered toward the carriage, their black and blue scales shimmered in the bright sun. They were juvenile, about an arm's length. All his serpents had appeared that way, even after the slicing and regrowth. It was like they worked together too, with one mind, controlled effortlessly by their master.

The slimy pair parted ways around the carriage.

As predicted, the horses side-stepped in an attempt to avoid what was tickling their hocks. The carriage veered into the long grass, and the driver leapt out. His footsteps must've alerted Soren's beasts, or the control he had on his magic was just that good.

Greeted by slithering shadows, the driver had no time to retaliate. They launched.

The serpents wrapped around his head and neck, occluding all air. Collapsing to the ground, the driver clawed at his face and kicked his legs for mercy he wouldn't find.

Thessa swallowed, recalling the look on the last driver's face—the one from the remaining carriage at Emiel's property. Soren had opened the door and was greeted with begging.

There'd been no use.

Part of her wanted to run then. Pull away from the vicious shadow-wielder and never look back. Except one thought had lingered, as if it were engraved inside her mind. Her purpose, it turned out, was a necessary evil.

End the culling.

Soren and Thessa eyed each other, their unspoken plan intact.

Stop the fire-spewing witches.

"Now," Soren shouted, charging forward atop Ares—as fearless as he.

His bellow had sent Hades flying.

When they reached the carriage and dismounted, things were quiet. Too quiet.

Breath steadying, she conjured enough magic to protect them both. She was a ball of night, and he was her fury.

Gripping the handle, Soren swung the door open.

29

LECTURE NOTES FROM IMMORTAL GENETICS:

All witches are born with magic in their veins. It remains colorless and undifferentiated until their Summoning Day—when it bursts to life.

Blue-flecked, Elemental blood seeped out of the carriage.

Wayland, the eldest McPorter brother, was crouched in a defensive position, then relaxed at the sight of Soren. Behind him were lifeless bodies in scarlet uniform, which meant all the soldiers were now dead.

Thessa withdrew her magic.

"Look who finally showed up," Wayland said.

Soren rolled his eyes at Wayland. "I'd compliment your efficiency, but we'd risk your head getting larger."

Wayland flared his nostrils. "Did they kill her?"

Sorrow filled Soren's expression, telling them without words. There were shades of pain behind his dark eyes, layers

Thessa could not begin to understand, but the thought of losing everything ... she shook her head.

Francis audibly wept, wrenching her heart, but Soren's face shifted—turned cold—as he began relaying orders like a rehearsed script. Without a question, the McPorters began working, unhinging the two horses from the carriage.

Soren dragged the dead driver and slung him inside the cabin with the dead soldiers. Wayland slammed the door shut, then the five of them hauled the carriage off the path.

Thessa had the honor of sifting dirt. She did her best to fluff up the grass too, then headed toward the males. A moment later, Wayland and his father set the carriage ablaze. The youngest of the McPorter brothers, Neremiah and Brinkley, were each side hugging their father with tears streaming down their innocent faces.

She shivered at the thought of their mother's violent death. Her stomach turned with all the loss and heartache. Excusing herself, she ran to a nearby tree and retched.

There wasn't much to expel, but she heaved until her body was satisfied. Unscrewing the necklace she never took off, Thessa breathed and pressed her other hand to her heart— like Soren had taught her.

As the carriage burned and the males mourned, she felt ashamed to be reminded of Kellan. Emiel's family dynamic was shifting her entire perspective. Not in a hundred years would she believe an Elemental would wed and have children with a demon. If there was a plane of existence where they could explore a future together, she wondered if she would.

Would he?

She looked up to see Soren gesturing her over. After cleaning herself up, she joined them around the fire. There was a late and awkward introduction when Francis asked Soren who she was.

A simple, "Thessa," was all he said.

She waved.

Despite their grief, all the Mcporters smiled politely at her—except for Wayland.

Soren continued, "I know this is a difficult time Francis, but you must go back. Burn the remaining carriage on your property, and all that remains. Everything. Pack only what's needed and leave. Let them think we're all dead. And do me a favor, warn the others."

Francis nodded solemnly.

"We'll rebuild, like we always have." Soren moved his gaze to the eldest brother, a speck taller than his father. "Wayland, we'll need you to come with us, for Emiel."

He was bathing his dagger in his own finger-flames as he said, "Yes, sir. Which horse am I taking?" There wasn't a whisper of sorrow in his tone, instead, his eyes burned with revenge.

Soren swept his gaze toward the four horses and paused before turning back. "Miah and Brink, you'll ride together on one of the carriage horses, and Francis, you'll take the other. Wayland, I'm sorry, that means you're riding Hades."

"Excuse me?" Thessa objected. "Hades is *mine*."

"Hades can't hold two riders," Soren countered. "Ares might be larger, but Wayland and I together would break his back. Besides, I'm not riding with Wayland."

"And where does that leave me?

Soren's lips twisted as he said, "You're riding with me."

She scowled.

"If you want to help Leora, this is how that happens."

Wayland scratched his head. "Leora?"

Huffing, Thessa turned her gaze to Wayland and snapped, "Treat my horse well or you'll have me to deal with."

Wayland scrunched his brows. "Please."

Thessa lifted her nose at Soren. "He's putting your arrogance to shame."

Back at the horses, Francis helped his two sons mount, before swinging himself over the other carriage horse. He gave Soren a nod, and the family of three took off.

Wayland mounted Hades, who flipped her ears back at the onslaught of his weight, while Thessa stepped into Soren's interlaced fingers and hauled herself atop Ares.

Soren grunted, "Move as close to the pommel as you can," before hoisting himself onto the saddle after her.

The thud of his body against hers, and the arm he threw around her waist, sent heat flooding through her. Before she could make an emergency dismount, the horses were flying north. Between his fingers gripping her, tighter than they needed to, and the rumbling hoofbeats beneath her seat, she wasn't cooling off.

She needed to think of something ... and anything but the way Soren's jaw flexed when he was angry, or the part of his waist that tapered down like a dagger.

When a soft moan escaped her lips, she knew whatever was happening between her legs shouldn't be.

Not among so much death, and certainly not with him.

Thessa bit her lower lip all the way back to Mabelton.

❧

Clopping on cobblestones indicated their arrival.

With varied strides, they'd made good timing. Pulling off-road, under an elm tree and next to one of the many streams coursing through Mabelton, they offered the horses a break.

Thessa's legs wobbled upon dismounting. Her thighs weren't accustomed to an entire day of riding, or *whatever* that was. She was so incredibly tense, every bone in her lower body ached.

Meanwhile, Soren's thighs were all muscle. Her curious eye marked every outline on display in his riding leathers—every single outline.

She wanted water, now.

Each step toward the steady stream was a dreadful reminder of how unconditioned she was. Gritting her teeth through the pain, she knelt down and drank. It was ice-cold and exactly what she needed.

Soren crept up behind her. "Should we check the town-houses first?"

Thessa startled. "Hades, you're quiet." She gulped some more water. "No."

"Then where do you suppose we start?"

Thessa stood, spinning to face him. Ignoring the sting in her thighs, and the warmth that brewed between them, she said, "It's Tuesday."

Those muscles in his jaw started twitching, as if waiting for her to elaborate.

"There's only one place she'll be."

30

LECTURE NOTES FROM THEOLOGY, OUR GODS AND GODDESSES I:

Each face of Hekate points in a different direction; one for the Maiden, one for the Mother, and one for the Crone. She's the symbol for life's crossroads, helping those who seek guidance. The triple-nature is what leads so many to her for worship.

Walking through the crystalline gates and beneath a canopy of magnolia trees, Thessa wondered if this was what the heavens looked like. White petals littered the lush grounds leading up to the House of Hekate. Many were floating in the pond, filled with giant lilies and fish as golden as the domed building it sat before.

"He's known her for how long?" Wayland queried Soren—had been since they'd tied the horses in the woods. Thessa found Soren's lack of detail amusing. It wasn't so much the short replies, but how irritated they made Wayland. Their micro-feud had been her only source of entertainment during the mile-long trek to the place Leora frequented every Tuesday.

A clutter of starlings perched along the bronze banisters dispersed at their approach. She opened the white-painted door to find an empty entryway. A single wooden table in the center held roses bundled with leafy stems and curly, twig offshoots. There were prayer jars, candles, and a basket full of meditation crystals with a little sign: *take one*. Behind the arrangement were double doors, ajar, and through them a carpeted aisle flanked by wooden pews.

There were about a dozen witches within eyesight, some lighting candles and others praying in front of the gigantic statue of Hekate. Hanging firelight blinked around the three-faced goddess, reflecting light off the trickling pool of water she stood in.

Thessa said, "Wait here, let me handle this," and slipped through the double doors.

The domed ceiling within was full of stars intersected by bright lines. Refocusing, Thessa scanned the room.

Leora's long, lean frame was something Thessa could spot from afar. Living with her had only been a daily reminder of how short she was.

"Psst ... Leora," Thessa whispered across the room.

Like a crane, Leora's head turned. The smile that beamed across her face sent a jolt to Thessa's heart. Leora ran over, but her features turned hard. She scowled, "How dare you!"

"I'm sorry," Thessa replied. "I had to—it's a lot to explain."

"Where've you been?"

"Uh, Wilcrest. Listen, we need to talk."

"What!"

"Thessa!" Beatrix's familiar voice yelled across the pews,

sending every head flying in her direction. Thessa ducked in an attempt to look less noticeable.

Ivy tailed Beatrix and soon, all three witches surrounded her with their arms crossed.

Thessa started, "Listen, there's a lot going on right now, and I'm sorry for leaving, but I need to speak with Leora, alone."

"They know Tess. They know everything. Who else am I supposed to talk to if my best friend disappears in the middle of the night? We've been praying all day for your return. Thanks to you, I've mastered the Celestial Messenger Spell, and thank the goddess for listening, saving us another trek through town."

Thessa exhaled. "Everything?"

"Everything," Leora admitted.

She scanned Beatrix and Ivy for any sign of fear, trepidation, or concern. There wasn't any. "Let's go somewhere we can *all* talk then."

They sat in a small alcove arranged with floor pillows and prayer candles. Thessa swallowed and began, "The capital retaliated. Soldiers burned Soren's property down, his horses, and maybe his family with it. I don't know if they fled, or worse, but we know Emiel's mother was just killed and his family is in danger."

Leora's eyes were moving like she was scanning the pages of a book. Her mouth opened before she spoke. "What have we done?"

Thessa shook her head. "It's too late for that. Where's Emiel? We thought he'd be with you."

She stuttered, "W-waiting at The Pickled Radish, we're meeting for an early dinner. H-how am I supposed to tell him this?"

"You're not going to."

"Then who is?"

"Wayland plans to."

A fleck of curiosity skated across her chestnut eyes. "Where's Soren? Who's Wayland?"

Thessa jerked her head toward the entryway, "Emiel's brother. He's out there too"

Leora's curiosity shifted to confusion. "You need to start talking. Why were you in Wilcrest?"

She exhaled. "I left, okay. My magic is not like yours. Last night I accepted that it's not fair for any of you to be around me, so I grabbed my bag and left. I didn't expect to meet Soren on my way. It's a long story, the whole thing is, but we brought Wayland back to help."

Leora stared at her. "Tess, why would you ever consider yourself a burden? To any of us? You're our friend, regardless of magical status, and that's the way we plan to keep it."

Water lined Thessa's eyes. "Things are different now. I'm *too* different."

"And like I said, that's *okay* with us."

"More than okay," Beatrix added.

Three gracious sets of eyes met hers. The idea of witches helping demons was a concept she wasn't familiar with.

"But please, what else can you tell us?" Leora questioned.

"I don't think the soldiers know who helped Soren and Emiel escape, they didn't recognize me and didn't mention anyone else."

"They saw you?"

"Yes."

"And what happened?"

"What happened is precisely why I need you all to pretend I don't exist, and stay as far away from this as possible."

Leora exhaled. "I'm absolutely not pretending you never

existed, and the same goes for staying out of it. We've been praying all day, helping is what I'm meant to do. Let me. Let us."

Ivy added, "I can speak for both of us." She eyed Beatrix before continuing, "We've spent one too many days folding linens. We've needed a push to get out of the townhouse, and this is it. We want to help, however we can."

Leora stood and proclaimed, "Sounds settled then, let's go."

31

LECTURE NOTES FROM INTRO TO CULINARY ARTS:

<u>A Simple Pickling Liquid</u>
6 clove buds

2 star anise (whole)

8 coriander seeds

2 thyme sprigs

2 tbsp sugar

1.5 cups vinegar

1.5 cups water

Thessa blew out a long breath, sending a lock of her hair skyward.

The maple-smoked turkey on rye she'd eaten was her favorite sandwich at The Pickled Radish. Jars of pickled fruits and vegetables spread across the table were an added bonus of eating here.

Emiel had suspected something was wrong the moment Wayland entered the eatery. After forcing everyone to stay and eat, Leora had moved with the McPorter brothers to a quieter area—away from mead-swiggers.

Stabbing a pickled cherry with her fork, Thessa took another bite. Rather than eating, Soren had been monitoring the door and windows.

Ivy and Beatrix were still conjuring up their exit strategy, knowing the house matron wouldn't be pleased with losing them both. "We can say my uncle from Gravenport has become undone with swollen tongue; he'll need us to do his bidding."

"*Or,*" Beatrix countered, "my pregnant cousin in Greenshire is bedridden and will need us to care for her, and soon the witchling too."

Thessa gulped down the last of her sage water and pushed the pitcher toward Soren. "Drink, at least."

He'd not ordered any food, nor picked at the jarred goods. He just ignored her, and everyone, with his eyes fixed on the cobblestone streets.

So, she poured him a glass, scooting it close enough to force his attention. When his dark eyes met hers, there was no mistaking the plans of vengeance in them. She wasn't sure what happened to his parents, and didn't feel right asking, so she leaned in close to whisper, "What happened was awful and I know sorry won't do, but I promise I'll help you make this right, and not only for you ..." She shifted her gaze toward Ivy and Beatrix, then back to him. "This goes beyond us. All witches deserve to learn the truth about how the Elemental Army really serves Andera."

Soren took the glass and drank.

Leora scurried over to inform the table she'd be spending sundown praying with Emiel at the House of Hekate. Trying to contain the grief welling in her own eyes, she sniffled before adding, "There's no need to settle up, your meals have been paid for," and spun back around.

Wayland returned, scooting next to Soren before speaking into his ear. Neither one looked at the other.

Thessa couldn't help but think about how Leora lost her parents, tragically, and not long ago. The thought of her revisiting those wounds she'd worked so hard to mend, worried Thessa. Pushing out of her chair with haste, she chased Leora out the door.

Yanking her arm, Thessa twirled Leora into a massive hug. She squeezed for every bit of love and light she'd offered her, and whispered, "Thank you for being my friend."

Sinking into her, Leora whispered back, "Forever, Tess."

When she made it back inside, Ivy and Beatrix excused themselves to the washroom.

Thessa sat back down and stabbed another cherry with her fork.

Wayland and Soren were staring at her.

"What?" She asked, popping it in her mouth.

Soren's jaw worked as he said, "We have a plan."

✵ 32 ✵

LECTURE NOTES FROM SPELLCASTING
AND CURATION:

The success of a spell depends on the will of the witch. Phrases may hold importance, but intent speaks to our powers beyond words themselves.

Ivy removed nettle and thyme from her leather pouch of herbs, dumping a generous portion into her mortar. "Do you need a blade?"

"No," Thessa replied, reaching for the dagger she'd crafted before her life shifted into a bundle of chaos. She swiped it through the flames then sliced through her palm.

She was thankful the Celestials had snuck her into their room for a bath, and for the clean clothing they'd given her. She wasn't surprised they said yes when she asked for their help with a Guidance Spell. Thessa needed to reverse the mindset of an entire population and wasn't sure how to start.

While black-flecked blood pooled into the bowl of crushed herbs, she looked to Beatrix and Ivy for any sign of hesitation or regret—there wasn't any.

"Are you ready?" asked Beatrix.

Thessa nodded, wrapping her hand. After stripping off her borrowed tunic, she swiped her finger through the bloodied paste and drew the five-pointed star across her chest.

Joining hands with Beatrix and Ivy, she said, "Thank you," before closing her eyes and reciting her spell.

The swirl of Celestial magic grew around her like a bubble of moonlight.

Drawing in her focus, Thessa went to repeat her spell, but everything went dark.

THIS WAS NOT THE IN-BETWEEN.

Thessa knew this place.

Darkness swept around her, caressing her cheeks as her hair swirled with the wind. She was surrounded by her magic ... her depthless black sea of magic. It wasn't simply her soul that was dark, it was *her*.

"We've made progress, Thessa." The feminine voice without a body boomed.

"Hello, *mother*. Why couldn't you have told me all this without a riddle?"

"Thessa, *child*, you must walk the path of your own existence. I may be the blood from which you're made, but only you can see the truth. You weren't ready then."

Thessa agreed but wouldn't admit that. She still yearned to know who her true birth mother was. "You have to tell me everything."

The sigh of an ancient goddess rumbled through her. "When black-flecked blood splattered across the midwife's apron, she screamed in horror. Her shrills were louder than your laboring mother, who'd tried to hush her, promising her it would be okay.

It was of no use.

Infirmary guards—Elementals—barged into the delivery room. They saw the midwife coated in *my* blood and knew. Your mother had her arm raised, prepared to fight for you, but the guards threw flames down her throat before she could try. Her body convulsed until succumbing, and her final shudder delivered you."

Thessa was horrified.

The goddess continued, "But what the guards didn't know was I'd prepared for that moment for the past two hundred years. The womb which held you would have never survived your birth, with or without fire, and that sacrifice I will always carry with me."

Unable to speak, Thessa swallowed.

"I harvested enough energy from a thousand Shadow Moons, the funnel from which our magic transpires, to come back to life. The first time was to conceive you, but the last time was to protect you."

"How?" was all Thessa could ask.

"A Resurrection Spell paired with a Possession Spell. I traveled through the meshwork of souls and made the jump into your mother's body for conception, and then the midwife's for birth. I used her arms to cut your cable, her mouth to declare you stillborn, and her legs to rush you away —*to the furnace,* I told the guards.

You were not stillborn, Thessa, but you were listless. I pressed a borrowed finger into your heart and gave you another wisp of my energy. Truth be told, I gave you all I could manage. When you opened your eyes, they were so rich, like the sea. Just like your mother's. Her given name was Thessaly, so I named you in her honor. That was my final respect for her sacrifice. Then I wrapped you, tucked a piece of parchment with your name and the date of our moon inside, and bolted to the Central Divinity.

Your blood runs pure and potent, Thessa. The energy may overcome you at times. I suppose that's my fault, for giving you a gift I've given none of my other children, but you have the power to steal an element no sorcerer ever has."

"And what is that, exactly?"

"*Oxygen*, of course."

Memories of her magic consuming flame and air resurfaced.

"We are running out of time." the voice of her goddess-mother faded.

Thessa had so many questions, but selfishness prevailed. "Why leave me in Gravenport? Of all places? It's terrible there."

"There are seldom redeeming qualities, yes, but caring for their supposed-own, is one they hold dear. And it was there, *only there*, that I knew you would see."

Thessa gasped, popping her eyes open.

Ivy offered her a hand to sit up while Beatrix held a glass of sage water in front of her face.

After gulping it down, Thessa laid right back down. Shaking her head at the beamed ceiling of the townhouse, she said, "My magic stifles flame and air."

"Woah." Ivy's deep voice rang.

"My magic stifles flame and air." Thessa repeated it, over and over until air left her lungs in short bursts.

"Breathe, Thessa."

That she could not. The thunder of a thousand storms tumbled through her veins.

She'd mourned the death of her mother, the one she'd never known, many moons ago. Hearing her name, *Thessaly*, and her birth story, reignited repressed grief. To be told that her mother had been some sacrificial vessel was unfathomable. Not to mention how she herself had been the product of some goddess-given seed.

Shock eddied its way through her bones. She wondered why an eighteen-year-old, with barely a handle on her forbidden magic, had been chosen to end the conflict between witches and demons?

Ivy hovered over Thessa, shaking her shoulders. "Breathe! I said breathe!"

"Vy, let me."

Beatrix came into view next. "Tess, can you look into my eyes?"

Swirls of brown, green, and blue made up the warm hue. She'd lined her eyes in charcoal, adding a diagonal line along the outer corner. When she blinked, a heap of brown lashes sparkled with stardust.

"We're with you. Just take a deep breath."

She tried.

"A little slower ..."

Thessa exhaled, slower this time.

"Good. Like that."

I. Will. Not. Succumb. To. This.

Closing her eyes, Thessa reached for her magic. Not to conjure it, but to be with it. The sea of blackness that was once her enemy, had become her friend. So, she shared her relentless pain, ceaseless worries, and incessant thoughts to the current, letting them drift away.

She couldn't carry it all, not anymore.

When Thessa's eyes finally opened, the ones her birth mother had given her, Beatrix said, "I'm not going to pretend that I know anything about what you're going through, but if there's anything we can do to make it easier ..."

After a few steadying breaths, Thessa sat up. "You've both been more than helpful." She rubbed the blood-crusted star off her chest and tossed her tunic back on. "And thank you for the clothing, my bag ended up burned with everything else." She didn't want to think about her Cheltz. She had nothing tangible to call her own, except Hades and her dagger.

"That's what friends are for."

Ivy nodded in agreement. "So, what's going to happen tomorrow? The matron said we have to leave by first light."

After a sigh, Thessa began. "The plan is to split. In the morning you'll travel to Greenshire with Wayland, Emiel, and Leora. Soren said Wayland has set up countless camps and you'll be safe staying together. You should arrive at the Temple of Three Moons by the third day. You'll use your Celestial grace to spread our message there. Then you'll trek another day north until you breach the forest. Soren said there's an encampment that requires warning."

"We can do that," Ivy declared, squeezing Beatrix's thigh in either nervousness or excitement.

Beatrix asked, "But where are you going?"

"Back south. Soren and I will leave tonight, it's safer for us that way. You have to tell Leora goodbye for me, and that it's not forever. Promise me you'll say that?"

"We promise across the stars," they proclaimed in unison.

Ivy and Beatrix eyed each other before sharing a small kiss. "Our adventure awaits."

Thessa had one last favor to ask, "Do either of you have a spare cloak?"

Beatrix, the same size as her, sprang to her feet. After sweeping through the wardrobe, she pulled out a wad of black satin before unfurling it. "I have this under-cloak. Will it work?"

"It's perfect." Thessa stood, swinging it around her shoulders and tying it under her chin.

Ivy smiled. "It shines like your hair."

Thessa took Ivy's compliment with a slight bow, thanked them both for all their support, and left under the privacy of her new cloak.

LECTURE NOTES FROM REALM RULES & METHODOLOGY:

Blood Moon rituals are held at the Central Divinity Solarium to honor the Blood Sacrifices of our fallen Supremes. The Blood Moon rises two-to-four times annually and all students are encouraged to attend.

Soren and Thessa were riding back to Wilcrest underneath the midnight sky. She felt relieved to be back atop Hades.

Hours earlier, on their walk back to the horses, Soren had the nerve to murmur something about her waddling. He'd veered off their course, asking her to wait, before running off to a nearby tree. Assuming he'd been relieving himself, she turned away, but when seconds had turned into minutes, she spun around to see him peeling tree flesh like a he was mad.

"What in the realm are you doing?" she'd asked him.

He'd paced over, ordering her to, "Chew, for the pain." His

arched brow and all-knowing grin had been all it took for her to cave.

She'd smelt it first—*wintergreen-y*—then chewed. It had tasted bitter and disgusting, but unbeknownst to her, the pain in her pelvis and legs had subsided twenty minutes later.

A few hours into their ride south, she still felt good.

Soren threw his arm up, easing both their horses into a walk. Thessa didn't know these woods. He had them trailing deeper into the southern forest than ever before. Nothing but the sounds of hooves crushing leaves and night insects filled her ears.

Thessa caught her breath and looked over to him. "Remind me why I couldn't travel with my friends?"

His onyx eyes shimmered, drinking in the moonlight. "Because I need you."

She glared at him.

He paused, as if studying her.

"But why?"

His mouth curved. "To reawaken an army."

"An army of demons? I think not, serpent-wielder." Thessa drew back on her reins, halting Hades. "Death may come easy at your hands, but not *mine*."

Soren curled Ares around so their horses were nose-to-nose. "Call me a demon again, *demon*, and see what happens."

It *was* a dreadful title.

"A rebellion has long been in place, *Thessa*." Her name slithered off his tongue, sending shivers down her spine. "And your gift will draw hope. Shadow-wielders have suffered for centuries—forced to hide, and made out to be the enemy. Have you considered what it'll take to overcome the true enemy?"

Thessa ignored him, dismounted Hades, and stomped away.

"Where are you going?" Soren shouted.

"Anywhere but here," she grumbled.

Goddess help me, an army?

Hope?

She despised soldiers, and aside from textbook definitions, she wasn't sure what hope was. She'd not be forced into whatever *this* was.

Soren's hand snatched her by the waist, tugging her back around. He'd left nothing but breath between their bodies. Familiar, unforgiving heat coursed through her. She tried to move, but he held her tighter. "Stay."

Thessa gasped as a serpent slithered up her back and along her collarbones. She yanked the slimy thing off and tossed it on the ground.

He scowled, releasing her.

"I'm not joining your army of *demons*," she seethed.

Soren aimed his magic toward her. "I warned you."

What began as shadows, creeping around her neck, shifted into slithering beasts. A slight tug turned into a full squeeze as they took shape. Unable to breathe, she clawed, shredding their scales, but they wouldn't give. Her protruding eyes met his. "Stop."

Releasing his magic with a huff of breath, he mumbled, "Do what you want then."

Soren walked back to the horses, mounted Ares, and took off—leaving her there.

"Hades, don't you dare!" She sprinted, managing to grab the reins before her horse followed Ares. "I need you on my side," she begged. "I'm sorry for leaving you."

Hades dug her hooves into the dirt.

Thessa let out a sigh, thinking.

Why is Soren right?

He was wrong for choking her, very wrong, but right

about needing allies, right about the need for a rebellion, and right about the word demon being sickening.

All of it.

She'd come too far to turn back now. Shoving her foot in the stirrup, she hoisted herself atop Hades.

I did it.

Hades chuffed; even the horse seemed impressed. Thessa made a couple clicking sounds, and they were off.

When she caught up to Soren, he whipped his head back. "Change of heart?" The smirk on his face was as wicked as his magic. "Camp's a mile out, follow me."

He'd not given her a chance to respond, only kicked Ares onward.

Camp?

☙❧

THE CAMP SOREN LED THESSA TO WAS NOT A-FEW-PITCHED-tents type of camp site. It was an entire village. With their horses tied next to dozens of others, Thessa staggered behind Soren. She wasn't sure why she continually followed him into dark places, however he'd promised her a safe place to rest when they left Mabelton, and that was all she wanted.

With a few hours before dawn, the entire campsite seemed to be in the midst of their evening slumber. A crackling fire in the distance drew her attention, or was it the three males who stood before it, battle ready with their daggers poised?

Thessa froze. "Where've you taken us?"

Soren paced past her, shouting, "Stand down."

He was loud enough to wake the entire encampment. Without hesitation, the three men sheathed their blades. Two sat back down and the third approached.

Soren glanced over his shoulder at her. "Are you coming?"

Tiptoeing over, she asked, "You know these males?"

"We keep three on watch overnight, rotating. This campsite rotates too, the morning after every Blood Moon."

She scanned the tented village, "How long have they lived like this?"

"Some ... a very long time."

"Sir, you're back."

Sir?

A pale, burly male, with a beard that reminded her of Professor Shovak's, greeted them.

"Reginald, it's good to see you. Will you escort us to an unoccupied tent?"

Reginald eyed Soren, then Thessa, and smirked. "*Very well then.*"

Thessa stomped on Soren's boot.

Soren cleared his throat. "This is Thessa, she'll be needing a place to rest, *is all*."

"Ah, indeed." After a small nod, Reginald guided them through an alleyway made of canvas and cloth. A symphony of buzzing creatures hummed in her ears as she passed tent after tent. The ropes strung across them gave the illusion of a giant spider web, and Thessa was strolling into the heart of it.

Minutes passed before Reginald said, "Here's the one." He held a flap open, gesturing them inside.

Thessa went in first.

It was a simple set up. A stack of blankets lay in one corner and an ewer and basin in the other. The roof of the tent was untied, allowing moonlight to stream in.

Reginald added, "I'll have a proper tent prepared at first light, of course."

Soren stepped inside next. "Thank you."

"And I'm very sorry to hear about what happened, sir.

Your father's in Stenmeier's tent—twenty tents south. I'll let him know you've arrived."

Soren swallowed as if he'd been the one force-fed bark and nodded. "Tell him I'll meet with him in the morning."

His father is alive.

Reginald tied the tent flaps. "Of course. Sleep well, General Whitfield."

Thessa's eyes popped. "What did he just call you?"

Soren exhaled, facing her. "It's only a title."

"You mean to tell me you left out the part about you *commanding* this army of shadow-wielders?"

"It's not only shadow-wielders who fight, and this is more than an army. This rebellion protects the ones who've lost everything because of the blood in *our* veins. Families live here."

"You could've told me."

"It's not a title I wear on my sleeve, nor a position I wish to hold, but one out of necessity. The experiments were part of my father's master plan."

"Master plan?"

He paused, rubbing his temples. "This all began without a leader, so he created one."

Thessa shook her head, sitting down. She supposed she was an experiment in her own right; one crafted by an overzealous goddess. "I'm sorry."

"I'm not looking for your sympathy."

"But your father's here Soren. He's alive. That must mean your mother ..."

His stare went cold.

"Surely if your father made it out, he'd—"

Sighing, Soren took a seat across from her. "Remember when you fainted?"

Slightly embarrassed by the memory, she said, "Yeah."

"Well, my father left. He came here to review the grimoire with our council. When you and I took the horses out, my mother was still at the house … alone." He blinked, and silver lined his black eyes. "I knew they killed her."

It explained the terror he'd unleashed. Thessa's heart sank. "This is all my fault. If I'd not taken you away."

Soren exhaled. "Let it be your fight, but it'll *never* be your fault."

She groaned and began to unlace her boots. "I'm sorry, nonetheless."

He shook his head. "I'm sorry too."

After a moment of quiet, she leaned over to pour herself a cup of water. "Do you always keep unoccupied tents stocked with blankets and ewers?"

"At every campsite."

"Why?" she asked, taking a sip.

"For those like the McPorters, and those like *you*. This is our ritual—to make space for others, even those who aren't like us. As long as they accept us, we accept their allegiance. My tent will be ready in the morning, after tonight consider this one yours. That is … if you decide to stay."

"Mine?" The offer may have sounded simple to him, but to her, it meant everything.

He nodded and stood, turning around to unbutton his tunic. When it fell, her traitorous eyes took inventory of every strip of muscle lining his spine.

Reining in her focus, she said, "Thank you for the place to rest."

He looked over his shoulder. "To rest or *stay?*"

She rolled her eyes. "I'm not joining your army, *General Whitfield.*"

He spun around to face her. "I'm not asking you to join us."

"Then what are you asking?" She took a big sip, officially confused.

"I'm asking you to lead them."

Thessa's mouth burst, spitting her water across the tent.

"*Thank you*, for the shower," he said, wiping his chest dry.

With the moonlight streaming in, her eyes couldn't miss the ripples of his abdomen, gleaming with water droplets. Or, how realistic the scales of his tattoo were.

She stood, regaining her focus. "I'm no soldier, nor a leader."

He angled his head. "I'd beg to differ."

"Do me a colossal favor and beg not. What makes you think your rebellion can outmatch the Elemental Army anyway? Elemental populations have always surpassed the other branches of magic. They're the superior line of magic."

"And why do you think that is?" he asked the question like she was back in secondary school.

"I understand there's a fetish for fire. Inbred or not, they're powerful."

His dark brow rose. "And what are you, Thessa?"

"Weak." The pain in her hips and legs returning was an unpleasant reminder of just how frail she was.

He stepped closer to her. "This is where we disagree. You're unequivocally powerful, you don't complain despite what you carry, and you're the most brutal, beautiful thing I've ever met."

Thessa prayed he couldn't see the heat flushing her cheeks. "Now it's my turn to beg to differ."

He leaned down, and the pinpoints of his eyes sucked her in. Her instincts told her to look away, that he was a predator, but she couldn't.

"What are you doing?" she whispered.

He lifted the underside of her chin, beckoning her lips closer. "Kiss me, Thessa."

She swallowed, holding his stare. "After you strung your beasts around my neck?"

Soren pulled back, ran fingers through his wind-blown hair, then poured himself some water. "You're right."

I know.

She thought about how he'd just lost his mother, and how he mustn't be thinking straight.

Lead his army? Kiss him?

Thessa snatched one of the blankets and moved to the opposite corner of the tent. "Let's just get some rest."

Wrapping herself as tight as a caterpillar in a cocoon, she went to sleep—tried to.

❧ 34 ❧

LECTURE NOTES FROM REALM HISTORY:

Shortly after the creation of this realm, the Elemental heir established the Elemental regime. She announced her title as General of the Elemental Army, promising to always protect the land we live on.

Thessa awoke to the sounds of children playing. Rolling over, she saw no one tucked asleep in the other corner of her tent. There were only two pieces of bark and a note atop Soren's folded blanket.

She pressed up to investigate.

For the pain.

What a lovely breakfast, she thought, while simultaneously cursing him. She chewed the bark, knowing whatever magic it offered, she needed.

Stepping outside to orient herself, she drew in a deep breath. The warm air held a combination of pine and burning wood. After scanning the trees for the sides with the most branches—the southern side—she began her pursuit.

Children swept past her, weaving through tents while shouting about imaginary shipwrecks. Their innocence shook a small smile from her.

Pacing twenty tents south, where Reginald had said Soren's father would be, she heard hushed voices. Peeking through the tent flaps revealed three males and one female, seated around a table, mid-discussion. Soren and his father were there, as she'd expected.

Thessa needed to ask Soren if there was anything to eat around here besides tree flesh. She scurried to the front of the tent, which was opened just enough to reveal what they were all looking at.

My gift.

She burst through the flaps without a second thought—but didn't make it far. Instead, she was pushed back and thrown against the floor. Before there was a moment to recover, what felt like the weight of a horse smashed her into the ground.

Thessa thrashed, unable to breathe. A heartbeat later, the pressure from her chest eased and air filled her lungs, but what she beheld next, left her mouth agape.

Soren was holding her attacker by his throat, hoisting him in the air. His teeth were bared, revealing sharper than usual canines, which confirmed she hadn't imagined things at the festival.

Soren hissed, "Touch her again and I'll see to your death. Do I make myself clear, Brenneth?"

Dangling from Soren's grasp, Brenneth began nodding.

Soren clicked his tongue, raising him higher as his serpents began their pursuit. "I can't hear you."

Sweat beaded down Brenneth's brow. "Y-y-es, sir."

Dropping him, without grace, Soren warned, "Good. Now go tell the others we have a new guest. *If* there are anything but kind regards to *Thessa*, please deliver them to me personally."

There was a firm, "Yes, sir," before he hustled out of the tent.

"You'll not really kill him, right?" A soft, feminine voice asked from across the tent.

Soren ignored the question. He was in some trance with his fists clenched.

Thessa stood, attempting to fix her hair and tunic. "Sorry to have interrupted." Shifting her focus to Soren she asked, "Is that how you'll introduce me to everyone?" *Are you always a raging fool*, is what she wanted to say, but reminded herself the ill-tempered male had just lost his mother.

Soren ignored her too, slowly drawing in his magic.

Tension lingered in the tent, as thick as the air before a storm.

Jussal cleared his throat, breaking it. "Welcome Thessa, just in time." He waved her over. "Have a seat."

Soren was a replica of his father, the only difference being a few strands of silver hair, the addition of facial hair, and lines around his eyes and mouth. They had the same sun-bronzed skin, obsidian eyes, and angular jawline. Even their mannerisms were similar: tense shoulders, slight furrow to their brows, and jaws that never seemed to stop working. She knew it took immortals five hundred years before showing their first signs of aging, which begged the question in her mind, how old was Soren?

As Thessa sat, Jussal said, "This is Silanthe Stenmeier."

"Call me Sila, my mother was Silanthe," Sila clarified, swiping her long wheat-colored hair behind her back.

Thessa managed a smile and took her seat, eyeing Jussal. "Thank you for having me. I'm truly sorry ... about everything—"

Jussal raised a hand to silence her. "What happened was a tragedy, but we'll be with Maradine again."

He was just like Soren. His eyes wore grief, yet there was seemingly no time for mourning.

Jussal continued, "Now's the time to act. All we've worked for, will be lost otherwise. We'll respect the fallen by defending our honor—our home. Just like the last time."

Ignoring the cries of her empty stomach, she asked, "The last time? You mean the UnResting?"

He shook his head. "There's a lot *not* taught in primary school, and a lot that happened before the UnResting. This realm was built by the Blood Sacrifice of our fallen Supremes, that much is true, but they won't dare mention who else was required to complete the energy exchange."

"Who?" Thessa blurted the question.

"The Blood Sacrifice of *our* Supreme."

"What? There was a Shadow Supreme?"

"We call her the *Forgone One*," Sila added. "There's a reason night falls in this realm, and it's thanks to her sacrifice."

Jussal went on, "After this world was forged, we really thought it was a sanctuary. Just as we were promised. Thousands of us had crossed over from the Mortal Realm, with all the other witches, desperate for escape. But our freedom didn't last long. When the Supremes' heirs stepped into power, everything changed."

Thessa listened intently.

"The Elemental heir, General Valstrom, was threatened by our bloodline," Jussal explained. "The power to smother—a blanket of death as they say—was never one carried or *judged* lightly. You've heard the folklore, I'm sure. She laid claim that shadow-magic had no place in the new world, preaching it would only cause harm. Her motives were effective enough to dethrone our Supreme and banish our bloodline from the world we helped create. Formally, after forging their Troika, the Supremes agreed to demote the line of shadow-wielders to demon status."

Thessa didn't understand. "Why would they do that?"

Soren chimed in. "To incite fear; to justify their claim."

Sila tapped her pointed nail on the table between them. "The same type of fear the mortals instilled," she added. "Fear which led to witches burning on stakes, I'll remind you."

Thessa remembered what the voice had said upon their visit.

What you see is not the darkness to fear.

Jussal cleared his throat. "But there's more. Banishing our Supreme and redesignating our line caused an uproar. As you can imagine, we demanded a throne and respect. However, it turned out there was no room for negotiations, so General Valstrom gave the order for a mass execution instead." He shook his head. "The few of us that survived the flames, fled."

"So the UnResting was a retaliation." Which was not at all how she'd learned it. She'd been taught that demons wanted to dominate the Immortal Realm, but it was the other way around.

"Yes. Except the UnResting took place a century after the realm was forged. That's how long it took for us to rebuild and restrengthen our bloodline after so much loss." He eyed Soren.

"But it wasn't enough," Thessa said, shifting her eyes between the younger and older versions of the same male.

"No, it was utter defeat," Soren said grimly, "and history is set to repeat itself."

"But the Hidden Grimoire of Eiliana could hold the answer that saves us all. The way it found you both. This was fated." Jussal tapped the grimoire between them.

Sila twirled a black-tipped finger along the cover. "That is, if we can get it to cooperate, it seems to like Soren though." She winked. Her turquoise eyes reminded Thessa of two gemstones.

Thessa asked, "Cooperate?"

"It's not responding to anyone's shadow-magic, only Soren's," she said, flipping it open.

Empty pages.

Thessa swiped a finger along the parchment, letting her magic spark. Text appeared instantly.

Jussal eyed Thessa, then Soren, and said, "Looks like you two have work to do."

"I don't take orders from you, father."

"You're still my son," Jussal pressed, before seeing his way out.

Sila grazed Thessa's shoulder and said, "It was a pleasure meeting you," before sauntering out of the tent.

Thessa smiled, waiting for the flaps to close before finding her familiar frown. "You need to work on your temper."

He leaned across the table. "Who says it's anger simmering in my veins?" The dark glimmer in his eyes was undeniably attractive. As was the twist of his lips, like he knew her heart was pounding.

Despite her disloyal organ, her voice remained calm as she said, "If you want my help, then we have work to do."

"So, you've considered my offer?"

She raised a brow. "Which one?" He'd not only asked her to lead his army, but to also kiss him last night.

"*Both*, if you're talking."

"I said I'm no leader, and I meant that, but I do want to help—I have to."

Dropping his hand on the book between them, he said, "Deal." His fingers crept along the page until they met her fingertips. "And the other offer?"

His touch was as magnetic as finding her gift. She forced her hand back and sat a little taller. "Still no."

Lips pursed, Soren sat up and slapped his palms on his lap. "Then let's get to work."

Work. You are thinking about the grimoire. You're not thinking about his lips—

Desperate for a distraction, Thessa asked, "What are we looking for, and why does it like you? I assumed it would respond to all shadow-magic."

He exhaled. "Another long story."

"Another experiment?" She resisted the urge to use air quotes.

He cleared his throat. "Goddess, no."

"Then speak up because you've left out some rather important details so far."

Soren's jaw ticked. "It must've been part of her charm."

"But why would it work for you, and not the others?" He paused long enough for her to tilt her head. "Go on."

"Eiliana was my wife."

35

MENTAL NOTES FROM THE SCHOOL HEALER AT CSA:

Many herbs have calming effects but consider the source, too. Take a stroll through the woods when you don't feel well. Not alone, of course.

Thessa didn't remember slamming the book shut or chucking it across the tent. She didn't register bursting through the flaps or storming down the alleyway of canvas and cloth. She ignored the children screeching past, kicked an empty bucket in her way, and cursed the goddess of night, loudly.

Next thing she knew, the smell of fresh moss and salty air occluded her senses. Massive arms were restraining her. One hooked around her chest, while the other pinned her waist back.

Soren held her close as he whispered, "You'll not run around here like a feral feline, scaring children. Do you hear me?"

"Get off of me!"

"Or what?"

Thessa wrapped her leg around his and tripped him. Dipping out of his grasp, she sprinted for her tent.

It was a useless measure of security. Soren hurled himself inside a second later, tackling her to the ground.

Beneath him, her chest heaved. Every breath she took inadvertently pressed her closer to him. She couldn't take another lie, yet she couldn't deny the heat building between her legs, or the ache of her breasts beneath his solid weight.

"*This* isn't fair," she eyed the minimal space between their bodies for clarification.

"Maybe, but your existence hasn't been fair to me."

She wasn't sure what he meant. "You can't expect me to lead your army, to kiss you ... I'm not some reincarnate of your late wife," she chided. "Why do you keep lying to me?"

He huffed, rolling off of her and onto his back.

"How do I tell someone they were gifted the grimoire of my late wife? That I lead a rebellion? That I was given a title I don't identify with? If you have any conversation pointers, I'd love to hear them."

She rocked to her side, facing him. "Let's start with *you*, like the experiment you keep mentioning." A part of her had been desperate to know.

Soren's eyes drifted to the roof of their tent. "My father is sick, and not in the physical sense. The order to execute our kind led to a century of conflict and fear that molded him. After he guided shadow-wielders and our allies south, that became the very beginning of this rebellion. But his numbers were weak, and there was pressure to rebuild, so he asked all the males and females to ..."

"Procreate?"

"Yes."

"And then what?" she asked.

"One storm-battered night, he rushed my very-pregnant mother to a sea cave. He hunted a Black Sea Serpent successfully, and unleashed its fangs on her womb while reciting a Manifestation Spell. In the days that followed, whatever I am, was born."

Thessa was horrified. "Why would he do that?"

Soren rolled to his side, facing her. "He was desperate for an heir to all of this; someone to lead. After I turned eighteen —after he saw what became of my magic—he tried to repeat the experiment again ... and again. Every other pregnancy failed. My poor mother. She did *everything* my father asked, including allowing him to have another wife—you met Sila. And my half-brother Brenneth."

Her eyes widened in shock. "Brenneth has your powers too?"

"Hades, no, that would be a nightmare. He has no aim."

She sniffed, holding back a laugh. "Do you hate him, or something?" Last she saw, his serpent-fingers were strung around his throat.

"No, I envy him. His powers don't turn into *things*. He doesn't hold the weight of this entire rebellion on his back, and he was raised by a father that I never knew, one that was ... kinder." It was like he had a hard time admitting the change he saw in his father.

Thessa exhaled. "I'm sorry."

"Stop apologizing."

She swallowed, unsure what to make of his honesty, but appreciated it. "What made Brenneth different?"

"He wasn't an experiment."

"Sila didn't go through with it?"

"She did, but her pregnancies failed. Twice. And she wouldn't allow my father to try again. She left him, moved out of our house, and stayed with the rebellion instead."

"I don't blame her."

"Me either. My father spent months begging for her forgiveness. After Sila made him promise to never perform the experiment again, on any female, she eventually forgave him. Then came Brenneth. But she's lived with the camp ever since, and prefers it here—says the woods are *healing* and all that. If it weren't for my mother, I would've stayed here too."

"It sounds like you were bred, not born."

"Yes," he said with certainty.

They were much the same in that way. "Me too."

He shot her a curious glare, and she sighed before unraveling her own truth. All of it. Matching his honesty wasn't as hard as she'd thought it'd be.

When Thessa finished, he said, "If my father finds out about your magic, you may as well flee."

"He'll be allowed nowhere near my womb, thank you very much."

Soren chuckled, and there'd been something about that sound, so light and different from the rigid male she'd come to know.

After staring at him for a moment she asked, "Could you tell me about Eiliana now?"

She watched his throat bob before he answered, "Our marriage was arranged."

That was not what she was expecting to hear. "Did you love her?"

His voice shifted, there was anger in it. "Madly. And I hated my father for what he forced, then destroyed. Losing her in battle ... I almost lost myself."

She shook her head, feeling sorry for him. "It was your father's idea?"

He groaned, answering that question.

Thessa wasn't sure why she was so curious, but had to ask. "Why her?"

"She was the heir to the Forgone One. He presented my *unique* skill set to her father and they forced our hands—to help restore hope after the exiles."

She wondered how anything forced could do such a thing. "And did it?"

"Yes, even in myself. She was as righteous as she was stunning. Falling for her was as easy as it is falling for *you*."

Thessa blinked. "You can't mean that."

"I mean it with every drop of magic in my blood."

He couldn't. He was a mourning mess. One question still lingered in her mind. "I don't even know how old you are."

"I'll be two hundred this year."

Thessa's jaw unhinged. His eyes and perfect skin held nothing but youth. "And Emiel?"

"The same. Father's orders, remember? We grew up together. He's my best friend."

"Does lying come easy to him too?"

Soren snorted.

"I mean it. You weren't going to tell me you fought in the UnResting? That I was gifted the grimoire of your late wife? That your father was a fanatical scientist? That you were created? That you want me to lead your army? At any point during our time together, were you thinking, *hmm should I tell her anything?*"

The inches between them seemed to disappear entirely. "I haven't been able to think about anything since I met you. Nothing but those sea-blue eyes and sharp tongue." He tucked a lock of her hair behind her ear.

"I can assure you, your thoughts are skewed."

"Far from skewed, *Thessa*," he purred her name, tracing a line from her jaw, down to the top of her tunic.

She grabbed his finger the moment it touched her heart. "Don't do this."

His magic flared in her grip. "Release my finger."

She did not. "Do you really think I'm afraid of your *little* serpents?"

"You seem to be the only one who isn't."

Smiling, she locked eyes with the serpent-wielder and brought the tip of her tongue to his finger.

He shuddered.

Without another thought, because her mind had won too many times, she pushed Soren flat on his back and straddled him. Pressing her hands into his shoulders, she said, "Every time you touch me, my body responds."

His gaze drifted from her eyes to where their hips met. "Do you have any idea what I was thinking about doing to you when we rode Ares together?" Thessa felt him swell beneath her, and the pressure was undeniably perfect.

Goddess, help me.

"Well," she breathed. "I appreciate your restraint."

He groaned and said, "When will you kiss me?"

She bit her lip, but her rumbling stomach had other plans. "Maybe after we eat, I'm starving."

"You're joking."

"I never joke about food," she said, hopping off of him.

Soren pouted, then grumbled something about having meetings anyway.

36

LECTURE NOTES FROM IMMORTAL ANATOMY:

Despite popular belief, the tongue is not the strongest muscle in the body. However, it is made up entirely of muscle, with considerable range of motion.

Over the course of an hour, she'd been fed, taken an overdue bath, and was finishing a full tour of camp. The dress Sila had loaned her was made of a white cloth material. It had no sleeves and was cut with high slits, *for walking,* Sila had said—although her wink had said otherwise.

Back in Sila's tent, she wasn't expecting to see Soren. His dark eyes hovered from the grimoire to what she was wearing. "You look … different."

"That's what you're going to say to her?" Sila threw a hand on her hip.

Soren's father shuffled into the tent. "Ah, good. I

wondered when you'd both get to work." He moved beside Sila, kissing her cheek.

Soren slapped the book shut. "Well this would be a lot easier if there were less distractions."

Sila, not much taller than Thessa, lifted her chin. "I'll remind you General Whitfield, your tent was prepared at first light, twelve lanes south and thirty-four east.

"Did you forget you left *your son* guarding the book in *this* tent?"

"Where *is* Brenneth?" she asked.

"I told him his canine services were no longer needed. I'll keep it with me from now on."

Sila sighed. "Fine, less fuss for us."

Jussal nodded once.

Soren stood with the grimoire tucked under his arm. "Now that you know the book was not stolen, and that your son was relieved, rather than disposed of, I'll be going." He paced toward the tent flaps before eyeing Thessa over his shoulder. "Are you coming?"

She skittered behind him.

No more than three steps outside he whirled around to face her. "Why are you wearing that?"

She loved the dress. "You don't like it?"

"I can't think with your shoulders that bare."

"Oh."

A moment later he threatened to rip it off entirely.

Thessa's eyes widened. "You'll do no such thing."

"Then I suggest you get inside my tent, and fast."

"What?"

Soren flashed his magic and purred, "Run," as several serpents slithered toward her.

Is he mad?

Heart racing, she took off.

The tour around camp had proved itself useful; the lane system they used was easy to navigate. She dodged the children whisking past her, ignored the curious glances from strangers, and stumbled inside Soren's tent. She took in the thick rugs, overstock of candles, rolled up maps, and fresh-cut table as she caught her breath; it was a tent fit for a general.

Soren fled in a moment later, grabbing her from behind. "You're faster than you look."

She squealed in his grip.

He loosened, but only enough to toss the grimoire and spin her around. His arms draped around her low back, pulling her closer.

She traced her finger along his chest. "What's all this about?"

Soren growled. "You."

She rubbed her lips together, then smiled.

He angled his head. "You look different when you do that."

"Do what?"

"Smile."

"You don't prefer my usual face?"

He huffed a laugh. "I *prefer* when your eyes light up."

She blushed, drawing her head down.

One of his knuckles found her chin, pulling it right back up. Thessa flicked her gaze to meet his. She felt weak, tingly even. "I haven't felt like this around anyone since my ex," she admitted.

Why am I bringing up my ex right now?

Soren backed away a little.

Thessa shook her head as an apology formed on her lips.

"Me either," he blurted.

"Then maybe we shouldn't." The last time she fell for someone, her heart fell apart too.

He stepped closer, wrapping his arms back around her.

She eyed the distance between them and breathed, "This is incredibly selfish." Her voice had betrayed her like she was some seductress.

"You're right." He loosened his grip.

She tugged him back. "I didn't finish what I was going to say."

He quirked a brow.

"This is incredibly selfish ... but not once in my life have *I* been the selfish one."

"So what are you saying?"

"I don't want to wait."

He grinned.

She clutched his tunic, drawing him closer. "Just kiss me already."

And Soren did. Their lips molded into one in some desperate attempt to consume the other. She didn't want air, or space. She wanted something other than the world around her.

Opening her mouth, she welcomed the push of his tongue. It was as decadent as his magic.

Soren gripped her thighs, hoisting her onto his hips. She moaned at the contact as he walked them across his tent. He sat her atop his table, then laid her down. Only when her back hit the smooth pine, had he released his mouth from hers.

She drew in what felt like her first true breath, but her body buzzed for more.

"I need to touch you," he said.

"Please." The word had just escaped her.

He made a guttural sound before yanking her sleeveless dress down with a single tug. While his mouth devoured one breast, his calloused hand massaged the other.

When his other fingers trailed lower, sliding between the slits of her dress, her back arched alive. Finding a very sensitive peak between her thighs, he pressed and twirled until she was moaning. By the time he slid a finger inside her, she whimpered his name.

"Tell me what you want." His warm breath atop her battered breast was too much.

"More," she breathed.

Soren growled something indiscernible as he added another finger. What started as slow and gentle strokes, easing her into his touch, had turned fast enough to rattle the maps off the table.

She reached her forearm across her mouth to bite back her moans.

Soren's grunt was her only warning before he pulled his fingers from her and dragged her to the edge of the table.

She clawed at the wood for purchase. "What are you doing?"

He knelt before her, propping each of her feet up. "I said I need to touch you, Thessa, and I plan to do just that." His tone had her toes curling.

After clutching her thighs and drawing his face against her center, the unthinkable happened. His mouth was upon her. She'd tensed on instinct, pulling her knees in closer.

Boxed in, he stopped and met her gaze. "You okay?"

"What are you doing?"

"You've never done *this* before?"

She shook her head. "No. Only the other way around."

He bit his lip, then nudged her inner thigh with the side of his head—a silent command.

As Thessa opened, his breath sent shivers up her spine, and kept them there as he snaked his tongue up the length of her. She cursed when he kept doing it, wondering if *this* would send her straight to the underworld. Once he added teeth, she had her answer.

Thessa dug her nails into the wood the moment he buried his tongue inside her, doing things tongues shouldn't have the capacity to do.

❦ 37 ❧

LECTURE NOTES FROM IMMORTAL ANATOMY:

A female's cycle lasts three months. During the middle of their cycle is when they're most fertile, though there is no guarantee as cycles may vary. Abstinence is the most effective method of birth control.

The fields of wildflowers were her favorite part about Wilcrest.

Thessa and Soren were lying on their stomachs amidst the multi-colored blooms with the grimoire splayed between them. The past week had been a blur of Soren's tongue and spell-searching. She'd yet to cross *that* line with him, but her patience was wearing thin. Every time they got close, he'd insist they had to wait, but he'd never tell her why.

"We should focus," Thessa said, removing Soren's roaming hand off of her rear.

"I *am* focusing."

She smirked, flipping another page. "Everything we've

found so far is simple spellwork, secondary school stuff, what exactly do you think could be hiding in here?"

He slapped the book shut. "Perhaps it's not the spells I spent a century searching for, but rather *you*."

She blushed.

"I think that's enough for today," he said.

Thessa arched her brow. "We've hardly looked."

His eyes churned like the contents of a cauldron. "But I *need* to touch you."

"You've *been* touching me," she countered.

He growled, rolling her over and settling himself between her knees.

She gasped at the feel of his hands pushing up her dress. "Soren."

"Saying my name like that isn't helping your cause."

She laughed. "Fine. If you must."

He winked a dark promise before tearing her undergarment—another gift from Sila destroyed.

Goddess, help me.

Wrapping his arms around her thighs, Soren pulled her flush against his mouth. He grazed his teeth over her flesh, just before plunging his tongue inside her.

She moaned loud enough to startle the flock of starlings nearby; the hum of their wingbeats filled the sky. There was nothing holy about the way his mouth moved, and she was at his mercy. Stretching her arms wide, Thessa gripped bunches of stems for purchase. The way he sucked on her sensitive peak, while battering it with his tongue, left her legs trembling in his grasp.

It'd been minutes of bliss before he lowered her hips back down. Soren palmed her thighs wider and purred, "You're exquisite," before slipping two fingers inside her.

His hand worked with unrelenting determination to make

her finish. When he dropped his mouth back down, it took her over the edge.

Her body shuddered while the audience of birds dipped and danced above her. The way they flew so carelessly, without fear, was exactly how she felt.

Soren's wicked hand remained put while he trailed his mouth up to meet hers, one kiss at a time. The moment their lips met, something shifted inside her chest. Little wings of her own fluttered, carrying a song of hope.

38

MENTAL NOTES FROM THE SCHOOL
HEALER AT CSA:

Exhale for a count of three, pause, then inhale for a count of three. Repeat as needed until calm. Don't forget to replenish the lavender once it loses its scent.

Thessa had abandoned her tent for Soren's days ago. Staying away from him had become increasingly more difficult than she anticipated.

Seated in one corner was Brenneth, and in the other was Soren. Pacing between them, their father spoke. "You two need to work together, find our weaknesses and strengthen them."

Soren eyed his half-brother, who curtsied for Thessa every time he greeted her now. "Brenneth, formalize combat training. I want protocols and drills established for review by morning."

Jussal's eyes darted between the brothers who looked like

polar opposites. Brenneth took after his mother with the same pale skin, blue-green eyes, and wheat colored hair.

"Will Thessa be joining combat?" Brenneth asked. "Or does she only serve other purposes here?" His salacious grin was unmistakable.

Soren hissed, "Protocols and drills, Brenneth. Now get out before you choke on those words."

The tent flaps fluttered in Brenneth's wake.

"If you can't get along with the head of our combat unit, you'll destroy everything I built."

Soren cleared his throat. "While I appreciate your concern, father, I'll deal with Brenneth. You and I need to discuss something else."

On their way back from the flower fields, she and Soren had a long conversation about her powers. She knew she couldn't hide this part of herself for much longer. If she could help the rebellion by offering a little hope, then she'd do just that.

Jussal's black eyes lit up. "You've found something?"

"Not yet. It's about Thessa."

Thessa was perched on the foot of Soren's bedroll. "Stop talking about me like I'm not here."

Jussal tilted his head. "What is it?"

Thessa stood. "It's about my magic."

"Yes?"

"It's ... different."

His dark brows narrowed. "Show me."

Thessa breathed in, conjuring her magic to a single fingertip. She let one dark wisp escape, dancing toward the corner of Soren's tent. A lone candle sat atop a tree stump there.

The flickering light gave way to her shadow in an instant.

Eyes wide, Jussal ran out of the tent.

"Is he okay?" she asked Soren.

Shaking his head, Soren muttered, "Likely not. I told you he wouldn't take it well."

A few minutes later Jussal sprinted back inside with Emiel's father. The last time she'd seen Francis, chaos unfolded.

Out of breath, Jussal panted, "Francis, go on please, like we discussed."

Soren stood, facing his father. "What exactly do you think you're doing?"

"Finding out *exactly* what Thessa can do. Have you bothered, *son?*"

"I've seen what she can do. She doesn't have to prove anything to me." Balling his fists, Soren huffed one syllable at time, "Do not push her."

Thessa intervened. "I'm fine." She eyed Soren to say, *we talked about this.*

He stepped back while those muscles in his jaw clenched to restrain his mouth.

She ignored him and gave Francis a nod. "Well met, Francis."

Francis nodded back, holding out his palms and conjuring fireballs atop each. After perfecting his swirling flames, Francis asked, "Now what?"

Jussal cocked his head toward Thessa.

Soren stepped in front of her, facing Francis. "Throw those and they'll be the last ones you conjure."

Thessa shoved Soren, unsuccessfully, so she walked around him and said, "No need to throw them Mr. McPorter, I can come to you."

Hovering her fingers in front of Francis, she couldn't help but see his russet eyes still plagued with grief. Had he slept at all? She shook off the thought and let her magic go. Not too much, but enough to smother each fireball.

Smoke fizzled in the air between them.

"What are you?" Jussal questioned, shifting closer to her.

Soren side-stepped, blocking his path. "Orphaned, she doesn't know anything, and just got her powers."

A partial lie they both agreed to.

Jussal peered around Soren, looking directly at Thessa with a sly grin. "What else can you do?"

"If Mr. McPorter could conjure air, I—"

Soren spun to face her. "You don't have to do this."

"Now, now, son. Let Thessa show us."

Thessa eyed Soren to say, *it's fine.*

He yielded, begrudgingly.

She gave Francis an encouraging nod and he quickly conjured two small spheres of air-magic. The aquamarine color reminded her of Sila's eyes.

Repeating the same process, Thessa let her magic flow toward him, devouring his air on contact.

Francis snatched his palms back, inspecting them. "I've never—"

"Seen anything like it," Jussal finished.

Thessa lifted her chin to Jussal. "If hope is what you wish to restore, then you have my permission to restore it."

Jussal's lips curved. "You're remarkable. Thank you." He shifted his focus to Soren, flattening his features and said, "Train her."

Then he left, summoning Francis along with him.

Soren plopped on his bedroll, palming his face.

"Is it that obvious?" Thessa asked.

"That my father is spiraling?"

She let out a small laugh. "No. That I'm untrained."

He slapped his hands on the bed. "*Train her* was code to exploit you. He'll want to know more and more until you exhaust your magic. How can you not see that? I won't allow it."

Thessa sat beside him. "He said *you,* you're to train me. Not him. Not Brenneth. You."

Soren breathed, clenching his sheets. "You're right."

"Have you ever exhausted your magic before?" she asked.

"Once, during the war."

"How long did it take you to recover?"

"It was three days of sickness, and not something I can ever forget, but unless you deliberately do it, it's preventable. How'd you learn how to control your magic so well?"

"I suppose I owe it to the healer at CSA, he taught me how to breathe when I forgot a few years ago."

Soren's face warped with confusion.

"I know you don't usually *forget* to breathe, but when the air is ripped from your lungs you'd be surprised."

He nodded, listening.

"Well, I learned to use my breath to steady my thoughts, which in turn steadies my heart. So I applied the same method with my magic."

"It works well."

She toyed with the necklace she wore, realizing it'd been a while since she needed it. "The goddess said something about how the energy may overcome me at times. I'm not sure what she meant, but I feel the magic inside me, it's endless."

"You may be powerful, but all powers give way ... eventually."

Thessa exhaled. "I just hope it's enough."

He tapped his forehead against hers. "It will be."

"You can't promise me that," she whispered.

"I know."

Thessa sighed and stood. "We should get to it."

Across the room, beside the now flameless candle, sat her

grimoire. Well, the rebellion's grimoire, she supposed. She paced over and sat down.

"I have a better idea," Soren crooned from the bedroll.

"No, absolutely not." She glanced over her shoulder to witness the pitiful look on his beautiful face. "Come sit. And bring your tinderbox." Thessa patted the rug beside her after crossing her legs.

Opening the book, her fingers tabbed worn parchment until arriving on *Illusion Spells*.

Soren lit the candle, illuminating the text.

They'd been going page by page over the week. Three-quarters of the way in, these were the first set of spells worth saving.

Thessa asked, "These are impossible, was she able to get them to work?"

"Of course, she was a master of spellcrafting. Well, forbidden spells."

"She must've loved you, a Multiplicity Spell interwoven with your magic is ..."

"Is what?"

She eyed him. "Captivating."

"That is the first compliment you've given me without my mouth on your—"

Thessa put her finger over his lips. "Don't."

Soren removed it, grinning.

"Are you truly unable to think of anything else?"

"Is it such a bad thing?" he countered.

Undoubtedly, yes.

Her body was molten around him. And worse, her heart was becoming the same. Thessa scratched the thought and said, "We have work to do." Flipping the page, there it was. The dark feminine figure with raven-like wings she'd seen with Leora. "Who is that?"

"The goddess of night, of course."

Thessa leaned in close, inspecting the image. "How do you know it's her?"

"*They* may obsess over Hekate in this realm, but *we* were raised to worship Nyx. Eiliana drew this, she always drew her."

"You mean to say our goddess had wings?"

"Some think she flew. Others say she drove a horse-led chariot. You know how legends go."

Thessa stared at the drawing of her make-shift mother for a little longer before flipping the page. "Another Communication Spell," she murmured.

Soren flipped the next page. "Another Enchantment Spell."

Thessa groaned, gesturing for him to flip.

Soren paused, tapping the page. "This Protection Spell could be useful. Especially for the Botanical and Celestial witches with us."

She worried about Leora every single day. Sure, she had *distractions*, but every sighting of the McPorter family had reminded her of the others. "I should write them."

"You can't, they're moving soon. They rotate locations the morning after every Blood Moon, just like this one."

That's a couple days away. "Where are they going next? I'll write them there."

"A location was scouted closer to Gravenport, that's all I know. We keep our messenger service vague—in case of interception."

"So we've sent them north, just for them to hike back south?"

His eyes narrowed. "How else would we have warned the northern half of the rebellion about what happened down here? About the possibility of war?"

Her heartbeats rang in her ear. "War? Soren, they're trusting us. Trusting *me*. With everything."

"What did you think all of this would lead to?"

She shook her head in denial. She'd been led into a web of lies. "Why didn't you tell me sooner?"

He stood with haste, pacing the room. "I've been force-fed command and combat training since before you were born. I know how to mediate delicate circumstances, and not everyone has to like how I do it. Keeping our kind hidden, *this secret,* is my only priority. The less anyone knows, until they need to know it, the better."

Her blood was boiling. "Okay *General Whitfield,* the lying and conniving rebellion leader."

"What's gotten into you?" His voice was laced with anger.

Thessa stood on wobbly legs. "They deserve the truth. Everyone does."

"I instructed Wayland to share the necessary details before we left. Your friends are likely taking it better than *you.*"

Thessa huffed. "So they know it's a rebellion, and not just an encampment? About the possibility of war?"

He nodded. "Can you please sit back down now?"

"How long until the capital retaliates?"

"Considering a new carriage of soldiers arrives at my property and the McPorter's every third day, they're bound to suspect an uprising."

"Is that where you've been sneaking off to? You said you had meetings."

"Only to hear the reports from our spies. You didn't think the capital would just give up?"

She was unnerved. "So we're moving north, is it?"

Another nod.

"But what if we didn't have to fight? What if the Supremes were open to a negotiation?"

Soren let out a small laugh. "The Supremes don't want to talk, and I *do not* want to talk to them. I want to *kill* them."

"You wouldn't try? If they're expecting an uprising, then what's the difference?"

"I would be too busy killing them to talk, is the difference."

She rolled her eyes. "Then what about all the innocents in the capital? Will you at least warn them?"

Soren stood, towering over her. "No one is innocent in Gravenport."

"You can't possibly mean that. I'm from Gravenport."

"That's different."

Thessa crossed her arms. "It's entirely not different," she snapped. "There are Celestial and Botanical witches living there. Witchlings, Soren. What about the Elementals that are forced to stay and don't want to? Think about the McPorters."

He lifted his chin. "With every battle comes casualties."

Thessa scrunched her brows. "That's not good enough."

He tilted his head to the side and asked, "Are you sure you don't want to lead this army?"

"If it means being anything like you, then I'm positive I don't."

"Then you'll sit back down and do as I say."

She wondered who was standing across from her? All the warmth was drained from his face, his tone ... everything. She'd put trust into someone she barely knew. Too much trust.

Again.

She did this to herself, again.

Her lips trembled.

What have I done?

Without another thought her legs were moving. She was tearing through the tent flaps and pounding dirt beneath her bare feet. She flew through the center of camp, sprinted through an alleyway of canvas, and stopped short before the group of horses.

Hades was grazing beside Ares, as usual. Grabbing her leathers from a stump, she rushed over, threw the saddle on her and mounted. There was no time for a bridle.

Thessa grabbed the mane and roared, "Go."

Hades bucked into a canter, bypassing a walk. Thessa's mind buzzed while they flossed through trees and into the never-ending fields of Wilcrest. She knew this land well by now. The ground shifted from blades of green to a honeybee's dream as she neared the sea.

The sound of strong hoofbeats thundered from behind her. A peek over her shoulder revealed Ares closing in. Thessa cursed the setting sun.

Reaching the cliff's edge, she dismounted, tied Hades as quickly as she could, and started scaling the rocks. She needed to be alone. Soren was controlling and arrogant, and most of all, a liar.

"Thessa, stop," Soren shouted down, seated astride a restless Ares.

"Why are you following me?"

"Why are you running away?" he countered.

"Just leave me alone. I need space," she yelled as her feet landed on the smooth sand. "And don't follow me." He needed to let her have this.

Soren yelled back, "You shouldn't go in there this late."

"Just go away," she bellowed from the shoreline.

He went silent.

Good.

Ducking into the sea cave Soren had taken her to when she first came to Wilcrest, Thessa crashed to her knees. Tears welled in eyes, but she'd be damned if they fell. Setting her forehead down, she formed a shell with her body and breathed. The cool, damp air soothed her, but the smell of salt air and fresh moss were too strong.

It reminded her too much of *him*.

She lifted her head, regretting her choice to come here. But it wasn't like she had many places to go. She eyed the back of the cave, where the walls tapered into darkness. Desperate for a distraction, escape, or whatever it was she needed, Thessa stood.

One step at a time, she crossed the threshold she was told not to, entering a cavernous tunnel. The farther she walked, the less light there was. Even the air was heavier as water dripped down from the walls.

She was careful, avoiding the sharp, stony deposits scattered above and below her. Bending with the cave, she followed the path into ... nothingness. Curiosity be damned, she kept going, running her fingers across the wet stone and dodging rocks along the way.

Eventually, the tight space led to steps.

Steps?

She ascended slowly.

They led to a chamber, but it was too dark to see anything. Thessa squinted, letting her eyes adjust.

Hundreds of thousands of tiny pearl-like eggs filled the space, and the largest serpent she'd ever seen—bigger than her—was curled atop them. Its forked tongue flicked once.

Then twice.

It launched.

39

LECTURE NOTES FROM REALM RULES & METHODOLOGY:

Keep your wits about you. The Immortal Realm may be a sanctuary for witches, but there's plenty of trouble to get into.

Thessa whirled around, bolting down the stairs and back through the damp tunnel of stone.

The creature slithered behind her, hissing its wicked song. She wouldn't dare look; the cave was full of sharp rocks that were just as threatening. She swept right, dodging the one to her left.

The thrumming in her veins had kept her feet moving, despite regret weighing her down. Bypassing another pointed rock, she swooped left, not seeing the small ditch.

Thessa stumbled, but the serpent had not. Fangs as sharp as daggers plunged into her thigh.

She collapsed on impact, swearing loud enough to rattle the cave, and the beast. It unlatched, slithering back toward its nest. Had she known verbal abuse would work, she would've tried shouting sooner.

Her thigh stung like a thousand bee stings.

An inspection revealed two finger-length punctures in front, and two small ones in back. Something yellow oozed from each, paired with her own dribbling blood.

"Great," she blurted, wondering why Soren had ever said this cave was safe.

Attempting to walk was a miserable failure. The pain was unbearable, and so incredibly hot. Using the slick wall for balance, Thessa hopped down the tunnel. The camp had a handful of healers, she just had to get there.

A cool blast shocked her foot as sea water puddled around her.

The tide.

She moved as fast as she could, gritting her teeth through the pain.

As the water swelled, Thessa was beginning to think the stairs had made a lot of sense. By the time she reached the end of the passage, the sea had risen to her chest. She would need to swim through the cavern and out the cave's mouth, and fast.

Thessa took a deep breath and dove in, but one kick of her marred leg sent pain jolting through her. She stopped, hugging the wall to recover.

Breathe. Just breathe.

The shrinking entrance was so close.

She tried hopping again, but the water was too high, and too dark to see the boulder that sent her crashing underwater. Beneath the surface, there was nothing but frigid darkness and the silence of the sea. For a moment, it was like things were peaceful.

Popping back up, she gasped for air. The tide had risen to

her chin; there was no choice but to swim. After cursing the Blood Moon for its role in this, Thessa took a deep breath and dove back in.

Every kick of her punctured leg was accompanied by shooting pain.

Knock, knock.

Panic was behind that door.

No.

She caught a breath and kept swimming, towards the light. The pain was excruciating, but the sea water was numbing it. She just had to move.

Kicking up for air, she was met with resistance. The top of her head smashed into stone as she pressed her palms into a surface that wouldn't give. Treading farther made no difference. Desperate for a breath, she pushed, scratched, and shoved the rocks above her.

Despite the salt burning her eyes, the pain in her leg, and the fear gripping her, Thessa swam as fast as she could.

Knock, knock.

There had to be a different door ... perhaps a window.

Her headmistress pointed her spindly finger toward the light. "*Yes, Thessa, you can open that little window there if you need some air.*"

Living in an overstocked attic at the age of six hadn't been all that bad. It was the first room she'd ever been assigned to that had a window. She'd sit before it for hours, wondering where the clouds went, and what the birds were saying. Thessa wasn't sure what happened to that child—the one without a worry.

"*Go on, it may be a smidge jammed.*"

Thessa pushed, and the window cracked. There wasn't a sky to see, instead it was some lucid dream. The first thing she noticed was Leora, smiling bright. Her true friend. Thessa smiled back, opening the window a little more.

Hades stormed through next, bucking in all her glory. Thanks to Hades, Thessa had learned what true freedom felt like.

Ares trotted in after her, with his fearless rider. Soren's gaze softened on hers like a siege to her soul. Not only had he helped her recognize who she was, but he'd helped her appreciate it.

Then, an unfamiliar female approached her, with eyes that matched her own. She stepped up to the windowsill and whispered gently, "Don't be afraid my brave daughter. You may rest now."

Thessa smiled softly, and let darkness sweep her out to sea.

⚜

A MAJESTIC VOICE BOOMED ACROSS HER MIND, OR PERHAPS her soul. "He will not help. I tried."

"Who?" Thessa asked.

"The god of the seas, of course."

"What?"

"Poseidon, my child. He'll let the water take you. He's very much into the, *the water decides* and *let the tides bring what may,* rubbish. You know the difference between male and female rulers, Thessa? Action. Hekate was willing to help me —help stop the hysteria her kind started. Not stand idly by. She had no problem visiting that friend of yours for me. To guide her to you. To help you, find him. Well, she wove the messages indirectly, but it worked all the same. After all, that's what the grimoire was for. I certainly tried. Let it all not be for nothing."

This had all been some constructed nonsense. "You lied too?"

The voice cut out.

⚜

THESSA SHIVERED AGAINST A WET, JAGGED ROCK. Something acrid dribbled from her parted lips while what had to be death coursed through her veins.

Muttering sounded, then a sharp, "Get out of my way."

She didn't care beyond her own skin. Misery had seeped its way from her thigh, and into every crevice of her body. Clawing at the rocks for mercy, her body shook in agony.

Something pressed her down, popping her eyes open.

A familiar face, dark and golden from the sun, hovered above her. Soren had straddled her, bracing a flat palm atop her convulsing chest. His mouth was against his other wrist, tearing flesh away until a river of black-flecked blood rushed down his forearm.

"Drink," he ordered her.

There was no room for protest. His arm smashed against her cold lips and the tang of metallic splashed on her tongue. When it pooled, she gulped. It tasted like a combination of copper and nutmeg, and her body solidified with each sip.

"More," she mumbled before piercing her teeth into his flesh.

Warm, thick blood burst in her mouth. Every swallow was as satisfying and strengthening as the last. She fed for minutes before Soren drew back his arm.

"Alright, that should hold you over."

Grasping his forearm, Thessa yanked him closer, drinking. She wondered, how long had the sea held her?

"That's enough for now, we need to get you back to camp."

Hissing sounded from behind her.

"She's had plenty," he snapped. "And you need to go, you've done enough."

More hissing.

"I said, go."

Withdrawing his arm, her lips quivered. "What happened? Who are you talking to?"

"Thessa, just breathe. You're safe now. I promise you're safe."

Safe.

He'd said that once before. "I don't feel so—"

Her eyelids fluttered before everything went dark.

40

LECTURE NOTES FROM IMMORTAL ANATOMY:

Similar to mortals, red blood cells replenish every 120 days. They are removed from circulation via the spleen and liver as the bone marrow produces more.

Amidst the haze in her sleepy head, Thessa could hear two things on repeat:

1. Growling.
2. "Do not touch her."

Searing, hot pain soared through her bones. The temperature was in clear competition with the sun, dotting her body with all the moisture her mouth lacked. Desperate to free herself from the unrelenting heat, Thessa thrashed.

Met with resistance, she blinked her eyes open to find worn, leather straps holding her down. She writhed in both agony and fear.

Above her, light shined through an unfamiliar ceiling of canvas, intricately painted with small herbs and flowers. Surely, someone who adored flora could not be evil, she thought. Then again, Quinnley was up for debate with her hemlock conjuring skills.

"Remove the straps, now." Soren's voice was unmistakable.

A kinder voice, one she couldn't place, replied, "Yes, General Whitfield, right away." Soft hands met the damp skin of her ankles. "Settle down dear, you'll only make it worse." One strap loosened before a female with heavy eyelids came into view. "Almost done, hold still, it was the only way to manage the tremors in your sleep."

Thessa's heart was racing. "Hot," she cried, "I'm too hot."

The unfamiliar female released the final strap around her chest and eyed Soren. "It's time."

Without hesitation, he knelt beside her, ripping into his flesh.

Jussal stepped into view, his face perturbed. "Son, there's daggers for that."

Soren snarled, "Get back." Blood dripped from the corners of his mouth.

Arms up in innocence, Jussal moved out of sight.

When Soren's bloodied wrist flashed before her, she clutched his arm to her mouth, as if practiced. His blood was as nourishing as it was intoxicating. An animalistic sound escaped her before she latched onto him. He didn't draw back, nor flinch.

More and more she drank, her discomfort subsiding with each sip. Breathing through her nose, she dug her teeth in and sucked.

Thessa peered up, drinking in silent gratitude. Soren's gaze, set with worry and fatigue, rested on hers.

Jussal's voice sounded from across the tent. "That ought to be enough, you'll need your strength too."

Soren's head snapped. "Get out. Everyone."

There were a series of footsteps and a whoosh of air before silence hissed. To Thessa's relief, there wasn't a serpent in sight.

Except for the snake himself.

Thessa eased off of his wrist, resisting the urge to lick her lips clean. "Do you have a cloth?"

"You're worried about a mess?" Soren got up and spun toward the table lined with healing trinkets and potions, then presented her with water and something made of cotton.

After patting herself clean, she sat up to drink. Finishing the water with a sigh, she asked, "Lemon?"

"Milanny said it would help balance the stomach ... from all the blood." Soren put her cup aside and settled on the foot of her cot. "How do you feel?"

"I still hate you."

He smashed his bloody lips together.

"Withholding any more lies?" she begged to know.

"I'm. Sorry." The words came out in pieces, as if he himself was broken.

"Do you even know why you're apologizing?"

"For not realizing sooner that I can trust you. It may not be a good excuse, but sharing anything, with anyone, is not something I do."

Thessa crooked a brow. "I've learned that."

"I promise I'll earn your trust back. The half-truths end now."

Why he wanted credit for telling partial truths was beyond her realm of understanding. "Your *lies* could've killed me. I thought I was dead."

"Trust me, I'm reminded of that every time you breathe."

He leaned closer but she drew back. "I should've warned you about Echidna."

"Echidna?"

"The serpent." He eyed her punctured thigh for clarification.

The oversized fabric she wore hung in layers like a slitted tent, exposing her leg to him. His fingers trembled toward the wound, but she pulled her leg away, embracing the throb it cost her.

Soren clenched his fists into the bed linens.

"So it's true then," she said. "If you knew it was back there, why ever tell me that cave was safe?"

"It *is* safe," he sighed. "I never thought you'd go back that far. Echidna only leaves her nest when the tide comes in fully. There's a lot more I need to tell you—should have told you."

Crossing her arms, she exclaimed, "Oh, this ought to be good."

"Echidna is the same serpent from the experiment."

Thessa's head tilted. "Why am I not surprised?"

He continued, "We're bonded, so as long as I live, she continues to live ... past her lifespan. With that, she continues to grow ... and mate."

Her head was spinning. "There were hundreds of thousands of eggs in there, Soren. Certainly they're bound to hatch and come slithering out of that serpentine tunnel at some point. I can't believe you didn't tell me."

The male who rarely slouched hung his shoulders heavy. "She said the same thing."

Rubbing her temples didn't subside her confusion. "Who?"

"Echidna. We can communicate with each other— through our bond. If I told her about you, none of this would've happened."

Told her? Soren had to be delirious.

"I'm not ill. The bond works similarly to the way I can hear your thoughts right now."

Her eyes bulged.

He waved his arms in innocence. "Please don't get mad. It's just that you've had so much of my blood. It'll wear off after the feedings stop."

Thessa stitched her brows together. *How?* She didn't bother speaking if she didn't have to.

"The bond was unexpected, but something to do with the Manifestation Spell during the experiment. For completion it required Echidna's blood, saliva, and venom. Right now, you've got a lot of all three."

Explain why I'm feeding like a leech.

"After the experiment, my body went through a series of adaptations to survive. In turn, I'm your personal antidote. It's why my serpents aren't venomous. Her venom needs to work its way out of your system, and my blood is the only thing that will help you survive until that happens."

"Then how did your mother and Sila survive the venom?"

"My father planned his experiments meticulously. He'd hunted the Black Sea Serpent before and gave its eggs to a healer. They developed the antidote, and he held a reserve—which is now burned."

Why does it taste so good?

"I can't answer for that." He dared smirk.

She scowled. "When will I need more?"

"Hopefully you won't. I fed you three times while you slept. This was the first time you opened your eyes in almost *twenty* hours."

Disbelief settled over her. She eyed his forearms for a shred of proof. There was more than that. One wrist was covered in bandages and the other was freshly ravaged.

Thessa muttered an apology she didn't mean. This was *his fault*.

Soren winced. "Stop. I'm going to make it right."

"If it weren't for that fanged beast, I would've gotten out of that cave. I thought I was dead."

He exhaled slowly.

"As much as I want to kill her, she's the *only* reason you made it out of that cave."

She didn't understand. "But you were the one to save me."

"That's not how it started."

Thessa sat up a little taller. "Then you better start from the beginning."

"Fine. You wanted space, remember?"

Thessa rolled her eyes at the memories of their argument. His lack of care for innocent lives had been her breaking point.

He shook his head. "If you want the truth, I was livid after you shouted, so I galloped Ares up the coast to cool off."

You were brooding while I was drowning?

"I should've never left."

"Well, you did. Then what happened?"

"Then I heard her," he said. "First, the call was distress."

"Echidna?"

He nodded. "When the signal shifted to fear, I knew something was wrong. By the time I got there, your body was bobbing on the surface of the water with Echidna weaving beneath you. I'll never unsee it."

Thessa was rubbing her temples in some desperate attempt to wake up from whatever nightmare she was having.

Soren continued, "I pulled you out from there."

"Why would Echidna help me? She bit me."

"She said your blood tasted *different*."

She scrunched her brows, still getting used to the idea that Soren had a personal relationship with a serpent.

"You'll get used to it. Sila should be here soon, there are few things I need to organize before the evening meal. She was coming by to help take care of you."

"Fine."

Soren rose from her bed, hesitated awkwardly, then left.

The female who'd untethered her tiptoed in a moment later. "Hi, you can call me Milanny, I'm the healer in this quarter of camp. Are you feeling alright, dear?"

"Better, thank you."

"I've never seen him like that, you know."

"Like what?"

"Troubled. He didn't rest once all evening, only ordered me to."

The tent flaps flew open as Sila jogged in. "Thessa, I was so worried. I'm going to help you get washed up. I'm sure you'd like to join us for dinner, you *must* be starving."

She wasn't, she was angry, but still offered Sila a small smile. Sila reached her arm around Thessa's waist, easing her onto her feet. Thessa could bear some weight on her mangled leg, but it still throbbed.

After a goodbye to Milanny, she rested her weight upon Sila, and hobbled out of the tent.

"So, you've met Echidna," Sila whispered as they walked through camp.

"Indeed."

"I've felt those fangs before, unfortunately."

Thessa often recounted the horrors about the failed pregnancies—the ones she tried to forget.

Three males passed by and greeted Sila, sparing her from a response.

Sila continued, "Aside from the healer, and council, no one must know about her. Do you understand?"

"Why?"

"For one, no one knows about her. It's just the way it is. From the council's perspective, when everything else fails, the serpents will be our final defense."

Thessa shook off the feeling of fangs plunging into her thigh. "So why not tell the rebellion about her, wouldn't that inspire hope?"

"When you've watched our kind retreat on a battlefield, talk to me about hope."

Thessa grew quiet. Sila was right. She knew nothing about battle. After a moment, she asked, "You anticipate we'll lose?"

"I anticipate what may happen. As does our council."

"Who, exactly, is part of this council?"

Sila hurled Thessa against a wall of a canvas as a cluster of children flew past them.

Thessa let out a small laugh. "Thank you, let's not add being trampled by witchlings to my list of casualties."

Continuing along the familiar path that led to the river, Sila said, "Aside from the general, myself and Jussal, there's Brenneth, Sinclaire, and Christof. Brenneth is in charge of combat. Sinclaire is head of weaponry—I'm not sure if you two have been introduced yet. He's a quiet male, keeps to himself, and his weapons. Then there's Christof—the leader of the northern rebellion."

"And what's your position?"

"Magical training."

Thessa's brow lifted.

Sila continued, "I teach our young Shadows, then assign the young Celestials and Elementals with their respective teachers. You'll have to help me recruit Francis by the way, he's adept with fire; very controlled."

"I've learned that."

"So you have. And so are *you*, Soren says."

Thessa blushed. Trying to rid the feeling, she asked, "And Jussal?"

"He's essentially the founder of all this." Sila looked across the encampment with pride. "My home. Well, we pack up at first light for the Blood Moon move, but it's home none- theless."

She quieted, unsure how Sila made a home for herself wherever she went. Thessa had been shuffled around her entire existence and never once felt comfortable enough to call someplace home.

When river mist tickled her toes, Thessa gripped the gravel. Sila helped her remove the oversized gown she wore, before pulling off her own dress. Thessa tried not to stare at the fang shaped scars across Sila's abdomen, at least not long enough for her to notice.

Thessa refocused on the white and blue ribbons of water rushing past while Sila guided her in. Once they were chest deep, Thessa scrubbed her face clean. Then she dropped her head back, letting her hair drift with the current. The water was *almost* loud enough to block out her thoughts about all the venomous lies she'd been told.

"You okay?" Sila cut across her thoughts.

Thessa turned to face her and sighed. "Is there a reason lying comes so easily to him?"

While finger-combing her golden hair, Sila said, "As a council member, I can say the secrets we keep are not ours to share. But if you're asking me as his stepmother ... he's nothing but a babbling fool around you. He would've lost his mind completely if the sea took you. Truthfully, I'm surprised he didn't strangle Echidna."

"He really likes that serpent?"

Sila smiled, then gestured for Thessa to spin. "They have an interesting relationship."

A smooth stone pressed into the grooves of her back, wedging into places she didn't know existed. Thessa curved into Sila's magical touch. "Your body has been through a lot in the last day."

"No thanks to *him*," Thessa countered. "I'm not sure why it took a near death experience to learn I'm trustworthy."

The stone lifted off her back as Sila said, "Me either."

She spun around. "Am I foolish for trusting him?" *For falling for him,* she wanted to say. She scanned Sila's face for the truth.

Sila swallowed before answering, "It's bold of any female to trust a male wholeheartedly." She glanced down toward her scars and added, "This I've learned."

41

LECTURE NOTES FROM GEOGRAPHICAL DISTRIBUTIONS:

The woodlands that make up a better part of Greenshire hold trees unique to the region. Not only are the trunks 2-3x the circumference of a typical tree, but the leaves remain green all year round.

Thessa shrunk in her seat. Rather than dining in shifts, the entire camp was present and bustling around the braziers. Hundreds squeezed around wooden tables, while the children found seats around the fire.

Jussal was in the middle of telling her how the tables and chairs here were made on sight. Woodworkers were responsible for rebuilding the dining space at each encampment, rather than carrying everything to a new location. Before the move, everything would be burned.

Instead of the usual frog stew or simple salad of nettles and ferns, tonight's feast was celebratory. She'd smelt the rabbits smoking from the river.

Jussal went on to tell her that almost half the camp had joined in on today's hunt, making the meal possible this evening—the night of the Blood Moon.

Thessa was seated at the table reserved for council, which she hated. It sat slightly higher due to the landscape, and tonight, hundreds of eyes lingered on her.

Sila nudged her to say, "Word's spread about your powers. Half the camp's fascinated, and the others deny it to be true."

"But it is true," Thessa said.

"Well, they haven't seen it with their own eyes."

"You haven't either."

"No, but I have," Jussal countered, passing her the bowl of cauldron-boiled corn.

Sila whispered to her, "Soren wouldn't have walked you into this camp if there wasn't something special about you."

Before she could reply, *he* showed up, sitting across from her with a grunt.

Tonight, casual attire was off the menu. Soren had swapped his usual black tunic for one with sheen. His chest peeked through too, showing off his slithering tattoo. Although his shoulders were pinned back, his eyes lacked their luster, like the night without its moon.

Fiddling with his empty water cup he flicked his gaze to hers. "You look nice."

Thessa scowled. Not because she didn't love the long skirt Sila had lent her, or the patches of net-like fabric covering her chest, but because she hated him.

Soren cleared his throat.

Can you really still hear me?

One look and she had her answer.

"Remind me to thank the hunters," Thessa said to Jussal, forking her portion of rabbit in an attempt to ignore the snake sitting across from her.

Trays of mead splashed on each table as if it weren't a question, rather an answer. She was drinking tonight.

"Son, when will you be delivering your speech?"

Thessa eyed Soren. Was this what he meant by needing to organize some things before dinner?

"I suppose, now," he answered.

Thessa blinked and he was up, weaving through the spattering of tables. After a few long strides, he was standing at the very top of a boulder. The Blood Moon hovered above him, casting a chilling spotlight. Chatter quieted and children were shushed, as every head turned his way.

"Good evening to all," Soren started. "I regret to inform you that tomorrow's relocation will not be in the southern forests."

The crowd murmured questions.

"We'll be moving north instead."

There were gasps. "But this is our home!" Someone shouted.

How'd you think they would react?

Soren went on, "This is all of our homes, but the capital continues to send soldiers to what *was* my family's property, as well as the McPorter's. I'm pleased to report the spies we dispatched were not harmed, but the capital will not yield until they claim what they came for. I can assure everyone, there is no more hiding, and the time for battle is swiftly approaching."

Half the crowd shuddered, and the others cheered for war.

Soren raised an arm, gesturing for silence. "Wayland McPorter was sent to warn the northern encampment a week and a half ago. They're moving south at dawn. Our combat units have been preparing, and council will meet shortly after our arrival to be sure our plans are intact."

"We'll sandwich the flaming bastards!" One oversized male called out while slamming his mug of mead down.

Soren cleared his throat, eyeing the crowd. "Which brings me to my second announcement. It's important to remember not all those who carry flame ... are *bastards*."

Giggles swept through the crowd.

"We'll be minimizing civilian losses by any means necessary. There will be no careless destruction either. You all know the Blood Moon calls for gathering. There will be innocent lives scattered across Gravenport the next few days." His eyes met hers before continuing, "Consider it a crime to disobey this order. We'll not give the Supremes another reason to undo our existence."

Thessa managed a smile. *Thank you.*

A voice called out, "What of our children?"

Another voice rang. "Our innocents?"

Soren swept his gaze across the crowd. "Those who aren't fighting will assist the healers and woodworkers. Gather whatever they need and as much they need. You'll hunt, you'll fetch water, and you'll keep moving as long as you're breathing. Our combat units are prepared to protect you. Which brings me to my third announcement; we have a new resource."

Whispers moved. Several sets of eyes even darted toward Thessa. She tried to duck but it was useless. If he was about to announce her powers in front of everyone here, she may truly die before eating her last meal.

"As some of you've heard, the Hidden Grimoire of Eiliana is now in our possession."

Cheers ripped through the tables before he could finish.

He waved for attention. "We're searching through it daily, and there is promise ... that I can say. We'll be distributing a powerful Illusion Spell before our trip north."

Thessa exhaled the breath she'd been holding.

"Lastly, I'll ask you all to remember." Soren tapped a finger on his heart—the same spot where the two serpent heads that coursed along his upper body met. "Remember why you're here and remember why we hide."

Heads began nodding in unison.

"Remember why we fight and remember those who died." His honey mead twinkled in the moonlight as he raised his glass high. "Remember."

Glassware all around her clinked.

⁂

WHEN THE MEAL CAME TO AN END, SOREN OFFERED THESSA his hand. "Shall we?"

"This doesn't mean I forgive you," she warned him.

He had the nerve to smirk. "Of course not."

A few goodbyes later, Soren was leading her to his tent. She limped along, using his calloused grip for balance.

"Echidna says, *Hello*, by the way."

She frowned. *I'm not talking about your pet right now.*

A small laugh escaped him. "You made my father's night when you agreed to finish reviewing the grimoire."

"Well, he was persistent enough." She'd taken one bite of her loin before Jussal had pressed them, as if she hadn't just drowned.

"That, he's always been."

"Why would you tell the entire camp the book held promise?"

"It does," he said. "We found the Illusion Spell, haven't we?

"That's hardly promise," she replied.

"They needed something. I know you'll call it a lie, and

call it what you will, but this is *my* role to fill. Maintaining the *illusion* of hope is better than offering none."

Thessa quieted, unwilling to argue. It wasn't her place to extinguish the hope of others, whether or not she disagreed with his tactics. "Why didn't you mention my powers?"

"That's not my announcement to make."

She exhaled. "Thank you for not bringing it up tonight. It's been—"

"A hard couple of days. You don't have to explain," he finished her thought.

Soren's tent was set so far from the bulk of the camp. They were less than halfway there when weakness prevailed. She groaned, slowing a little.

"What is it?"

"It's just sore. I'll be fine."

"Your leg doesn't need any more damage," he told her. Without room to argue, he scooped her up like she was a child.

Thessa prayed the moonlight concealed her reddened cheeks. "Again, this doesn't mean I forgive you," she reminded him.

"Acknowledged," he said, biting back that smirk.

Her muscles relaxed a bit, and she spent the rest of the walk listening to the hum of night insects.

"We're home," Soren blurted, breaching the threshold of his tent.

After setting her down she rolled her eyes. He had no idea how she felt about that word. "Let's just get this over with."

The old spellbook was perched on its tree stump.

"I'm surprised you left it unguarded."

His eyes fixed on hers. "I've already found what I was looking for."

She frowned at him before hobbling over and easing onto

the floor. Soren tried to help her down, but she'd swatted his hand away.

Seated beside her, he opened the grimoire to their place-holder. Thessa shook her head while reading the page. *Glamour Spells.* "It's a shame these only work on mortals, imagine glamouring the Elementals to burn themselves to a crisp? How simple."

"You're terrifying."

"Thank you." Flipping the page, she muttered, "You know ... my spellcasting professor said the success of any spell depends on the *will of the witch* ... I think Eiliana is what made this spellbook special, above anything else."

"You may be right, but you've got more will than Hades."

"Are you comparing me to my horse or a god?"

He flicked his gaze to meet hers. "Both."

"I'm not sure if that's a compliment."

He chuckled.

She shifted to a serious tone. "Is talking about Eiliana difficult?"

"Not as much as I thought it'd be."

She refocused on the book, unsure why she'd bothered to ask. *Cloaking Spells.* "Forbidden, but useful."

"Illusions will work better."

She agreed. "There's got to be more in here." Flipping to the next page, she was greeted with a pair of ravens, one on each side with their beaks meeting in the center spine. "While her art is lovely, it's also covering half the book. I'm not sure what everyone was fawning over for a century."

Darkness swelled in his onyx eyes, like something was trapped within them, itching to get out. "I meant what I said, Thessa. What if I wasn't meant to find the book, at all?"

Her brows twitched. "What do you mean?"

"What if I was meant to find its new owner instead?"

Vague memories of the goddess rambling from her stupor resurfaced. Was her gift meant to bring them together? She was not willing to admit this was all some fated attraction. Rejecting the hypothesis with the shake of her head, she said, "To be fair, I found you. Then saved you. Which, by the way, you've yet to thank me for, so I guess that makes us even."

Soren slapped a flat palm over the page. "Tell me you know how sorry I am."

"Yes, Soren, I know you're sorry. Does that make any of it okay? Does that make me feel better? It doesn't. Stop worrying about your petulant feelings and focus on the grimoire. If you're looking for support, perhaps your *pet* can provide that."

His jaw ticked. "Okay, maybe I deserved that."

"And more, although going on is only making my blood boil."

"I promise, no secret will ever be worth losing you."

"Why should I believe you now?"

He paused before whispering softly, "Because I'm falling in love with you."

The words hit her like a jagged rock. "Why would you say that?"

Soren's sigh sounded like a heartache in the wind. "There's a reason why talking about Eiliana isn't as hard as I'd thought it'd be. I spent a century searching for a shred of hope in the form of my late wife's spellbook, only to stumble upon something *far greater*. You can pretend all you want, but this ... us ... we were meant to find each other. It's not time that's healed me, but *you*."

Thessa swallowed, unsure how to control the bile working its way up her throat.

He continued, "Except I've been lying to myself too, Thessa. I'll curse myself for taking so long to see how much you mean to me—I'll do anything." Drifting his hand to her knee, he squeezed, sending a wave of heat through her.

She began shifting in her seat.

"Do not bolt out of here," he pleaded.

If she could, she would ... but something wasn't right. She felt *too* hot. Holding out her trembling fingers, she muttered, "I don't feel so good."

In an instant, pain shuddered through her. She screamed as her torso flew back. Soren swore, managing to catch her head before it crashed to the floor. He pinned an arm across her chest, while ripping open his other.

Warm blood dribbled onto her parted lips.

"Drink, Thessa."

One taste and she instinctively pulled him closer. A few gulps in and the heat subsided ... then the pain ... then the trembling. She closed her eyes, drinking him in.

Slurpy, breathy sounds escaped her.

You taste so good.

"I'm going to need you to think about anything else, please."

It's impossible to think of anything else. Stop listening to my thoughts.

"I don't actively try but when you're attached to me, it's *impossible* not to hear."

Teach me how to hear you. I can focus on that.

"Part of it is quieting your own thoughts. The other part is accessing your power and channeling it to who you're connected with."

It wasn't possible. The taste was too intoxicating. She moaned on his forearm.

Soren groaned, "Please, try harder."

Thessa breathed through her nose, but slower. She really

tried this time. After a few rounds of controlled breathing, she felt her mind ease.

How do I channel my magic to you?

"You have to let me in."

She tapped into her well of magic. A dark, depthless sea.

There's nothing here but my magic. No doors. No windows.

"Focus."

Thessa squinted to see something caging in her sea—so tall and dark she hadn't seen them before. What she'd thought was infinite, was trapped. She'd been desperately keeping him out—everyone out—she realized, spending all this time, and all this energy, on *walls*.

"Let. Me. In." He bit out each word.

I'm trying.

He was her antidote in more ways than one, had been. He not only deserved her forgiveness, but perhaps love in return.

Water splashed as her walls crumpled into the sea, and what felt like the weight of the moon lifted from her chest.

Something immediately caught her eye, rippling through the water. Her magical sea eddied along each side of the black serpent swimming up to meet her.

Its red tongue flicked once. *You found me.*

Why are you in this form?

Your mind manifests a sea. Mine manifests this.

You're a giant. Way larger than Echidna.

Thessa, I need you to listen.

I'm listening, aren't I?

There's no other way for me to tell you this so I'm just going to say it.

You're making me nervous.

If I wanted to exhaust my magic, I could shift into what you see here, but my mind would shift too. I'd become a full serpent.

Is this how you exhausted your magic during the war?

His serpent head bobbed. *You're not afraid of me?*

Never of you.

Thessa opened her eyes, gently pushing his bloodied arm away from her mouth. "Thank you for telling me."

He nodded.

"So, what happened to make you shift?"

"Eiliana had just been killed, and we were running out of options. I did what I had to do. My father and a group of fighters managed to capture me before the Elementals did ... leaving me inside a carriage, wounded and alone, for three days."

"Three days, as a serpent?"

He nodded. "My father would open the door long enough to toss rabbits inside. That's it."

Thessa exhaled, listening.

"That's when I finally accepted my bond with Echidna. I refused it up until that point. But she's the one who helped me shift back. I'm not even sure how, but she helped me remember I was not meant to be a beast ... at least not forever. Without her help, I'd be dead. I haven't felt trapped like that since I was in the capital's dungeon. I thought about shifting while I was in there—surprise the guards and go out with some dignity, but I'd given up all hope at that point. A hundred years of searching for a spellbook, for nothing, and my best friend was going out with me. I wanted to die."

"So why leave with us? Why not stay and shift?" Her tone was sharp. She was aggravated that he cared so little for his own life.

"When I bled in that cell, you remained."

"That's because we share the same blood."

"Well, it shook the nonsense out of me. You reminded me what I was searching for. Forgetting may be kinder to the mind, but it's just another lie."

Thessa agreed.

Leaning closer, Soren lifted her chin and asked, "Please, may I kiss you?"

She rubbed her bloody lips together, inviting a soft, press of his lips.

Soren pulled back and said, "One moment," before gathering a slew of cushions, and bundling them around her. Afterwards, he poured her a cup of lemon water. "Drink."

"You're fussing, Soren." While she sipped, her eyes danced between the damage on both his forearms. "Maybe we could fetch a salve from Milanny?"

"She gave me one."

"And why haven't you used it?"

He shrugged.

Self-loathing fool. "Get the salve, Soren."

"And I'm the one fussing?"

Thessa burst out a laugh, sputtering blood-tinged water.

Soren laughed too, spinning out of view. It wasn't long before a damp cloth dangled in front of her eyes. "Clean yourself up."

She did, then scooched over, pressing some cushions aside. "Come sit with me. And bring the grimoire."

"We don't have to finish tonight. My father will deal with it."

"No. I want to."

Setting the spellbook beside her, Soren sat and unscrewed the canister of salve. He dug a finger through the paste and waggled it before her. "You first."

Sliding the fabric of her skirt up, Thessa exposed her punctures to him. They were healing and no longer oozing, which she supposed was a good thing.

His calloused fingers, so rough and deadly, nursed her

wound gently. "Holes this deep will still scar, salves can't help that, you know."

"I know."

I missed this.

I missed you, too.

Stop listening to my thoughts.

Stop listening to mine.

Thessa laughed again.

Soren spoke through his teeth. "You don't know what that noise does to me."

"When I'm feeling better, you can let me know." Her lips curved.

He grinned, but it was short-lived. That serious, general face returned. "I want you to feed in the morning before we move north. If we're separated and your symptoms return, I won't forgive myself."

"No need for theatrics, I'm fine with that." She never wanted that pain to return.

"The venom shouldn't last much longer."

How it was possible for someone to be her death and savior at the same time, she wasn't sure. "I know."

Spreading the book between them, Thessa read aloud to quiet her thoughts. "Healing Spells, how fitting."

Rubbing the salve between his wrists, Soren said, "If it comes to battle, spells like these aren't possible time-wise. It's best to shuffle the injured back to camp and let our healers take over."

Thessa flipped the page. It was a map of Greenshire forest. "Eiliana knew this area well?"

"She grew up in those woods."

"I hear it's peaceful there."

"It is."

Flipping the page, Thessa muttered, "This can't be real."

She read the two words once more, *Astral Projection.* "Soren, this could work. This could actually work."

He leaned in, scanning the spell with scrutiny. "But for what purpose?"

"What if we don't need to fight? What if I could speak with the Troika to demand change before conflict?"

"Thessa." He shook his head. "We tried talking, they decided incinerating us was easier."

"Not with this you didn't. It'll show us how they'll react."

"I refuse to speak with the Supremes."

"That's fine because I will."

He clenched his fists. "I won't let you do this."

She raised a brow. "You may lead this army, but you do not lead me. I'm speaking to them, and that's that."

"It's foolish and you know it."

"We'll have an army waiting and ready, won't we? I need to try."

Surrendering with an exhale, Soren gave up. "Fine."

Thessa smirked in victory.

Head tilting, he asked, "What's going on in that head of yours?"

"The will of the witch, Soren."

"Explain yourself."

Shoving a palm against his chest, she said, "Sit back then, you're making me tense."

42

LECTURE NOTES FROM THE ART OF BLACKSMITHING III:

In simple terms, sharpen your dagger or fail.

Soren shifted to his side, facing her. "Good morning, my love."

The edges of Thessa's mouth curled hearing the last two words. "When did I fall asleep?"

Rubbing his face, he said, "I was going to ask you the same thing." He scanned her. "How are you feeling?"

"I feel fine, considering." She sat up and lifted her skirt to inspect her wound. The edges were coming together, and it no longer throbbed. It wasn't warm to the touch either.

"Morning, is Thessa in there?" Sila's voice sounded from outside, startling them both to their feet.

"Hi, Sila!"

Sila popped her head in. "I tried your tent first, I should've known."

Thessa's cheeks flushed.

"I wanted to make sure you had something clean to wear."

She set a pile of clothing down on the floor. "I'll leave these here."

"Thank you, for everything." Thessa meant it. To be taken care of, so kindly, was something she'd never forget.

Sila nodded. "No trouble at all. I'll see you both at The Burn." And as quickly as Sila had come, she left.

Thessa eyed Soren and asked, "The Burn?"

"That's just what we call it. Burning everything before we leave symbolizes our resilience to rebuild. It's a bit celebratory."

"Got it. Should we pack?"

"No. I'll arrange to have our tents sorted."

Thessa reached for the bundle Sila had left her. It was a cream tunic and riding leathers, which wasn't Sila's typical fun and flirty attire, but Thessa knew why. Today marked the precipice of change. Her blood usually thrummed at times like this, but today it didn't. She'd slept well.

After dressing, she tucked the book under her arm and asked, "What else do we need?"

"Nothing. The carriages will be stocked."

When they arrived at the burn site the cooks were passing around oats that had soaked overnight. They were surprisingly pleasant when topped with honey. Hades would love it, that was for certain.

Soren helped chuck a few stumps into the massive pile of wood furnishings. Children ran around the emptied campsite in circles, while hundreds gathered around the pile, strapped in burlap sacks.

Sila passed copies of Eiliana's Illusion Spell through the crowd, and Jussal gave a quick speech reviewing their two-day route. Afterwards, Francis and a few other Elementals torched the pile.

The flames were mighty, and hot. Thessa shoved the

grimoire and oats into Soren's chest, and said, "Find somewhere to put these."

"Are you sure you want to do this?"

"We want the spell to work, don't we?"

His eyes softened.

Last night Thessa had told Soren she was not a fighter. She believed her purpose was to work toward a possible agreement. He'd not argued with her, only issued a small warning that they were long past agreements, and followed it up with a kiss for encouragement.

Thessa paced toward the flames, standing beside Francis.

When it all was well and burned, she held out her arms, nodding to the Elementals to step back.

Jussal was salivating as he called out, "Everyone, give her space."

Whispers rippled through the shifting crowd.

What is she doing?

That's the one the general keeps.

The fire-snuffer.

Do you think it's true?

I hear she's injured.

Dark tendrils escaped her fingertips, silencing the whispers. Her magic had passion and spark, soon blooming into a mountain of shadow.

Gasps sounded as Thessa stepped into the blaze.

When the fire ceased to exist, the rebellion roared. Hope gleamed around her in the form of tears, cheers, and admiration. As everyone closed in to celebrate, Soren dashed through the crowd. His arms wrapped tight around her waist, lifting her swiftly off her feet. When his fierce, black eyes found hers, the world disappeared entirely. She was falling into a chasm only to see something dark and lovely at the bottom, beckoning her to fall a while. He tipped his nose to touch hers and grinned so broad his sharp canines sparkled in the sunlight.

I'm going to need you to kiss me, Thessa.

It was hard to resist smiling back before she crashed her lips into his. Thessa held the will of this rebellion in one hand, and the serpent-wielder in the other.

❦

THESSA ASKED, "WHY ARE HADES AND ARES LEADING THIS carriage?"

"Because we're riding in it."

"Your bags and the grimoire are inside, sir."

"Thank you, Reginald. You've been more than helpful."

Reginald dipped his head and moved to speak with the driver.

Thessa narrowed her gaze at Soren. There were only three carriages and hundreds of travelers. "Why? You said the carriages were for storage."

"Your leg." His tone was sharp and left no room for argument.

"I said I feel fine," she snapped. It was true. Walking was no longer a burden.

"And I want to make sure it stays that way," he pressed.

Even if he had a point, it wasn't fair.

Thessa, argue with me in the carriage then.

Caving, she stepped into the wood paneled cabin. The opposing benches were draped in a dark floral print, matching the window coverings. She plopped down with a sigh before Soren shut them both inside.

He sat beside her and asked, "Why are you so stubborn?"

"I don't want special treatment. Resentment is the last thing that'll help us," she said.

"They were cheering your name. That's far from resentment."

Thessa tried to hold back her grin. "They were pretty impressed, weren't they?"

His gaze drifted from her eyes to her mouth as he spoke through their bond. *I almost ripped your clothes off in front of children.*

Her body hummed for him, especially as his knuckle nudged her chin.

"I suppose ... they'll understand," she whispered, closing the distance between them.

Soren, the victor, smiled and kissed her. It was soft, though the press of his lips held something formidable. "They most certainly will," he whispered back, moving his mouth to her neck.

Every peck and scrape of his teeth had her shriveling in her seat. She palmed his thigh, squeezing it to rid her own tension.

"You should feed," Soren reminded her, cutting right through her bliss.

When he brought his wrist to his mouth, she kicked her leg up, unsheathed her blade, and thrust her dagger at him. "Please. Use this."

After slicing through his skin he noted how sharp her blade was.

"Thank you." She took the compliment with a smile before sliding down to settle down between his knees.

She looked at him, then his bleeding forearm draped over his thigh, and latched on. Each sip was more divine than the last. As her feed turned into a feast, all she could think about was how delicious he tasted.

Soren swore.

When her hands traced his chiseled waistline, her name slithered off his tongue.

In response, she lifted her mouth from his arm, rubbing her bloody lips together. She was satiated, yet not at all. Looking up, she met Soren's darkened glare.

He grinned, ordering her to undress while wrapping a cloth around his wrist with expert speed.

Getting out of Sila's too-tight leathers had proven to be just as difficult as squeezing into them. Soren had already stripped down and was threatening to rip them off of her, and she was about to let him until they finally gave.

A shift of Soren's arms and he'd pulled her astride his lap.

"I wasn't done," she teased, jabbing his shoulder with the point of her nail.

"Done with what?"

She couldn't say it out loud, and didn't have to.

Tasting you.

Releasing his grip on her hips he threw interlaced hands behind his head and smirked. "Oh, by all means."

Thessa knelt back down, kissing his knee first. Then the other. She moved her way up his bare thigh, slow enough to torture him. Though she was only torturing herself, she loved the taste of him. His skin. His magic. His blood. His—

Thessa, I'm going to destroy you.

Me first.

When her mouth met the base of his length, he moaned. Forgoing kisses, she licked her way up.

Soren shuddered.

Bracing his thighs, she slid her mouth around him and sucked. Slow and deliberate movements shifted into a hasty game of making him finish.

At some point, his fingers had woven through her hair,

helping guide her up and down his length. When he slammed his tip into the back of her throat, she moaned.

That's what you want?

Seated deep inside her mouth, she nodded in answer.

Soren gripped her head and thrusted hard enough to make her gag, before growling and pulling her off. He jerked his chin to the opposing bench and said, "Sit."

Never taking her eyes off of the male tinkering with her heart, she slid back and up to her seat.

His voice was low and rumbling as he said, "Now put your legs up how I like them."

Seconds passed and she hadn't done what he asked. Instead, she was doe-eyed and rubbing her knees together.

"Thessa," he breathed. "Are you going to behave?"

She swallowed her rebuttal and set one foot on the bench at a time—utterly exposed. Soren grumbled his approval before leaning forward and ordering her to touch herself.

Heat flooded through her

Do what?

Go on.

Soren's eyes shifted to her center as he stroked his length.

To do something like *this* in front of each other was unthinkable. Although, if she cared to admit it, watching him come undone was making her entirely weak.

Starting easy, she cupped and rubbed her breasts.

His approval didn't last long. He flashed his pointed canines. "Lower."

Soren.

Lower.

Her fingertips trailed down her stomach, landing between her thighs.

Soren's hand was roaming brutally over his tip. By the

looks of it he wasn't going to last. "Do you see what you do to me?" His voice was rough.

"Yeah," she breathed, finding her most sensitive spot and pressing down. "You do the same to me."

Soren's predatory grace gave way to wild hunger. He flew across the carriage and landed between her legs.

He groaned on her skin, as if starved.

Thessa gasped as he became a blur of tongue, teeth, and feral heat. Clutching the window coverings for leverage, she writhed, whimpering a string of curses. Every time she'd try to slide back, he pulled her closer. When her hips would lift, he'd shove them down. If her knees dared press closer, he'd tear them apart. He was a serpent, suffocating his prey in the most brilliant of ways.

Through their bond, she asked, *why won't you let me have all of you? I need you. Every part of you.*

Soren swore as his body shook. His mouth hovered over her center as his hot breath came out in bursts. The feeling sent waves rippling inside her. With his head down between her thighs, he whispered, "You've thoroughly destroyed me."

Thessa sighed, thinking how his mess could've easily been solved.

Still crouched between her legs, he eyed her. "Not even the elixir you keep taking will help your campaign. Even the best ones have their faults. If you were to fall pregnant, do you understand what that means?"

Did he think she paid no attention in Immortal Anatomy lessons? "I understand pregnancy leads to a child, but the elixirs are effective, at least for a majority."

"See. You admit it."

Thessa closed her legs, shoving him out. "You've taken the fun out of this."

He exhaled, sliding up to sit beside her. "It's not the chance of a child I'm concerned about."

"Just tell me why then."

He paused, running fingers through his silky, black hair. "I wish to never pass my powers on. To be this different ... is a burden. Living in a world where we are hunted, is a burden."

This form of nobility was frustrating and although she understood, her eyes rolled anyway.

He toyed with her breast while nuzzling into her neck. "Forgive me."

"For now."

❧ 43 ❧

LECTURE NOTES FROM ANIMAL HUSBANDRY:

Horses require a substantial amount of feed and water. The addition of oats to their diet will keep them full, while salt blocks ensure they stay hydrated.

Hooves clopping on cobblestones chimed in her ears. After camping in the forest just south of Mabelton overnight, the second leg of their journey began early the next day. The three carriages rode through town while the rest of the rebellion avoided it.

The majority continued north on foot, protected under a canopy of trees, while some families chose to stay in Mabelton, unwilling to travel farther, or take part in battle.

Thessa couldn't blame them. Soren hadn't either.

Through the window, she eyed the bay until it was out of sight. Not far past it was her favorite tea shop and the library where everything began.

"There'll be a time when you can enjoy it again."

"Are you listening to my thoughts?"

"I don't have to."

How long had she been staring out this window longing for a slice of normalcy? She sighed. "This better work."

Soren gave her an indiscernible look.

"Once we make it to Gravenport, how will the rest of camp know where to find us?" she asked.

"I'll send two of the drivers on horseback, they'll find them."

"But this is different. They'll be farther north than ever before."

"We've moved as a group hundreds of times, we'll track them."

"There's children, Soren," she reminded him.

"And I'll do my best to protect them. We all will."

Thessa shook her head. War was brewing in a cauldron she held the spoon to.

❧

A FEW HOURS LATER THE CARRIAGES ARRIVED AT THE border between the southern and northern territories.

Thessa wasn't expecting to get harassed. Every other crossing had been as simple as the driver stating their comings and goings.

Thankfully, all the drivers Soren had assigned were Elementals. There'd be no other shadow-wielders crossing the formal border. The woods would protect them—as they had for centuries.

Soren shot off his bench faster than lightning.

Thessa groaned, "Sit down. You think they don't have an illustration of your face by now?"

His nostrils flared. "I can't just sit here. They're ransacking my carriage."

"I'll deal with this."

Thessa slammed the door shut behind her and stomped over to the first carriage. The corner of her eye caught Hades, who had her ears pricked back.

Canvas, poles, and cloth were flung in every direction. To her credit, the driver of the first carriage remained calm.

Approaching the mess, Thessa spat, "You can't do this."

"Excuse me?" A soldier, wrapped in a scarlet bow, whipped her head to face her.

"Says who, exactly?" Another guard stepped up, glaring at her like she was dirt. This one had a chin as pointy as her red-painted fingernails, with black, beady eyes.

"You'll damage my tents before the festival even begins," Thessa proclaimed with a face the portrait of innocence.

The guard tossing canvas paused. "What festival? And where's your cloak?"

"Southerners," the other guard sneered. "No respect."

"The festival that *my* tents were ordered for, in Greenshire. How will I make it in time if I'm here cleaning up your mess? And why would I wear that thick thing in this weather?"

One guard asked, "All these carriages contain festival materials?"

"Tents, dinnerware. Precisely," Thessa answered.

Both guards stepped back. "Then you wouldn't mind if we checked?"

"Well, we don't need your permission, now do we?" The second guard snickered.

As they approached carriage number two, the driver eyed Thessa warily. Unlike the first driver, this one was visibly shaking. Swallowing the lump in her throat she formed what she hoped was a reassuring look on her face.

Thessa joined the soldiers amidst their sloppy inspection. "See anything of interest?" she asked, poking her head in between them. "Oh, please do be careful with those ewers. The porcelain was imported from Sanabria."

Both guards ordered her to step back.

Thessa complied, knowing better than to push them too far. After they'd made a decent mess, they moved to the final carriage—her carriage.

Ignoring the pulse bounding beneath her skin, Thessa managed a flat smile.

On their pursuit, the first guard asked, "Where'd you say you were headed?"

"Greenshire."

"Specifically?"

"T-three miles west of the Anderan River." She'd stuttered and they heard it. "We better be going. Thanks for your blessed service." Thessa signaled the drivers to reboard.

The beady-eyed guard sneered, "Not until you tell us what's hiding in this carriage. Or should we find out for ourselves?"

No.

Thessa wanted to scream it.

They're coming.

In a panic, Thessa blocked their path.

The guards tossed their flames in the sky, warning her.

But their magic flickered to nothing as the air was choked from their lungs. Serpents had snuck up behind them, slithering up and around their necks. Just before they collapsed, clawing at their throats, Soren opened the carriage door. "They were awful anyway."

She sighed, stepping over the struggling soldiers and into

the carriage. Soren ordered the drivers to take care of the rest before slamming the door shut.

Thessa sighed. She was falling in love with a monster. "We won't win the Troika's favor if you keep killing their soldiers before we attempt a truce."

"They've taken everything from me. They won't take you too."

She crossed her arms. "Spare me. If they thought there were whispers of a rebellion, consider this shouting."

"Oh, it's about time we shouted."

Thessa went silent, focusing on the shapes woven into the window covering instead. A few lavender-infused inhales later, the carriages were moving again.

"And the horses?" she asked.

"We'll let them rest somewhere more secluded."

"Good."

Grabbing her dagger and the bag of supplies someone packed for them, she began gathering everything she needed.

"What are you doing?" he questioned.

She ignored him, slicing the blade across her palm.

LECTURE NOTES FROM REALM RULES & METHODOLOGY:

Forbidden spellwork includes, but is not limited to, Astral Projection, Cloaking Spells, Illusion Spells, Multiplicity Spells, Resurrection Spells, Torture Spells, Love Spells, Possession Spells, Memory Spells, and Wisdom Spells. These will not be taught in your Spellcasting and Curation course, rather discussed.

One moment, she was in the carriage, and the next she was in her old room at the townhouse. Her body felt exactly the same, despite being a tad translucent. But it was unsettling how her footsteps left no sound—almost as unsettling as the scrunched-up faces peering back at her; twin faces with blood-red eyes and moon-white skin.

"Mira, Mona, hi. Sorry to barge in like this."

"It's Mina."

"And Mora." Their high-pitched voices sounded exactly the same too.

Mina continued, "Please don't tell me you've died and come back to haunt this room. I can't deal with another ghost." She moved, stomping toward the wardrobe.

"What are you doing?" Mora barked at Mina.

Mina spun and spat, "Packing. I'm moving across the hall. You're welcome to stay here ... with that *thing*."

"Excuse me?" Thessa interrupted.

"Do ghosts usually talk?" Mina questioned Mora.

"Mostly in moans or riddles, so this is peculiar."

Thessa was shaking her head. "I'm not a ghost."

Mina sighed. "Poor thing is still in denial. She can find some other witch to help her cross over because it's not going to be me." She whirled around from her wardrobe with a bundle of clothes in her arms before waddling out of the room.

Thessa was two steps from stopping her until she stopped herself. Let them think she was some trapped spirit, she figured that would take care of one problem.

When Mina disappeared, Thessa turned to see Mora flipping through her grimoire and snuck a look.

Goddess.

"While you decide which Banishing Spell to try, may I ask if Noam and Rhetter still live in the other townhouse?"

Mora's red eyes flicked up to hers, along with a bright, red glow on her cheeks.

Thessa smiled. "Are you sleeping with one of them or both?"

Mora's eyes widened before scanning the page once more. Her finger moved faster, as if in a desperate hurry to memorize the spell.

Thessa laughed before leaving her old bedroom.

Stepping down the townhouse stairs felt nostalgic, although the absence of smells she missed. As much as she loathed the angry chef, her breads and pies were delightful.

Thessa wished pie making would channel her unrelenting thoughts the same way a hammer had. Baking only angered her. Some souls were simply not meant to combine milk, sugar, and butter.

Crossing through the shared dining hall, she ignored the witches staring her way. There were more than a few gasps, and lingering comments.

That's the one that got kicked out.

Why does she look like that?

Is she a ghost?

Thessa could've been more careful about walking through tables, chairs, and walls, but it was her first time casting an Astral Projection Spell and it was too tempting not to try.

After threatening to haunt several males for the rest of their lifetime, Thessa was escorted to Noam's and Rhetter's workstation—garbage duty.

"This is disgusting. Why haven't you requested a different work assignment yet?" Thessa asked by way of greeting.

"Thessa. I'd ask why you're here but I'm more curious as to why you're flickering?" Rhetter spoke for the pair.

"The spell is running out of time. I didn't use much blood."

"What spell?"

"Did I say spell? I'm a ghost, I mean. Dead as dead comes," she said, correcting herself. They weren't buying it. "You've known me for eighteen years, please just roll with it."

They eyed each other in silent conversation before Rhetter asked, "What's going on?"

"Are you two still playing that board game of yours?"

"You came back here to mock us about Dungeons & Serpents?"

She bit back her laugh. "Not a terrible idea, but no." Shifting to a more serious tone, she said, "I need your help bringing it to life."

Noam's ears must've perked up because he spoke for the first time. "Hello ghost of Thessa's past, how may we be of service?"

She grinned.

❧ 45 ☙

LECTURE NOTES FROM SPELLCASTING AND CURATION:

Both Illusion and Cloaking Spells are forbidden because they play tricks on the eyes. Illusion spells are far more complex, holding the power to condense a body into the proportion of the illusion desired. Despite this, both spells could be overcome, potentially leaving the spellcaster in grave danger.

The location Soren scouted was just shy of the capital. It was large enough to hold what remained of the southern half of the rebellion—those who'd continued farther north—but it was nothing like the dense woods of Wilcrest.

It was temporary, at best.

Two drivers had left on horseback already; they'd find those on foot from Mabelton and lead them back here. Meanwhile, Thessa had helped Soren and the remaining driver set up tents in preparation.

It wasn't long before he'd asked her to rest. She'd refused the first few times, until the pain in her thigh returned. Sighing, she took her leave.

❦

"Stop doing that," Soren scowled at her.

Thessa shoved him away with a bloodied palm. He'd been an inch from her face when she awoke from the Astral Projection Spell—again.

He pulled back, scanning her.

There was a five-pointed star drawn across her chest, Eiliana's grimoire sprawled to her right, bloodied paste to her left, and her dagger beside that.

"Are you okay?" he asked.

"Yeah, it worked."

"Where'd you go this time?"

"I went back to *haunt* Mina and Mora again." Thessa wiggled her fingers for ghostly emphasis. "They're absurd and it's too easy. I just wanted to practice."

"Tell me next time. I don't particularly enjoy finding you unconscious with bloodied breasts. Well, the former—the latter is markedly attractive. It almost pleases me as much as my blood on your lips."

The sight of his half-smile was enough to make her blood simmer, like that pounding silence between lightning and thunder.

But that fanged grin she loved so much disappeared as realization struck his features. "Please don't tell me you were unclothed?"

She pressed up to her hands. "And if I was?"

Growling was the answer to her question.

She rolled her eyes. "No. It all works the same way. So I could be wearing whatever I picture, wherever I can picture it. But it can't be anything or anywhere. The spell says a memory of each must already be held."

He handed her a damp cloth, as well as her tunic. "Brilliant."

"She was, wasn't she?"

Soren sat beside her, keeping his hands busy by cleaning up her mess. "Eiliana was a master of many forbidden spells. Her father would've locked her in their library if it weren't for her determination to be outside. Christof was just as sick as my father."

"If only he noticed how much she loved the woods. And to sketch. And ravens. It seems like those things pleased her very much."

"You're right."

"Is her father still alive?"

"Christof leads the northern rebellion."

Thessa went quiet. She hadn't realized Christof was her father—the husband of the Forgone One. She knew Jussal had approved of whatever it was going on between them but what if—

"Who cares what he thinks," Soren answered the question she'd not spoken.

She frowned. "When will this mind-blood-bond thing wear off?"

"When your body recycles my blood and replenishes yours."

"But that could take months."

Soren grinned. "I quite like hearing your broody thoughts."

Thessa backhanded his chest. "Anyways. We need to talk

about the Supremes."

"Right. Tell me what you'll say."

"I'll tell them the truth, of course. That the lies they've spread will not be buried like our fallen. That we refuse to be forgotten, and we deserve a place in the world we helped create."

"And where is this discussion going to take place?"

"In the Trial Room, I think."

"And what if they're not in the Trial Room."

"Then I'll walk through walls until I find them, making every guard in the Central Divinity wish they never met the ghost of Thessa's past."

"The who?"

"Never mind, it's a mortal saying that my friends use."

"What?"

"Never mind."

"Sir." Their driver sounded from outside their tent.

"Yes Oleander, what is it?"

"The first group is arriving now, I've spotted them."

"Thank you, be right out." Soren pressed a kiss to her lips and said, "Put your shirt on before you kill me," then ducked out of the tent.

By nightfall a majority of the remaining rebellion had made it, and the rest would trickle in overnight. They'd told stories of how the Illusion Spell proved useful when the trees grew sparse. They'd camouflage themselves as rodents and insects until they were protected again.

After a brief evening meal, Soren led Thessa away from camp. "Bring your dagger," was all he'd said.

46

LECTURE NOTES FROM SPELLCASTING
AND CURATION:

Astral Projection is a far worse spell. Not only does it play tricks on the eyes, but it's impenetrable. There's no stopping the spellcaster unless their body is found. Due to its nefarious nature, it's strictly forbidden.

Thessa pivoted, dodging Soren's blow, and kicked his stomach. He curled on impact while simultaneously grabbing her foot. She was hopping, hopping ... she was down.

At least all the dirt and dead leaves had softened her landing.

"For someone so concerned about my leg, it doesn't seem like it." He didn't need to know it was feeling good today.

Soren bent over her, offering his hand. "We're running out of time, and you've hardly trained in combat."

She took it and stood.

"Don't kick unless it's below arms reach, or your opponent

is facing the other way." Soren stepped farther back and said, "Unsheathe your blade."

Thessa bent down and freed the dagger from her boot. Poised and ready she asked, "Where would you like to be scarred, general?"

He smirked, charging her without warning.

Thessa bent her knees, preparing to strike until her head whipped to the right and her blade was on the floor. Soren had driven his palm into the side of her face, while blocking her striking arm.

"Now what?" he asked.

Stuck between his arms, she answered with a question, "I die?"

"Thessa." He shook his head and released his counter-attack. "Never hesitate. It gives your opponent the chance to disarm you. If someone's charging at you, run to meet them. Make them think you're mad. Dodge at the last second to regain the advantage." He picked up her blade, handing it back. "Try it again," he said, flicking his hand in silent command.

Thessa had left a decent gap between them before bolting. She ran hard, meeting him in the middle, but not before dipping down and barreling into his knees.

Soren tumbled over her, groaning. "That works too."

Before he could find his footing, she slammed her body onto his back, thrusting her dagger into the crease of his neck. "Do you yield?"

He huffed a laugh, and then they were both laughing. She rolled off him, placing her palm beneath her ear to rest. Soren shifted to his side, meeting her.

"I'm not a fighter," she pleaded.

"If I'm not mistaken, you've been fighting one battle or another your entire life."

She blushed beneath the moonlight, unsure how he managed to truly see her.

"Get up, we're doing it again," he said, rising in one swift motion.

For three hours Thessa was ducking, pivoting, and rolling. She figured out how to wiggle out of most holds, and even managed to stab Soren in the arm. By the time she'd landed in their tent, her eyes slapped shut.

※

THE NEXT MORNING, THESSA AND SOREN HAD TAKEN Hades and Ares on a leisure ride to clear their heads. While tying them back up with the other horses, an unfamiliar rider trotted into camp—appearing from thin air.

The bright sun gave her a clear picture of his ice-blue eyes, a vivid contrast to his complexion, which was as dark as the night itself.

"Christof, welcome." Soren called out, marching toward him. "Your tracking skills are remarkable, as always."

This is Eiliana's father.

Transfixed, Thessa leaned into Hades' sturdy rear, observing their exchange. As Christof dismounted, his black cloak flowed to the ground. "General Whitfield, nice to see you this far north."

"If it were under better circumstances, I'd be quicker to agree," Soren responded.

She'd known the council meeting was soon, but she hadn't realized it entailed the *entire* council.

"Indeed." Christof's hard features softened as he said, "We're very sorry to hear about your mother, be sure our soldiers are ready and willing to fight in her honor."

The bob in Soren's throat was visible from afar. Not once

had he stopped to mourn his mother, not unless killing several Elementals Soldiers counted for something.

Most likely to change the subject, he asked, "Cloaking Spell?"

"Does the trick in a pinch."

Soren looked over his shoulder and gestured her over. "I'd like you to meet someone."

Thessa waved, stepping forward.

"Christof, this is Thessa, she'll be joining our meeting. You've met her friends, yes?"

She brushed a hand along Soren's back, the touch as soothing as steel, and asked, "Please tell me they're doing okay?"

Christof nodded by way of greeting. "The Celestials are fine, training mostly." He looked to Soren and added, "Wayland's blade skills are remarkable; he's been training our combat unit."

Questions danced on the tip of her tongue, but Christof moved on to talk strategy with Soren. As a flock of children flew past them, Soren said, "Let's continue this conversation elsewhere." He tied Christof's horse off with the others and spun around. "Follow us."

Inside the tent set up for council, Thessa took her seat across from a golden-eyed male she'd not recognized. He was seated beside Brenneth, who was next to Sila and Jussal.

Sila gave a brief introduction. "Sinclaire, this is Thessa, Thessa meet Sinclaire—head of weaponry."

Jussal added, "He's spent centuries crafting daggers. Every blade in this camp has crossed his hands."

Thessa's ears twitched. She ogled the smith with a glint of admiration. "If you need my assistance with anything, I'm happy to help," she offered.

Clearing his throat, Soren sat beside her.

Still fixated on Sinclaire, Thessa held tight for his response.

Sinclaire asked, "You know your way around a blade?"

Soren shot a heated look towards Sinclaire, then back to Thessa—she ignored him. "Very much so. I've taken the Art of Blacksmithing I, II, and III—by choice." Thessa bent down to unsheathe her blade, then slid it across the table. "I made this in six hours."

His roughened hands handled her dagger delicately, tracing every groove with his fingertip. It reminded her of Professor Shovak's ministrations. Thessa waited earnestly for his approval, scanning every line of his face until finally, his eyes flicked up to hers.

Passing her dagger back, the corner of his mouth curved upward. "It's well made."

Thessa beamed.

Sinclaire's foxlike eyes glimmered with interest. "I could —" he started, until he met Soren's lethal stare and quieted.

Thessa grimaced, knocking her knee into his. *What's your problem?*

Soren's jaw was working. *I'm not sharing you, Thessa.*

Her cheeks burned.

Christof interrupted their voiceless conversation, his eyes darting back and forth between them. "Are you two, together?"

They'd never talked about what they were, so that answer was a *no*.

"Yes," Soren said. The word had come out crisp and clean.

Thessa swallowed. *We need to talk.*

Later.

Lips smashed, she held her tongue. This was the last place she wanted to discuss the matter anyway.

She was no mood-reader but the shift in Christof's expression was undeniable. His ocean eyes were muddied with discontent. After an indiscernible noise, he looked to Jussal. "Let's begin, shall we?"

"Son." Jussal gestured to Soren.

Exhaling something other than pure air, Soren began, "Tomorrow can go one of two ways. The Supremes can take an overdue stance against their own brutality, or we can continue the hundred-year cycle and fight for our freedom. It's their choice to make."

"Choice?" Christof questioned him.

Thessa eyed Soren before addressing the table. "The general and I have gone back and forth on the matter, but we're in agreement. I'll be speaking with the Supremes first."

A sharp, intimidating laugh escaped Christof. "Do you wish to die?"

Soren had warned her the council would consider her mad for trying, but she'd made up her mind. He let out a low growl in her defense and said, "If we need to remind them of what wicked, dark things are waiting in the woods, Christof, we'll do just that."

Thessa cut in, "Eiliana's Astral Projection Spell will help me *not die*, actually." She'd perform the spell while Soren watched over her body.

Christof went still, his eyes bouncing to Soren. "So you finally found her grimoire?"

"It was Thessa who found it."

"It's a long story," Thessa said, "but your daughter was brilliant."

Christof grumbled, "Sometimes. Other times, foolish enough to get herself killed."

Soren's nostrils flared as wide as his eyes.

Thessa pressed a reassuring palm onto his thigh before

speaking. "Fear isn't something I'll let trap me anymore." She eyed Soren before continuing. "I say it's worth a try."

His hand drifted atop hers and squeezed.

Jussal spoke. "She's right." His tone was bright. "It's a chance worth taking. Thessa, when will you depart?"

"Tomorrow, at sunrise."

Christof shook his head. "This will only give them time to prepare."

"They've had decades to prepare," Soren said coldly. "And so have we."

"So what's your plan, general?" The disrespect in Christof's tone was not lost on Thessa.

"We'll be ready if Thessa's discussion goes awry. Hiding is what we do best, so we'll show them how well we do it. He took his finger to the map before him—an outline of the capital. Thessa recognized every corner. "All of our soldiers will make their way toward the gates and wait in these alleyways while Thessa performs the spell."

Brenneth nodded while rubbing a hand over his fist.

"Hardly inconspicuous, General Whitfield." Christof's tone was bold, as usual.

"Which is where this comes in," Soren countered, sliding Eiliana's Illusion Spell toward him. "Masking not only shape, but *size,* will be advantageous to hide us properly. Here's your copy."

Christof countered, "Fire won't protect an Illusion Spell."

Jussal grinned. "That's where Thessa comes in."

"I can't protect everyone," she interjected.

Christof scrunched his face at Jussal. "What does the female have to offer?"

Soren stood, slapping both his hands on the fresh-cut table. "Her. Name. Is. Thessa."

Thessa's eyes bulged. *Sit, please.*

He didn't. Soren glared at the leader of the northern rebellion with an obsidian storm brewing in his eyes.

Brenneth palmed his face.

Soren spoke through his teeth. "If you have a question, you may ask her directly."

Christof swallowed before shifting his gaze to Thessa. "My apologies, Thessa." His words held reluctance, but they landed. "What is it you do?"

Only once she accepted his apology had Soren been willing to slide to his seat. From that moment on, his eyes never left Christof.

"My shadows don't yield to flame," Thessa said.

A single dark eyebrow on Christof rose sky-high. "Is that right?"

"Yes," Soren hissed.

"Interesting." Christof's tone was skeptical. "We'll see how well then, won't we?" He stood, disdain stitching his brows. "If there's nothing more to discuss, consider the northern rebellion ready for battle, we'll be waiting in the alleyways at first light."

"Sinclaire has your weapons." Soren jerked his head toward the silent daggersmith, an unspoken order to retrieve them.

Sinclaire obliged, scurrying out of the tent like he was on fire.

"I'll show you to Sinclaire's tent," Brenneth offered Christof, escorting him through the flaps.

"Well, that went well," Sila muttered with sarcasm.

"Sila, dear." Jussal reached for her hand. "There's much to do. And son ... save that temper for our true enemies."

"Thessa," Sila said. "Thank you for trying to speak with them first. It's very brave of you."

"I'll try my best."

When Thessa and Soren were left alone, she rolled her eyes and started, "You remind me of a child sometimes."

His jaw clenched. "Christof has me on edge."

"I'm aware. Everyone is aware."

"And I learn you have a thing for daggersmiths?"

She scoffed. "Daggers, Soren. Not the smiths."

He quirked a brow. "Sharp objects, is it?"

"I like those fangs of yours, don't I?" She winked for the first time in years.

He leaned closer, swiping his tongue across them. Her body pulsed when he did that.

Soren smirked. "I thought you were angry."

I am.

Your eyes are telling me otherwise.

Scowling, she said, "Why'd you tell Christof we were together?" As if a council meeting was the best time to define their relationship.

"Are we not?"

"We never talked about it."

Soren moved closer, hovering his lips an inch before hers. "If I haven't made myself clear, Thessa. I want nothing but you."

With her heart practically thumping out of her chest, she said, "Then, I suppose, we're in agreement," and her mouth met his. It was a simple, yet defining kiss.

"Come on," he said smiling, "I'll show you to Sinclaire's tent."

Thessa squealed.

47

THESSA'S PRIVATE NOTES:

~~Thessa and Kellan, forever.~~
~~Does he even love me?~~
Did he ever love me?

The Trial Room was as she'd remembered it. Cast in sleek marble from floor to ceiling, the oval-shaped space held three empty thrones.

Thessa grimaced, padding past the podium and through the domed door in back.

Urgh, where are they?

They're not in there?

No. Empty.

The fact that she and Soren could still speak through their bond in her astral form was not something she'd expected. She wondered if it had something to do with her feed last night, amplifying their connection.

Let me focus.

And then he was gone.

Walking down the empty hall was discomforting, at best. Sconces flickered firelight, but there were no guards in sight ... which led her to believe the Supremes felt safe behind these walls.

Must feel nice.

Noise set in and Thessa followed the sounds. There was clinking and chatter. When the voices rang loudest, she paused before a door, listening.

"May I get you anything else, General Valstrom?"

"Not at the moment."

"And for you, Madame Hearthling?"

"The same, thank you."

Enjoying a meal, it seemed. Thessa stepped through the intricately carved door, a warm contrast to the cold marble walls, and said, "Blessed be, Supremes."

They gasped in unison.

Madame Morganna's fork dropped, the sound echoing off the smooth floor. There wasn't a carpet to be found in this miserable fortress.

General Valstrom slammed her fists on the table. "Guards! Seize her at once."

Madame Hearthling pursed her lips, setting her uneaten scone down. "How'd you get in here?"

Thessa eyed the soldiers. "Oh, I wouldn't bother." There was nothing to collect. Apparently, the more blood she used, the less translucent she appeared. She slipped through their arms and sauntered over to the dining table.

General Valstrom was seething. "Astral Projection is banned in this realm, when we find you, and trust me, we will, you'll be locked in the dungeons until there's nothing left of you."

Thessa sighed. "How typically extreme."

"Why do you look so familiar?" Madame Morganna asked quietly.

Thessa amused her. "You were the guest speaker at my graduation this year. Great speech, by the way. What was it you said about my future? *The possibilities are as unique and infinite as the stars?* You got me there." Her tone was nothing but satirical. She hadn't planned to act this way, but undeniable anger coursed through her veins. She understood now why Soren wouldn't have been able to form any sentences here. "And of course, you might recognize me from the recent trial ... do *serpents* sound familiar?"

Another round of gasps.

General Valstrom's face was etched with undiluted hatred as she whispered something to her guards.

Thessa began to pace in an effort to appear unworried. "I've already sent the message across Andera, fixing your lies. Shadow-wielders exist and were executed cowardly, by you three. And continue to be."

The room fell silent, all attention creeping toward her astral form. Madame Morganna and Madame Hearthling eyed each other, and Thessa could've sworn guilt swept across their faces, if only for a heartbeat.

Thessa went on. "Death is not to be feared, so why fear it?" She spun to the Elemental Supreme and pointed a dramatic finger her way. "Who will hold your hand, on your last breath, General Valstrom?"

No answer.

Thessa reclaimed her astral appendage and went on, "Unless you learn to accept our kind, and restore our rightful place in this world, the respect you hold will wither."

General Valstrom barked out a laugh. "There is *no place* in this world for demons, or their sympathizers."

"Our magic created this realm right alongside Celestial,

Elemental, and Botanical magic. Is it not darkness that balances light? For even you can see that, Madame Morganna, can't you? It's *your* Celestials who so quickly understood. We'll come peacefully. We deserve that chance. That is why I've come here." She tried not to beg.

Madame Morganna's lips parted but General Valstrom's glare had her mouth snapping shut.

The Elemental Supreme huffed, taking a sip of wine before speaking. "No. Absolutely not. If you try to walk these streets, you will die."

"Then we'll have to call this battle the ReAwakening. Hopefully it's written up correctly this time."

Madame Hearthling's eyes shot wide with worry.

"They've re-bred," General Valstrom spat, red wine dribbling from her thin lips.

Thessa backed through the wall and booked it down the hall.

She had one last conversation to have.

⚜

"How'd you get in here? Again? And why are you flickering?"

She shook her head. "Long story."

"Thessa, is this some spell?"

She sat on the foot of Kellan's cot. "Listen, I don't have much time left. I just need to know something."

He sat upright, scanning her with confusion. "What is it?"

"Do you really believe all shadow-wielders are bad? That just because someone told you they were, you believe it to be true?"

"What are you saying? Their magic is deadly by nature."

"And what is yours?"

"Not the same."

"That's not true."

Kellan rubbed at his eyes. "I'm going to ask you again, Thessa. What are you saying?"

She swallowed before speaking. "I'm a shadow-wielder. And there's many of us."

"What?" He looked around.

The guards that weren't sleeping were preoccupied, and she'd dodged the ones that had chased her here between flickers. "There's a rebellion," she said quietly.

His demeanor shifted.

"We've been exiled for centuries, for no reason other than control and power. You could help us spread the word."

Scratching his head, he said, "I don't believe this."

"Which part?"

He stood, gathering his uniform. "That I ever slept with something as filthy as you."

A soldier stirred from behind her. "Who is that?"

Kellan answered, "No one."

Her astral form was useless against feeling like she'd been stabbed in the heart. Flashing beyond resolution, Thessa disappeared.

HER EYES POPPED OPEN.

Soren was perched over her. "What happened? You were twitching this time."

Thessa sat up, scowling. "Nothing. We fight."

48

LECTURE NOTES FROM REALM RULES & METHODOLOGY:

Celestial power arises from the moon and stars—
light is what fuels their magic.

Wearing the black cloak given to her by Beatrix, Thessa and Soren rode through the mist-ridden capital. Despite the weather, her magic cast a perfect sphere of protection around them, warding off the onslaught of air-wrapped fireballs thrown their way.

Soldiers flooded the streets like a scarlet wave, no doubt a preparation order that had been placed by General Valstrom.

They'd managed to corral a majority of the soldiers on their way toward the towering gates.

Halting Hades, Thessa spoke to the crowd. "I have a message for your general."

One soldier among the rest inched forward. It was Kellan. "What do you think you're doing?"

"If this is the type of regime you wish to uphold Kellan, then by all means, fight for it."

The soldiers murmured while Soren kept quiet, though she'd felt his eyes snap her way after addressing the soldier by name.

"You're a demon," Kellan announced, as if it weren't wholly evident. Her shield may be translucent, but it was definitely black.

"Surprise." She wiggled her onyx fingertips for effect.

Soren grinned beside her.

Kellan conjured his own magic, molding it into a perfect sphere. As the air-wrapped fireball hovered atop his palm, she wondered if he'd ever cared about her—the difference between lust and love wasn't evident until she'd found it.

"You've been practicing," Thessa crooned. "As have I." She spread her arms, casting her magic wider. "You can tell your general her reign ends now!"

Kellan, among the rest, ignored her, tossing their fireballs into her sphere of night. Except, they had no idea how her magic worked, and it showed on their bewildered faces.

Thessa sat taller, shouting, "You've all been lied to—bred to hate something you know nothing about. Our kind were incinerated for your general's pleasure. Let today serve as a reminder that we'll never be forgotten. I suggest you leave now, or fight against us!"

Only a dozen soldiers scattered, ripping off their jackets and running down the graveled streets. Kellan remained, with his usual smug expression.

She lifted her chin and spoke softly to Soren. "Shall we?"

His thick whistle rang through the air in response, signaling the host of insects hiding in the alleyways. In a series of bursts the crawling creatures transformed into a full-fledged rebellion army, poised and ready to fight.

The Elemental soldiers startled back, tossing out a defensive wall of fire. The blast of heat felt all too familiar. With a single finger, Thessa cast a line of magic just as powerful, negating it.

"It won't be that easy, not this time," she seethed.

A slithering heap of darkness shot towards the gates as serpents poured from Soren's fingertips. Hundreds. The ones that weren't fried to a crisp wrapped around their targets' throats.

Soren yelled, "Charge!"

An onslaught of shadow bloomed across the graveled streets, smothering the choking soldiers within reach. Thessa paused to watch Kellan struggle for air he wouldn't find. She'd never told Soren about the gluttonous male who chewed up her heart and spit it out. If she *had*, his death wouldn't have been so quick.

Meanwhile, the Elementals on their side fought fire with fire and air with air. It was a meticulous game of who had better aim, and more power. But it wasn't enough. Fireballs were flying higher than blasts of air-magic could deflect, and farther than Thessa's magic could protect.

Screams roared as the rebellion burned. Their war cries shifted to pleas for help; pleas for death. The ground was a tangled mess of scarlet, flame and shadow. Thessa looked down, focusing on her breath and her shield. Her magic still pulsed strong, protecting as many soldiers as she could.

"Thessa," Soren shouted, pointing up.

Her eyes drifted to a massive cloud of Celestial magic growing overhead. Its glorious plume of white shimmering stars halted every soul in the streets. Countless Celestials appeared through the alleyways next, casting a sphere of magic so large Thessa wondered if there'd be any stars left in the sky.

They came. Why?

Thessa scanned the crowd. Leora's warm eyes flashed into

view. Both worry and determination laced her brows. Beside her was Ivy, Beatrix, and so many others. There wasn't time to tell them how stubborn they were, or how perfectly kind and compassionate. Celestial magic wasn't defensive, only distracting—but distracting enough to cease a war.

If only it'd lasted more than a moment.

The group of Celestials were forced back by the rebellion as the battle ensued. "We need to move," Soren shouted.

Thessa agreed, letting Hades follow Ares. Turning in her saddle, she hurled her shadows back toward the gates, then all the way around until she faced forward again.

Soren unleashed more serpents on enemy targets; his specificity was unmatched. But the Elemental Army had shifted to destruction mode. Fires burned everywhere. Flames were launching beyond her veil of darkness. Serpents fizzled. The smell of burnt skin was piercing her nostrils while the acrid taste of smoke coated her tongue.

It wasn't enough. She wasn't doing enough.

No, no, no.

Thessa closed her eyes, to find her sea within. She dove deep into its depths with every speck of strength she could muster. Anchoring down, down, down ... until she exploded.

The scream that escaped her was akin to a banshee. Hades reared in protest just as the sky went dark, and stayed that way. The world was cast in shadows like a sustained eclipse of the sun. Enemy soldiers may outnumber the rebels, but to what advantage do they hold without fire?

The rebellion roared, reigniting their fight as the Elemental soldiers called for a retreat.

Hades stomped her hooves into the earth.

"Thessa, stop!" Soren wailed. At some point he'd hopped off of Ares, because he was bracing her leg.

Sure, she was swaying a bit, but she was focused. This was working.

No, I'm concentrating.

"But your nose is bleeding. Your eyes. Your ears. You have to stop." He was pleading.

I won't.

You're bleeding too much, something isn't right.

I can end this. Let me.

No. Not like this.

With a flash of night, Soren shifted into the predator he was.

❧   49   ☙

LECTURE NOTES FROM IMMORTAL
ANATOMY:

Major arteries branch out from the neck, traveling into the shoulders, and down through the arms. They feed our fingertips with a healthy supply of magic. When our supply diminishes, kidneys will stimulate the production of new cells alongside red blood cells in the bone marrow, which can take a few days. The spleen and liver help recycle everything.

One heartbeat Soren had been by her side, begging her to stop, and in the next, he was a serpent.

Losing focus, Thessa's veil of darkness collapsed. Nothing remained of her shadows, but a small, sputtering sphere around her.

Something warm coated her face and neck. A finger inspection revealed fresh blood. A lot of it. Thessa dismounted, smacking both Hades and Ares on their rears, leaving bloody handprints behind. "Run!"

The enemy had ended their retreat at the abrupt return of light. Fireballs already streaked across the sky, and more of her army burned. This far away from the gates, a cluster of soldiers formed a wall of protection around her, despite her pleas for escape. She was desperate; her veins pounded with worry. She pushed and shoved the rebels, trying to get to the massive serpent thundering through enemy lines.

Elemental soldiers scattered at the sight of Soren, tossing frantic fireballs, while ally Elementals were using their air-magic to blast them away. Soren's tail looped through legs, tripping soldiers off balance while his fangs shredded their calves into ribbons. He'd taken down three soldiers in approximately three seconds, until a single blast of air sent him tumbling out of sight.

Thessa screamed, "No!" And as if the sky cried with her, rain began to fall. Her view was cut off, as was their fire—at least not without their energy-sucking air wraps and shields.

Then, like a red sea parting, General Valstrom waltzed through her army, dragging Soren by his mighty tail. An air-shield big enough for the two of them protected the fire-cuffs encasing his throat. Any relief Thessa had felt, was replaced with pure horror.

"Stand down if you want your companion back," General Valstrom ordered.

Anger rippled through Thessa, enough to breach her wall of protection.

Her allies fended off the Supreme's guards, leaving the two of them boxed in alone with Soren. Her magic wasn't strong enough to absorb the general's air-shield. There was hardly enough left to protect herself.

"Aren't you done yet?" General Valstrom crooned.

"Let. Him. Go."

General Valstrom pouted. "Why? I'd quite like something I can lock up and poke when I feel like it."

"I'm going to kill you," Thessa promised.

"And how's that? Your shadows don't smother like the rest." The Supreme tilted her head in observation. "I've been watching you, what an interesting *variation*."

Never hesitate.

Thessa unsheathed her blade and charged at the Supreme. She'd prepared to tumble into her legs, but the general side-stepped and laughed. Thessa fell, scurrying back to reassess her shield.

Intact.

Hissing drew her attention.

General Valstrom's face was twisting with sick pleasure as her fingers bore holes into Soren's flesh. Thessa could hear the searing and popping of his slimy skin.

She rushed toward the revenge-struck Supreme.

Anticipating her side-step, and playing into it, Thessa managed to stab her straight in the thigh before skidding out of reach.

General Valstrom roared, yanking on Soren's tail in retaliation.

Soren no longer hissed. He was limp.

Thessa snapped at the sight, releasing a force of rage she'd not known existed within her. She was all limbs, trampling the Elemental Supreme to the ground. Swinging in arc motion, the one she'd rehearsed with her forging hammer, Thessa stabbed. Her muscles delighted in the memory.

First, she pierced the general's shoulder. Ripping her blade free, she sunk it into the other shoulder, cutting off the blood supply to her arms. Then she stabbed her neck—right through the center to shut her up. Blood pooled but Thessa bared her teeth and continued, stabbing both her flanks. She stabbed and stabbed until massive, hairy hands tugged her away from the macerated corpse.

A familiar voice sounded. "That's plenty."

Thessa whipped her head left and right, realizing Soren wasn't in sight. "Where is he?"

She was being hauled away without an answer.

Thessa turned her head farther than she should be able to. She met Reginald's worried eyes and said, "I need to find him."

When his gaze shifted, she followed it, landing on the tree Soren was staked to.

"No!" Her voice cracked at the same time thunder clapped.

Thessa froze, unable to think as Reginald scooped her up and ran.

The rebellion was calling for a retreat.

No.

Just as they made it past the fighting, and towards the Celestials and healers, a flurry of screams broke out.

Reginald paused and turned back. "I'll be damned."

Soldiers in scarlet uniform were collapsing and thrashing. Poisonous fangs disabled every limb in their path. The enemy was falling, one by one.

Soren had called Echidna through their bond the evening before. She'd taken the river north with her newest hatchlings, crossing into enemy territory at last.

Reginald tossed Thessa into a group of Celestials like an empty barrel of mead before advancing. As war cries rang out once more, she sobbed. "Help him. Help him, someone help him!" She crumpled to the ground, pleading.

"Tess!" Gentle, yet strong hands caressed her back. "We need to go."

She was being dragged away again—from where she needed to be. Thessa dug her nails into the dirt and screamed, "No!"

"Stop! We need to get you somewhere safe." That voice. It was Leora. She'd been so consumed with Soren she'd forgotten that Leora had come.

"We need to run, now!" Leora shouted, as two enemy soldiers broke through the lines and hurtled directly towards them.

Thessa managed as much magic as she could muster right before two Celestials jumped in their path—a white-haired witch with violet bangs and one with a triple pigtail. They cast a double ray of moonlight so bright it blinded their attackers.

She'd never seen Celestial magic used defensively. It was working brilliantly.

Leora and Thessa gasped in harmony as Wayland crashed into the soldiers. He slit one throat on impact before whirling around to snap the neck of the other. Where the capital had gone *very* wrong was not training their soldiers in hand-to-hand combat. Elemental hands were always too precious to be bothered.

"Get out of here," Emiel demanded of them.

Thessa did just that.

"Damn you, Tess!"

She was aiming for *him*, dodging anyone in her path. Rebels surrounded the tree and fought in a frenzy to protect what remained of Soren. Without a second thought she funneled through them, shoved her dagger into the bark for leverage, and climbed.

Soren's serpent head was dangling, yet he managed a low hiss when she arrived.

"I'm going to help you, *please* don't waste your energy on biting me." She wasn't sure if he understood her.

Are you in there, Soren?

No reply.

Using her dagger, she plucked all seven arm-length bolts from his scales, marring him in the process. He had no skin left. She threw each one as far as she could, hoping and praying to impale the soldiers who'd done this to him.

Once freed from all his bolts, Soren's body crumpled to the ground.

I'm Sorry.

Jussal was there, alongside Christof, and others, to catch and carry him away. The vantage point from the treetop gave her a view of the entire scene. Serpents had swarmed the capital. She couldn't tell Echidna's from Soren's but there were too many to count. Bystanders were fleeing in fear with hopelessness and confusion etched across their faces. She blinked, focusing on a group of rebels escorting a handful of townsfolk away from the bloodied streets.

Her mouth fell open in horror at what she saw next.

No, no, no.

Echidna was surrounded by enemy soldiers, bathing in fire. Without her, Soren's bond was broken, and her serpents would roam uninhibited.

"Get down from there! You're a target."

Brenneth had climbed the tree to meet her.

She'd clung to the branches in shock. "Take me to him."

"I will."

Brenneth helped her down, then tossed her over his shoulder. As he ran through fallen bodies, their cries filled her ears.

50

MENTAL NOTES FROM THE SCHOOL
HEALER AT CSA:

Despite breathing and herbs, there's no cure for this type of wound. Healing takes time.

After Brenneth had carried her back into camp, Thessa faltered at the sight of Soren's serpentine skin, seared beyond recognition. She'd sat there for however long, watching the healer's work.

Her mind was in a silent fury, while her heart screamed. Although her eyes were opened, she couldn't see. Without him, the world was uninhabitable; her mind was once again, uninhabitable. So, she'd drifted away. Not even the gurgling pain of others, or the tears of the mourning could steal her attention.

When day faded into night, Thessa still hadn't moved. She had no purpose to. Familiar faces passed by, trying to free her from her torment, but nothing would help her escape this.

At some point, someone carried her away, into a healer's tent and atop a cot.

"Perhaps a head wound," the healer said.

A series of hands cut every piece of muddied fabric from her, inspected her skin, and cleaned her. There were mumbled uncertainties as to why she'd remained in such a daze, but Thessa didn't care to listen. Afterwards, someone had dressed her, laid her down, and covered her with a thin blanket. Maybe it was Sila, or some other aqua-eyed female. She wasn't sure.

The healer, who'd introduced herself as Pennique several times, stayed awake all night to observe her. When morning broke, she wagged her thick finger, mapping a shape Thessa had no energy to track. "Follow my finger, go on," the healer repeated.

She couldn't. Her sleep had come in waves, her eyes closing for a bit, then popping back open. Unseeing death was not an option, she learned.

"Grab me a Celestial, please," Pennique asked the child who'd been staring at Thessa like she too was a corpse.

Leora tumbled in a second later, landing at her bedside, as if she'd been waiting for an opportunity to come in. Thessa wanted to reach out to her, to slide her fingers across Leora's skin, and let her know she was here ... but she was just too tired.

"How can I help?" Leora asked.

The healer hovered over Thessa's face. "Conjure your magic please, just to one fingertip," Pennique requested.

Leora did so effortlessly.

"Now, bring your finger closer to her right eye."

Thessa heaved a breath as Leora's opalescent fingertip shined bright. As exhausted as Thessa was, and unable to voice the pain inside her chest, she was proud of her friend.

"And the other eye, please."

Leora's bright finger dipped from one eye to the other.

"Pupils are responding well, good," Pennique noted. "That's enough, thank you."

"Will she be, okay?" Leora asked.

"There's no active bleeding, anywhere. There's no wound to her head that I can find, no swelling either. Her breathing remained steady all evening. There's not even a scratch on her skin. I think this may stem from the mind, which would require time, and rest. There's nothing more I can offer her."

Thessa felt Leora's warm hand squeeze her shoulder before asking Pennique, "Could you leave us, for just a moment?"

"I have to get some water anyway, I'll be back soon." She gathered a bucket and looked over to the child. "Come."

When they were alone, Leora began. "Tess, I think you're in shock, or something. Whatever it is, I'm here. I've been here, and I'm not going anywhere."

Thessa's chest swelled and settled, like a tide flowing in and out of sea.

Leora continued, "You're the strongest witch I've ever met. Do you know that? You can push through this." Leora shook her head. "Is this about Soren? Sila, who I really like by the way, told me how close you two were getting. He'll be okay, the healers said so. In fact, he's doing so well they had to move him into a carriage. He was becoming too alert, and aggressive, which they said is a good sign. This way, they can keep him safe. All everyone wants is to keep you both safe." Leora tucked the blanket tighter into her sides.

The act was so small, yet so comforting. Thessa wondered if that was what it'd felt like to be tucked in as a child. Her voice was scratchy, but she managed to say, "Thanks for coming."

Leora squeezed her hand. "Tess, always."

She cleared her throat. "So, it's true, he'll be, okay?" She wanted to hear Leora say it again.

"It's true. Emiel's driving the healers mad with questions, but it sounds like the burns and wounds are responding well to the salves. They said he'll be scarred, but nothing more."

"Emiel's okay? Beatrix and Ivy too?"

Leora smiled. "Yes, they're all alright."

"And Hades, Ares?"

"The horses? More than alright. Emiel's been caring for them."

"Good." She was scared to ask but had to. "How many are ... not alright?"

Leora paused. "Many."

"And dead?"

After dropping her head, Leora said, "Many."

Thessa sighed, rolling to her side. "There's no point in leaving this tent. It was a fool's dream to stand a chance against them."

"That's not true. Their forces retreated as fast as ours, thanks to Soren's serpent friend."

Echidna.

Her last memory of the serpent was not one she wanted to remember. She wondered if Soren could feel her loss. He must. Thessa groaned into her pillow, feeling unworthy of the soft reprieve beneath her cheek.

"Come on. Let's stretch those legs of yours. I know quite a few people who can't wait to see how you're doing. Pennique is really strict, she wouldn't allow any visitors overnight." Leora stretched an arm around Thessa's back, helping her off the cot.

Ivy and Beatrix were only a step away from the tent, shooting to their feet when they saw them. Beatrix opened her arms wide before pulling Thessa into a giant hug. There wasn't room to object, especially not as Ivy did the same, squeezing her from the other side. Thessa would've stumbled had they not been holding on so tight. Leora couldn't help herself, stretching her long arms around all of them. The ball of Celestials infused her with enough energy to shake a small smile from her.

"I love you all, but I can't breathe," Thessa said. After they released her, she zipped in a breath and asked, "How'd you all do it?"

"Do what?" Beatrix asked.

"Gather enough Celestials to distract an entire army?"

Ivy answered, "Have you met Leora?"

A genuine smile escaped Thessa's lips. "And that slice of moonlight? Amazing."

Ivy smirked. "The Celestials in Greenshire taught us." She eyed Beatrix before saying, "We're planning to move up north and learn more."

Beatrix reached for Ivy's hand. "You're not just saying that for me?"

"No. I think you're right. We should do it."

Beatrix squealed before kissing Ivy hard enough to knock her back a few steps.

Thessa remembered the mountains and trees Eiliana had drawn. "I hope you both love it there."

"We'll write of course," Ivy added.

Thessa was grateful for friends that saw the light in the darkest of places—friends like them. A rough throat cleared from behind her, and Thessa turned to see Jussal eyeing her with concern.

Sila smiled and said, "I'm glad you're feeling better."

Jussal inclined his head toward the tent. "We should talk inside."

"Let's go get Thessa something to eat." Leora steered Ivy and Beatrix toward the braziers while eyeing Sila.

"What?" Thessa asked as she moved back inside the tent. "He's going to be okay, right?" Hearing it again would help. She scanned Sila's face for the truth.

Sila answered, "That's what the healers say, but—"

"But what?" Thessa interrupted her.

Lips pressed flat, Jussal said, "He won't eat."

"Not yet, you mean." Thessa looked to Sila for reassurance.

Sila nodded. "Not yet."

Shifting her gaze back to Jussal, Thessa asked, "What have you offered him?"

He rubbed his forehead. "So far, we've snared some rodents and river trout. He's not interested in either."

"Well, try something else," Thessa snapped at him.

"We're working on it," Sila said softly.

Eyes still fixed on Jussal, Thessa asked, "How *many* did we lose?"

Jussal sighed, "The numbers aren't for certain, somewhere between 170 and 180 are unaccounted for, but I can assure you the Elemental Army lost more."

It didn't make her feel better. "And children?"

"None harmed."

Thessa let out a breath. "What are we going to do about him?"

"We wait," Jussal said, as if his son wasn't trapped. *As if* it weren't every bit his fault for cursing Soren with this burden. "For now, there are things that need to be settled, and you're the only one who can do it."

Thessa snarled at the founder of the southern rebellion. He may be reformed, but his heart was made of stone. "You don't have to tell me. Where's *my* horse?"

"Thessa, let's get you fed first," Sila offered.

The haze threatened to take over her head again. Thessa spotted her boots and moved to slide them on. "I'm not hungry," she muttered, and stomped out of the tent.

51

LECTURE NOTES FROM SPELLCASTING
AND CURATION:

Only a Supreme's blood is pure enough to perform the Blood Sacrifice. The release of undiluted power is so grand, it can be cast across the land—in exchange for their life.

Thessa rubbed her eyes dry, repressed the pain that was deep inside her chest, and rode Hades back to the Central Divinity.

Rain had fallen all evening, washing away most of the blood from the streets. However, it'd done nothing for the rotting corpses. The reek of decay lingered in her nostrils as she approached the iron gates.

Her magic swelled around her in a thick, shadowy sphere, having regained its vigor overnight. The row of guards securing the gates didn't attack Thessa, learning the hard way that their powers were useless against hers.

"I've come to speak with your Supremes," she shouted. "And I believe now they will listen."

The guards eyed each other before one stepped forward. "If it's a message you wish to share, I will share it." Her white hair and soft features reminded her of Ivy.

Thessa reached into her saddlebag, retrieving the agreement she'd configured and shook it in her hand. The female guard approached, snatching the parchment faster than necessary.

"I'll wait," Thessa said, then watched the witch scurry down the courtyard and into the Central Divinity.

Putting on a mask was easier than settling into despair. Here, anyway. She stroked Hades' mane for comfort.

"Are you going to summon an army of insects and serpents this time?" A soldier barked the question.

"Do I need to?" she countered, nostrils flaring.

The soldier stayed silent.

There'd been no winner in their battle. There was no victory in so many needless deaths. Killing their Supreme was a long-standing message—their lies would no longer be tolerated, and her kind were here to stay.

It'll be that, or chaos.

Shadow-wielders had endured torment over centuries. The level of cruelty shed was similar to that of mortals—burning witches on stakes. Denouncing the shadow line of magic to demon status, then eradicating it, had been a misstep that would require acknowledgment.

To generate a prosperous society, the bloodlines would need to work together. There would need to be respect for the framework of all the souls that made up their realm, and a position of power should never be strong enough to eliminate an entire population. Importantly, the children of Andera deserved an accurate portrayal of their history.

So that's what Thessa had written ... in a desperate attempt to forge an agreement.

The creaking of iron gates stirred her to attention. Flanked by guards were two Supremes in billowing robes, one glistening white and the other shining green.

Madame Morganna approached first, signaling her guards to stay back.

Thessa sat taller atop Hades, lifting her chin with a false sense of pride.

"We received your message," the Celestial Supreme said. "However, the display of Celestial magic yesterday spoke to me well enough. Their subsequent demise was only a taste of what your kind have endured for centuries, and for that, I am indefinitely regretful." The Celestial Supreme dropped to one knee.

Guards shuffled on uncertain feet.

The Botanical Supreme, Madame Hearthling, set her knee down too. One scowl from her lips and all the guards knelt. "Will you accept our two-century-late apology?"

Thessa shook her head, confused by the sudden changes of heart. "Apologize to Andera," she countered.

Madame Hearthling met Thessa's eyes. "It's going to take a lot of time and grace for Andera to accept the rise of one Supreme and the loss of another."

"It's our fault we let our power-hungry sister carry on for so long. That is blame we accept, and now wish to correct," the Celestial Supreme added.

Madame Hearthling continued, "There were things we couldn't stop. Not fully. You have our word; we'll help undo what's been done."

Squinting with speculation, Thessa asked, "I'm supposed to accept a sorry and promise?"

"As fellow Supremes, that is what we offer," Madame Morganna said simply.

Thessa's lips parted. "Fellow, what?"

"Having enough magic to cast night over this entire realm tells us exactly how potent your blood is—exactly *who* you are. That type of power would have ended in the Blood Sacrifice had you not stopped."

"I am no Supreme," Thessa snapped. She was the offspring of an overzealous goddess, yes, but no Supreme.

"After darkness swept over this fortress." Madame Hearthling eyed Madame Morganna briefly before continuing, "We knew you'd risen. We looked deeper into your file after you so *politely* visited us." She paused to raise an eyebrow. "Were you aware Skiafer translates to shadowbringer? It's an ancient language."

"Latin," Madame Morganna added. "The mortals call it Latin."

Digesting the information, Thessa quieted. *Shadowbringer?* All those years of searching, trying to learn about her non-existent family, not once had she sought out the origin of her surname. To be called Supreme was not something she'd ever expected to hear, especially not with so much blood on her hands.

"And when will the Elemental heir take her position?"

Madame Morganna said, "She is protected within the walls of this fortress and will remain so until she turns eighteen. Then, she will rise."

Thessa wondered how long a potential truce could last. "And what of the lives lost? The remains of this city?"

Madame Hearthling placed her fingertips on the ground in answer. She released the greenest magic Thessa had ever seen, sending emerald tendrils of life spiraling towards the dead.

The power of Earth Rendering was unique to the most potent of Botanical witches. Her magic wrapped around dead bodies like cocoons, coating each one. When it dissipated, what remained were grassy beds, full of herbs and wildflowers.

Inch by inch, the gravel-ridden streets of Gravenport transformed into a blossoming city of hope.

Madame Morganna stood first. "Come, we have much to discuss."

52

LECTURE NOTES FROM ANIMAL HUSBANDRY:

Rodents, reptiles, and amphibians require specific diets and housing structures. Rodents will eat something similar to bird feed, while reptiles and amphibians prefer insects and small rodents or mammals. Their housing requires frequent tending to; no creature wants to sleep in their own filth.

After she'd been escorted through the gates of the Central Divinity, Hades was led to the stables, while she trailed the Supremes on foot.

Guards eyed her warily.

There would be revolts, that was expected. When, she didn't know. How often, she couldn't think about that.

She was brought to the Supreme's private dining room, rather than being chased from it. Seated at the table set for three, beneath a chandelier of enchanted candles, they established the rules of the New Regime.

The term demon had been stripped, for starters, and any citizen of Andera that unjustly took the life of another, would relinquish their own life. The army would welcome all four types of magic, working together, and enrollment would not be mandatory.

Importantly to her, the Supremes would no longer be barred to the capital, and the checkpoint between territories was no longer required.

The last topic they discussed was the Troika—which would be dissolved. It was agreed to replace them with a few members of each bloodline, selected at random for each trial.

Regardless of positive progress and dire change, she felt sick without Soren.

By the time she was leaving, Noam and Rhetter had arrived at the gates with a basket of eggs in tow. They'd found the cave she described, collected hundreds of Echidna's eggs, and were depositing them to healers from Wilcrest to Gravenport.

A mixture of a common neutralizing serum with the serpent-specific yolk would yield the antivenom everyone needed, according to Jussal.

Ignoring the horror and confusion on their faces, all she could mutter was a simple, "Thank you," to them, before mounting Hades and taking off.

❈

THESSA CRACKED THE DOOR OF THE CARRIAGE OPEN. IT WAS still parked in their temporary encampment, just south of Gravenport.

A quick survey of Soren's scales told her his burns were healing well. She knew he felt better, it's why they'd contained him—alone—for the past two nights and three days.

"Soren ... you won't let the healers help you anymore, you won't eat these rabbits, and you won't drink. You'll die in there. Do you understand that?"

Ducking beneath his coils, he hissed.

He'd done this for her—shifted into a beast. It was the only thing capable of distracting her enough at that moment.

Somehow, he'd known she held the power of the Blood Sacrifice. He'd figured it out and saved her by sacrificing himself instead. Maybe it was all the blood spewing from her face, but he'd believed in her magic, in her, more fiercely than she ever had.

It wasn't right to give up on him, so she hadn't. She'd camped outside the carriage both nights, ignoring Leora's requests to sleep in her tent. Ares and Hades wouldn't leave the carriage either. The three of them refused to leave their friend—her lover, her *everything*. Thessa couldn't picture a world without Soren, and just the idea of it made her stomach knot.

"Damn you Soren, shift." She sighed, opening the door a little more. "At least eat."

He ignored her.

Infuriated, Thessa squeezed inside.

Soren launched, his snout halting an inch from her face. Zipping in a breath, she remained still as his red, bifurcated tongue flicked her neck, jiggling the necklace she always wore.

"Can you smell that?"

His tongue flicked her necklace again.

He must. "It's me. It's me." Moving her fingers frantically, she opened the pendant.

His black eyes blinked, as if in recognition.

She began begging, "You have to shift. Please. Do it for me."

Soren retreated, curling up beneath the bench.

"Eat. Drink. Anything." She tossed the dead hare closer to him.

He nudged it away.

Please.

The other end was silent. She wasn't sure why he couldn't hear her anymore. But it felt like he was choosing not to.

Unsure how to start persuading a serpent to change their mind, Thessa sat across from him and sighed. "I'm sorry about Echidna. I can't begin to understand the connection you two had. I know this has something to do with it, but she wouldn't want this. She lived longer than any serpent was ever meant to. She wanted you to live, as you were meant to. I know she helped you remember last time, but maybe it can be me this time."

You remember me, don't you?

Nothing.

Her heart wrenched inside her chest, but she spoke through the pain. "You are not the beast you were made to be."

You never were.

The serpent tucked himself in tighter, as if ignoring her.

She couldn't take this any longer. Thessa opened the door and murmured, "Come back to me," before slipping out.

Jussal was standing there beside Sila, his shoulders were tense. Several healers waited too, desperate to tend to him.

"Well?" Jussal asked.

She shook her head, holding the door shut. "He knows it's me ... I think. But it doesn't change anything."

"But the last time he ate." Jussal scratched his head. "It wasn't like this."

Her voice wavered. "I think we have to let him go."

"Don't be ridiculous."

Thessa opened the carriage door with trembling hands. "We have to."

Without hesitation, the serpent poked his head out and flicked his tongue. Like a mouse freed of its trap, Soren slithered out and into the woods, never looking back.

Jussal held up his hands, stopping Emiel and the healers from chasing after him. "She's right."

Thessa stood there, unwilling to look away from the scaled figure blurring into the distance.

❧

THE NEXT MORNING THESSA ATE A FEW SOUR BERRIES before packing her things. She never had much of anything, and now, she had even less.

"Are you ready?" Leora asked. A majority of their camp had left the day or two after battle, while the rest trickled out last night.

"I suppose. Thanks for waiting with me." Thessa had stayed one more night, just in case Soren would return.

Leora, Emiel, and Wayland had stayed too, helping pack up and burning what remained of camp.

"Of course. They're done harnessing the horses, we can go ... if you're sure." Leora held out her hand, the hand she'd always offered Thessa. Whether it was on her back, her shoulder, or drifting between them, without ever needing anything in return, Leora's hand was always there.

Thessa took it and stood. It was time to let him go. "I'm ready."

Hades and Ares led their carriage back to Wilcrest.

Emiel and Leora shared one bench, while Thessa squished herself beside a hoard of tent materials.

The barren path had been a persistent reminder of who

she'd shared it with, time and time again. Soren was gone because of her. She'd never let herself heal from this wound—it was pain she deserved to feel.

Somewhere between Mabelton and Wilcrest, a small plume of smoke filtered through the trees.

"My father's group probably stopped to eat, is anyone hungry?" Emiel asked. "The berry selection in Gravenport was horrendous."

Thessa agreed. "The horses should rest anyway."

Emiel knocked on the front paneled wall and shouted, "Wayland, pull off."

When the door popped open, Thessa was relieved for fresh air. The thought of Soren being alone in a carriage for three days made her heart sag a little more.

After crossing over the tall grass that flanked their journey south, the four made their way into the woods.

When scarlet uniforms flashed in the distance, she knew they'd not stumbled into a friendly campsite.

Ducking behind a row of dense trees, Thessa counted eight Elemental soldiers. Their uniforms were torn, and their faces were etched with anger—and grime.

"Hades," Emiel whispered, peering through the leaves.

Leora's mouth was fixed in that "O" shape.

Wayland mumbled, "Let's get out of here."

Emiel eyed him. "That doesn't smell like food."

"No," Thessa said. It smelled ... familiar. She couldn't see much. There were too many bushes and fallen trees blocking her view.

A voice snuck up from behind her. "Shh. If I can hear you, they're bound to hear you."

"Quinnley," Leora gasped.

Quinnley pressed a finger to her lips. "Shh."

"Why are you here? What's going on over there?" Thessa

questioned quietly.

"They crossed into *my* campsite late last night." Quinnley used her thumb to gesture over to the upturned tree trunk and small cavern within. "It goes beyond what you see, which is why they haven't found me. That poor thing they have with them. I have to help it. I've been preparing a sleeping agent. Burning it will keep them asleep. I just have to figure out how to—"

Thessa interrupted, "Quinnley. Do you understand there's been a war?"

"Oh my, well, that explains why they look so disheveled. But it definitely doesn't explain why they trapped an unusually large serpent. I've never seen one so big, or this far from the sea."

Thessa swallowed.

"Spies." Wayland mumbled.

Thessa shot him a knowing look. "I let him go, so they could track him. *I* did this."

He said nothing.

"The sleeping agent is almost ready," Quinnley pressed.

Thessa said, "I have a better idea. Everyone, stay back," before storming through the trees.

❦ 53 ❦

LECTURE NOTES FROM HERBOLOGY 101:

It was worse than a nightmare. Soren was there, encased in fire-cuffs. They'd not spared any part of his body, which sizzled with every breath he dared to take. They weren't just killing him, they were torturing him.

"Release him, or you'll die." The voice that had escaped her was not her own, but that of the monster within her.

The soldiers whirled around at her threat. The one in the middle grinned before saying, "Look who came to retrieve her beast."

Thessa stood tall, letting her shadows dance around her.

"Killing us would go against the *New Regime*, now wouldn't it," mocked the soldier.

She took a step toward Soren. "This is far from *just* behavior."

"I wouldn't do that if I were you." The soldiers tightened their grips on Soren's fire-cuffs as he writhed in agony. "We'll end this now."

Thessa snarled, sending eight wisps of her magic to float in the space between them: one for each soldier.

"Retract your shadows and this will be over soon. It's only *just* after what you did to our Supreme."

Knowing her magic stole a particularly useful element, she quieted. Her shadows were not a gentle blanket of death, rather a bundle of rage. Flicking her fingers, she willed them down the soldiers' throats.

As they clawed at their necks, Thessa held her focus—she'd die before letting her magic escape their lungs. When they all collapsed, the fire around Soren's scales faded, but only once the final soldier shuddered had she lunged for him.

Collapsing to his side, she sobbed. How long had they *hunted him? Tortured him?* His body was burnt, limp and without a hiss.

Leora burst through a bush. "Quinnley's going to help. She has supplies."

Thessa was shaking. "I don't think he's breathing."

Quinnley skidded over, pressing her palms atop Soren's scalded flesh. "His heart is still beating, I can feel it." A moment later, bright green magic escaped her fingertips, trickling over Soren like water. The lush color was as rich as the magic she'd witnessed in the capital.

"Quinnley," Leora gasped; her eyes displayed the same level of shock as Thessa's. "When you said you had supplies, I was thinking you meant potions and salves."

"I wasn't sure how to—" Quinnley stopped talking, shaking her head instead.

"Tell us you held the power of Earth Rendering?" Thessa chimed in, recognizing exactly who Quinnley was.

"How does it work?" Leora asked.

Her magic began forming intricate strings, weaving around Soren's body like a tapestry. It was patching and sealing each crevice anew. "We can grow anything from flora to fauna. Scales and body tissue aren't much different than algae and fungi. As long as the heart pumps and their blood moves, we can grow the rest."

"Why is someone with your gift living under a tree root?" Leora pressed her.

"It's not just a gift," Thessa muttered. "She's the heir."

Quinnley sighed before mumbling, "I never asked to be ... that's why I ran away. Living in the Central Divinity was awful —with all that fire. I like it much better here, in the woods. I have a purpose here. You won't tell my mother you found me, right?" Her vibrant, green eyes pleaded up to them both.

"Of course not, Quinn," Leora said, "thanks for trusting us."

A deep breath surged through Soren just as his skin began to shine, slick with slime.

Thessa sighed in relief. "Quinnley, keep working. Leora, let her focus."

Leora nodded and stood, backing up into Emiel's embrace. Thessa hadn't noticed it before, but Emiel was terrified. Worry laced his freckled face.

"He's going to be okay," she heard Leora whisper to him.

Thessa refocused on Soren, staring directly into his black eyes.

I know you're in there. I need you to shift. Find the strength and do it.

The bond was silent.

Please. Please, do it for me.

Nothing.

Thessa groaned.

Fine.

Pulling her dagger free, she sliced through her palm.

"What are you doing?" Quinnley asked.

"I need clove and mugwort, now."

Quinnley used a single finger to conjure the herbs for her.

"Thank you," she managed, dropping them on the ground and mashing her bloodied fist atop them. She opened the top of her tunic and smeared the mixture across her chest, drawing a five-pointed star.

"*Blood, herbs, heart, and soul. Take my gift, take this toll. Seek my mother, not another. Goddess be, please help me. Blood, herbs, heart, and soul. Take my gift, take this toll. Seek my mother, not—*"

Thessa met Quinnley's puzzled stare just as everything went black.

❧

"The least you can do is help him shift after lying to me for eighteen years."

"Thessa." The majestic voice boomed across the dark and airy plane of her soul. "I'm more than relieved you survived your slip in the sea. Look at all you've overcome."

Thessa shook her head, the blurry memory of her mother babbling about Poseidon resurfaced. "Spare me, and help Soren, *now.*"

"It won't be that simple. He's too far gone. In the mind."

"You said you're with all those who share our blood, so go to *him*. Save *him*."

There was a thunderous sigh, a dramatic pause, and then a response. "He'll need a tether."

"What do you mean, don't start with your riddles," Thessa snapped at the goddess of night.

"Something to tie him back to his immortal body. A *reminder*."

"But he knows it's me, I'm not enough."

"Make it enough, Thessa. You've worked so hard, let it not be for nothing."

Thessa's eyes shot open and she cursed.

"I take it that didn't go so well?" Quinnley asked, her hands still busy healing Soren.

Thessa grunted and sat up. "Useless, as usual." A swell of heat to her back had her glancing over her shoulder; Wayland was incinerating the dead soldiers.

Good.

Emiel was still wholly focused on Soren, and Leora wholly focused on him. Their connection was palpable.

Thessa turned to Soren's serpent form, now breathing steadily. Every scale was whole.

Alive.

"I'll never leave you again. I'm never leaving you again," she swore to him. She'd watch him in this form, from afar if she had to, forever—*after* killing his father for placing this curse upon him. Upon her.

Lying beside him, Thessa unscrewed her necklace. "I suppose now is a good time to tell you how foolish I am."

Soren blinked slowly, as if listening.

"Growing up, I used to be so jealous of the witchlings with homes. So much so that I convinced myself that if I worked hard enough, one day I could afford my very own." She laughed; the sound was more melancholic than joyful. "But I was wrong to think it was something you could buy, and I'm sorry for taking so long to realize it." She paused, swallowing the lump of fear in her throat. "The way my heart trembles when I'm near you, and the way you look at me, but actually see *me*, makes it clear. You brought light into my life that not even the stars could muster. My home is with you, and forever will be. I love you, Soren. *I love you so much*."

Then, Thessa kissed the serpent.

Quinnley gasped—from either the sight of Thessa's lips on the serpent's mouth, or the glistening veil of night Soren created while shifting back. Thessa sprang to her feet to meet him as Quinnley backed away, muttering something about fairytales.

From the corner of her eye, she watched Leora drape her arm across Emiel's chest, holding him back as Soren uncurled.

Quinnley was a powerful witch, was all Thessa could think about while staring at Soren's nude and unscarred body. Everything was perfect, with the exception of one missing serpent tattoo.

Soren followed her gaze, brushing a palm over his clear skin in recognition. What she'd thought was a tattoo was an imprint.

Echidna was *gone*.

Despite this, and everything he'd been through, Soren stepped closer, scanning her. He whispered, "Are you hurt?"

Thessa's heart crumpled. She shook her head—the weight of it suddenly so heavy. "Not physically." Her words broke as they came out.

Soren's strong hand cupped her face, lifting her watery gaze to meet his. His eyes glazed over like black pearls before crashing his lips into hers. Their tears mingled on her cheeks as he swept her off her feet.

Pulled in tight, she felt every emotion in his embrace—grief and anger, hope and longing, desire and need. But something lingered above the rest; it was so strong her insides melted.

Atop her lips, Soren said, "I love you too, Thessa. So very much," before shielding them both with his magic.

ONE YEAR LATER

Thessa beat the metal thin enough before shaping it. With so much to rebuild, she'd found her real purpose in Andera, but today was for a special project.

She paused, admiring the freshly planted lavender on her windowsill, thinking about how much Professor Shovak would love it here—her very own workshop tucked into the forest of Wilcrest.

Back to work, she hammered the metal along the edge of her anvil, curving it, until the two delicate ends met.

Next, she sifted through her unorganized bucket of tools for some sandpaper. "There you are," she purred, before plucking it out. Humming to herself, she smoothed out the ring—which was less time consuming than a dagger.

"Knock, knock," Soren blurted before barging through the door.

She spun around, wide-eyed. "Usually one knocks with their fist, not their mouth," she reminded him. A casual sweep of her hands behind her back, and she slipped the ring onto her thumb.

He sauntered toward her with a wicked smile. "Are apologies in order?

She lifted her chin in innocence. "I would think that's only appropriate."

Hoisting her atop the workbench, he nudged himself between her legs. "How would you like me to express my regret?"

She tugged at the fabric along his waistline before meeting his eyes with fervent intensity. "Undressing will do."

Soren obliged, and just the sight of him nude had her lips parting.

"Only *you* would forge in a dress," he noted.

She smiled, lifting her arms up. After he helped pull it off, he unlaced her boots and yanked those off too.

Settling his body against hers, he turned her soot-stained cheek and whispered something naughty in her ear. Her body buzzed for him, especially as he dragged his sharp teeth down her neck and pulled her undergarment to the side.

That day he'd shifted from serpent to Soren, he'd practically taken her in front of their friends. Later that night, there'd been nothing to stop him. Without the need to hide their magic or love any longer, he'd laid down all his walls and gave her everything.

Soren pressed the tip of his length against her center before asking, "Is this what you want?"

She bit her lip and nodded.

It was all he needed to ease himself inside her. When he filled her, she tipped her head back and sighed. But Soren backed all the way out, pausing.

Thessa frowned, begging for more of him. *"Please."* She'd

never tire of the beautiful male who held her heart on a string.

After watching her come entirely undone, Soren gripped her hips and thrust so deep she screamed.

The predator didn't yield, he unleashed.

His force had her wrapping her legs around him and clawing the workbench. The table shook so violently, her bucket of tools rattled off the edge. She ignored the crashing and clanking of metals, and watched him instead.

Soren's concentration was … commendable.

The moment she cried his name, his mouth latched onto her breast, sucking her flesh like he was going to swallow it whole. When he stretched a thumb to the most sensitive skin between her thighs and swirled, her body spasmed.

Warmth flooded through her aching core as her breath escaped in bursts. A few more of his wicked thrusts were all she needed—and without having to listen to her thoughts, he gave them to her.

As Thessa shattered, he took her deeper. He laid her flat on her back, drove her knees into her chest, and pounded through her orgasm.

"I love you," she whimpered.

Light was how she felt—there was no darkness, no panic, no fear, no loathing—nothing at all to weigh her down.

His hips crashed into hers as his own wave of pleasure crested. The feel of his length pulsing inside her had release consuming her all over again.

Soren kept thrusting, as if for good measure, while he whispered, "I love you, too." His words were a hymn, ones he'd sung to her every day.

"Enough to marry me?" she managed to ask between shallow breaths.

He froze and stared at her—then through her—causing her blood to crackle like wildfire.

"A measly soldier, marry a Supreme?" He eyed where their bodies met and grinned. "I was beginning to think you preferred me as your concubine."

She smacked his chest. "Yes, I'm asking you, a measly soldier, to marry me."

She'd not stepped into her title lightly. She was not only the symbol of change, but the enforcer. Soren and the rest of the rebellion had paved the way for this opportunity, and she'd not let it go to waste.

Holding up her thumb—the one wearing the ring she'd spent the better part of two days making—she awaited his reply.

He laughed. "I knew you were up to *something* in here."

Leora and Emiel's engagement had got her thinking—too much, evidently. Tilting her head to the side, she said, "This is when you do anything other than laugh at me."

"This is the easiest decision I've ever had the privilege of making. Of course I'll marry you," he vowed, stealing the ring and sliding it on his finger.

Sunlight sliced across the steel as he held up his hand, admiring it.

She squinted. "It's a little dusty, from the sanding."

He leaned down to press his lips atop hers before saying, "It's *very* well crafted."

Thessa smiled. Not so much about the compliment, rather, that his complimenting skills had improved over the year.

"Speaking of well crafted." She eyed him still fixed inside her. "I'd not planned to ask you like *this*."

"Well *this* is very much your fault."

She flicked her gaze up. "My fault? Why'd you come in here, anyway?"

"To see if you needed anything." He smirked, tucking a lock of hair behind her ear. "It seems like you did."

Thessa hooked her legs around him and smiled. "Carry me home."

In answer, Soren scooped her off the table, and into eternity they went.

Fin.

BEFORE YOU GO

Please consider leaving an honest review on Amazon, Goodreads, or any other site you frequent.

ACKNOWLEDGMENTS

Thank you to my husband—for your patience and time, to my son—for your light, and my mom—for your unending support.

To my friends who take reading so seriously they have entire social media accounts dedicated to it, thank you for your encouragement to keep writing. Your virtual support is palpable.

To my readers, I am truly grateful that you gave this story a chance.

To my editor and beta readers, thank you for your effort and care with my manuscript.

To my book artist, thank you for listening so well.

To all the literary agents who told me not to give up, thank you for lighting my fire.